FROZEN FREIGHT
IRON REACH

A Novel by
JR ELROD

Book One of the Frozen Freight Series

Mercer House Publishing
Mount Pleasant, Texas
2026

Print ISBN: 979-8-9938535-0-5

E-book ISBN: 979-8-9938535-1-2

Printed in the United States of America

First Edition

TABLE OF CONTENTS

Prologue

STEEL AND SILENCE

There's a sound a truck makes when the world's still asleep. Not the engine yet—just the slow tick of cooling metal and the whisper of a night that never truly ends. In a yard full of rigs, each one towers quiet in the dark before dawn, and for a moment it's church. The air's thick with diesel settled into the dirt, and the cold cuts through your jacket no matter how many mornings you've done this. A man learns to breathe different out here, slow, like engine oil before the first turn of the key. Dew beads on the fender. Chrome catches the first hint of light and throws it back lazy, like it's too early to shine. The yard smells like fuel, dust, and the faint ghost of a coffee spill. Every rig's got a story—busted latch, mirror that won't sit right, a trailer that's older than some of the drivers who park beside it. Out by the fence, the yard dog—what we call the yard truck—shoves trailers around the lot like a tugboat nudging barges in a crowded harbor. Short frame, big heart, all torque. It ghosts through the fog with its lights on, brakes hissing and fifth-wheel clacking as it hooks, unhooks, and keeps the place alive.

Folks who've never driven one think big trucks roar to life. They don't. They wake up. You turn the key halfway and the dash and gauges come alive—low air warning and low oil pressure buzzers split the silence.

When I bump the starter, she answers with a deep-voiced rumble that climbs through my boots and settles in my ribs. That's not noise, that's heartbeat. Air tanks breathe a long, patient sigh and the needles on the gauges twitch their way toward normal. I reach over and throw the light switches and the dash blooms white, amber, and green like Christmas lights.

People like to tell me these things have eighteen brakes. They don't. They've got eighteen tires and I've got one chance to get it right. Stopping isn't mashing the brake pedal; it's negotiating. You don't fight mass—you reason with it. It's an eighty-thousand-pound torpedo waiting on your right foot to decide whether you'll respect it or if it'll have to show you who's in charge.

Every mile feels to me like a conversation between steel and asphalt, and the pavement might win if you're not paying attention. I've learned the feel of my rig the way a soldier learns his rifle—by instinct. How she leans on an uneven road, how she feels if the load sits a hair off-center.

The steering wheel talks if you let it. Sometimes it hums steady and other times it trembles like a man remembering something he'd rather forget. The cab's not just a seat and a bunk, it's a world in motion. The dash glows soft amber. The CB crackles once, then goes quiet for a moment—that silence just before voices fill it. Coffee steams in a thermos that's seen more states than most people.

Some folks think you slam through gears and hope for grace. I've learned different. You listen to the engine, match the RPMs, ease out on the clutch. When you get it right, the gears slide together so clean you barely hear it. The first time I ever floated a gear—shifted without the clutch—it felt like the machine had decided to trust me. That kind of trust is earned one careful movement at a time.

Out the side window, the highway rises out of the dark. A lone rig slides by, chrome catching the first thin light of dawn. Somewhere a refrigerated trailer starts and settles into a low drone. A door slams in the distance. The crows complain. Then the yard goes quiet again.

Folks say trucking's about miles. They're not wrong, but they're not right either. It's the rhythm of white lines and the weight of promises. It's knowing the bridge height before you see the sign. It's repairing a hose with zip ties on a Sunday because the ship sails Monday. It's the stranger waving from an overpass and a kid in a passing car pumping their arm up and down, begging you to blare the air horns. It's the smell of hot brakes on a mountain grade. It's the way wind shoves at a tall load on a bridge, and how you pretend your heart's not in your throat as you hold that lane like it's the last piece of ground you own.

I can tell the state I'm in by the sound of the pavement—smooth hum in Tennessee, coarse growl in Virginia, slap-and-echo in Pennsylvania.

The mirrors don't just show traffic; they show ghosts. Every run I've ever made rides back there—partners who taught me more than I deserved, rigs that didn't come home, jokes that got me through nights so long I forgot what daybreak looked like. Out here, my life fits in the space between the wheel and the windshield. Tools in the box. Permit book in the side pocket. Lists on the clipboard, a lucky coin under the rubber mat, and somebody's picture taped above the radio, edges curled from too many summers.

To me, trucking's not a job, it's a language. The tires hum what words don't have time for. The CB is gossip; the road is truth. The logbook isn't a diary of freight, it's a ledger of hours traded for miles. The older I get, the more I understand the exchange rate.

I climb down out of the cab and walk a slow circle around my W900L, fingers sliding along cold steel like checking a pulse. Tarps pulled tight. Chains snug. Flags bright.

The name on the door—Mercer Hauling & Recovery—is faded but it's ours. I kick a tire out of habit and it doesn't tell me much more than the pressure is right. Good. The sun fights through the trees—weak, orange, stubborn.

In an hour, the day will take more than it gives. The phone will ring and the yard will come alive with engines starting, dispatch talking, paperwork sliding across hoods. But for now, it's me and the truck and that low promise in the air; ask her to roll and she will. There's peace in that. There's truth in it too.

Every man's got a place of worship. Mine's twelve feet tall, painted in road dust, and powered by diesel.

Back in the cab, I lay my hand on the shifter, watch the gauges hold steady, and feel the cab breathe with me. The yard dog is still out there notching trailers into place; the world clicks forward one gear at a time.

I check the mirrors, tap the throttle, and feel the horsepower and torque combine and shudder through the whole rig as if it's saying, "I'm ready." Easing out on the clutch first thing in the morning always feels the same, no matter how many years go by. Feels like God giving me one more day to get it right.

Sitting here in the silence reminds me of some of the prayers I often utter before trips. Nothing fancy, but they're true:

Dear Lord ~

Keep me sharp when I'm tired.
Let my actions be professional.
Keep me steady when the road turns mean.
Let my words be kind.
Keep me and the people around me safe.
Let my eyes and ears be in tune with my surroundings.
Keep my family safe while I'm away.
Let my work exemplify my love for You and for them.
Keep my equipment in good repair and running as it should.
Let me see trouble before it sees me.
When the day asks more of me than I've got left,
give me just enough to safely make it home.

Amen

I didn't know it yet, but this morning would be the last quiet one for a long while.

Chapter 1

THE CALL

Morning didn't so much arrive as drift in, slow and unde-cided. The house held its breath the way old houses do, wood ticking, pipes sighing, everything waiting to see if the day was worth the trouble.

I had been off the road five years now, ever since Maggie passed. Folks called it retirement, but that wasn't the word for it. You don't quit the road—you idle. The miles still hum in your bones even when the wheels stop turning.

I set two mugs on the counter—mine and Maggie's, and poured coffee from the dented pot on the stove. Hers stayed empty. A habit older than my grief, I didn't see any point in changing it now.

Through the kitchen window, fog pressed against the glass until the yard looked whitewashed. The dually—the nickname for a hulking, one-ton pickup with wide hips and four wheels supporting the bed to carry heavy duty loads—sat out there under the porch light, hood shining wet. On the other side of the fence, the flatbed gooseneck and the tool trailer waited in a row like patient horses hitched for a job that hasn't been called in yet.

Gus was snoring on the mat at the door, half-blind and half-dreaming, one paw twitching at something only dogs remember. I took a sip and let the morning jolt burn the sleep off my tongue. The radio on the counter murmured the morning report about weather and soy prices—white noise for a man who didn't farm but liked the sound of people still trying.

The signal faded to silence, then a new voice cut in—it sounded official like Walter Cronkite but the words coming out of his mouth sounded absurd, like he was reading the latest rag sheet claiming a UFO landed at the White House.

"…researchers in Antarctica claim they've uncovered several fully preserved woolly mammoths under the ice. Reports suggest a military transport plane is already on-site…"

I poured another splash of the hot stuff and shook my head. "Sure they did! Next they'll have Elvis ridin' one of 'em through Times Square."

The host rambled on about secret bases and government silence until I twisted the dial back to static. I don't own a TV, never have. Pictures told lies too easy. Sound makes a man think. Radio was plenty.

I scanned the kitchen. Boots were lined up by the door, invoices sat on the counter half-covered by a wrench, and the framed flag on the wall caught just enough dawn to glint red once. It wasn't grief anymore. The echo of it, quiet and steady like a heartbeat under metal. Tapping the rim of Maggie's cup once with the tip of my finger I nodded toward the window. "Another day. Let's see what it wants."

I finished my coffee, rinsed the cup, and set it back beside Maggie's. Habit fell like gravity, stronger than reason.

The door hinge groaned as I stepped outside. Gus followed me. Fog hung thick as wool, swallowing the fenceline and most of the world beyond it. The gravel under my boots was slick and cold, smelling of rain and diesel from yesterday's work.

I pulled my jacket tight and did what I do every morning—a walkaround—whether I'm haulin' or not. The hood of my dually was beaded with dew. Starting at the driver's side, my palm dragged the fender like greeting an old friend. Tires good, lights unbroken, no new leaks under the chassis. I checked the ball hitch, gave it a tug, then glanced at the gooseneck and tool trailer sitting behind the fence—ghosts of motion, standing by just in case. Gus followed halfway down the steps, tail thumping, then turned around and went back, deciding the porch was far enough.

I finished circling the truck, checking mirrors and tailgate latches for no reason except that not checking felt wrong. The habit wasn't about trust. It was about respect. Machines remember when you get lazy.

I opened the driver's side door, paused a beat, and looked back toward the house. Steam still curled in the kitchen window, two mugs in silhouette. "Hold the fort, girl," I muttered as I climbed in.

The dually started on the second turn of the key. The diesel grumbled low and even, like it knew its job. I let it idle a moment, watching the gauges come alive. Easing out of the driveway the headlights cut two narrow tunnels through the fog, bound for town.

The road into town was quiet, two lanes slick with mist and memory. I kept one hand on the wheel and the other resting on the shifter out of habit, though the dually didn't need guidance the way my Kenworth had. Fence posts slid by in ghostly rows. Every mile carried the same rhythm—diesel hum, wiper squeak, gravel at the shoulder.

Mount Pleasant's single stoplight blinked yellow in the fog, and beyond it the Rusty Fork Café glowed like it always did—neon sign buzzing, windows fogged from bacon grease and gossip. I parked in my usual spot out front, left the engine idling long enough for the turbo to settle, then shut it down.

The bell over the door gave its tired jingle as I stepped inside. Warmth hit me first. Coffee, fry oil, and a hint of bleach wafted through the air from the mop Chef rarely used unless Mona nagged him into using it.

"Morning, Buck," Mona called from behind the counter. Her hair was up, her tone already in mid-argument.

"Morning, Mona." I shook the damp off my jacket and hung it on the coat tree by the door.

"You're late! Chef said he thought you must've died in your sleep."

Chef leaned out from the food window, spatula in hand. "Told her if you were dead the dog'd still drive your truck in."

I grinned. "He'd probably park it better, too."

The regulars chuckled from their corners—same farmers, same mechanics, same line of muddy boots against the floor rail.

My table is in the back next to the window with the cracked frame. Thirty years' worth of cup rings marked the wooden table like old friends that didn't need small talk. The vinyl cushion sighed under me as I slid into the booth against the back wall, facing the front door.

Mona came over with an empty mug and steaming rocket fuel before I could ask. "The usual?"

"Unless Chef learned how to cook something edible overnight."

Chef's voice came back from the grill. "You want gourmet, go to Dallas!"

"Dallas doesn't open this early," I said, grinning.

Mona poured the coffee, smirked, and left me to it.

Outside the fog began to lift, but the café stayed the same—warm light, quiet jokes, and the sound of the spatula snapping against the griddle. I leaned back, hands on my cup, and let the morning settle in like a familiar road that never ended.

Mona came back a few minutes later with a plate that looked like it had fought a losing battle with the fryer. Over-easy eggs slid toward one edge, bacon edges curled like they were getting ready to run, and the toast glistened with enough butter to waterproof a barn.

"Here ya go, hero," she said, setting it down with a clatter. "Chef says he made it with love."

From the grill, Chef barked, "I said I made it with lard! She hears what she wants!"

I about choked on my swallow of joe with a snort. "Don't change a thing, Chef. Cholesterol builds character."

"Yeah?" Chef hollered back. "Then you're the most developed man in Titus County!" Laughter rolled across the room.

The café's old wall-mounted TV flickered above the counter, grainy footage of ice and scientists in parkas.

Mona pointed at it with the coffee pot. "You hear about that? Mammoths frozen solid—the military is involved."

"I heard it on the radio. Same folks said last week that little green men walked into a Walmart at two in the morning."

Chef grunted from the grill, "Long as they pay cash, I don't care where they're from."

"World's strange enough without help from TV," I muttered as I grabbed my fork.

A pair of old farmers at the counter simultaneously smacked the Formica top with the flat of their hands, one of them wheezing, "He got you there, Buck!"

Mona topped off my brew, leaning on the table like she'd been doing since the Clinton years. "Ignore him. Man couldn't boil water without burning it."

Chef shot back, "And yet you married me for my cooking!"

She didn't miss a beat. "No, I married you 'cause the other man in town had three ex-wives and a lazy eye."

I swallowed a bite of bacon and snort-laughed again.

"Keep talkin', woman," Chef said, flipping a pancake so hard it nearly left orbit. "One of these days I'm gonna run off with a waitress who appreciates me."

"Go ahead," Mona said sweetly. "But you better find one that's blind and can't smell."

Chuckles from around the diner filled the air. The clatter of forks and the hum of conversation folded back on another morning at Rusty Fork, where insults were affection and the coffee pot never emptied. Finally cutting into my eggs, grease pooled like a mirror. "You know, Mona, this plate's a cardiac event with a side of butter."

She winked. "Eat up, Pops. Keeps you outta heaven one more day."

The bell over the door jingled again, sharper this time. I didn't bother to look up until I heard her voice.

"You planning to walk that off or let your arteries file a complaint?" Katie stood in the doorway—all business before seven a.m., phone in one hand, jacket half-slipped off her shoulder.

Mona turned with the pot of java raised like evidence. "I told him the same thing. He won't listen."

Katie said, "You trying to kill him before I get him to a doctor?"

Chef called, "Lady, he's too mean to die!"

"See? Even Chef's optimistic," I retorted.

Katie sighed, "Optimistic or blind?" She leaned down and kissed the top of my head before sitting across from me. "You ever eat a vegetable that didn't come with gravy?"

I smiled into my mug. "Coffee's a bean. Beans are vegetables."

Mona chuckled and poured Katie a cup before she even asked. "He's been arguing that one for thirty years, sweetheart. Save your breath."

Katie grinned. "Thanks, Mona." She reached across, swiped a piece of bacon off my plate, and bit into it. "Still crunchy. I'll allow it."

I looked at her like a daddy who still couldn't figure out when his little girl had learned to run the whole world. "You look tired. You even sleep anymore?"

"Only when the universe allows. You eat this junk every day?"

"Every other. Doctor told me to cut back."

"Doctor meant quit," she said. "You need to move around more. You don't even drive anymore, just tinker and grumble."

A slow grin spread across my face. "Grumblin' keeps the gears from rustin'."

She rolled her eyes, sipping her liquid energy. "You're impossible."

"Runs in the family."

For a few minutes, neither of us spoke. The café hummed around us. Plates clattering, someone laughing near the counter. Then Katie leaned forward, tone softening.

"Dad, we got that offer again for the old ten acres. The one with the overgrown fenceline and all those busted truck parts. You don't even use it anymore."

My gaze drifted to the window, fog thinning outside. "Place still got good dirt under it. Just needs someone to care for it."

"It's been twenty years," Katie said. "It's not a museum."

I nodded, not arguing, remembering. Mona passed by with a tray and tapped the table. "You two want a refill or a referee?"

Katie laughed. "Just coffee, Mona."

Mona poured and moved on, humming something off-key. Katie checked her watch. "I've gotta run. Work stuff piling up already."

"You even eat breakfast?"

She snagged my toast and tore off a bite. "Yup. Yours." She stood, drained the last of her coffee, and headed for the door. "Try to eat something green this week," her voice trailing over her shoulder.

"Only if bacon counts."

She smirked. "Love you, Dad."

"Love you too, kid."

When she left, I stared at the empty bench. The cup still steamed where she'd set it down. Sundays used to look just like this—me and Maggie and a booth full of laughter. Maggie loved the noise of Rusty Fork. The way Chef and Mona bickered like clockwork. For a second, I could almost see her smiling across the table, shaking her head at both of them. Still lost in that memory, the bell over the door jingled again, quick and urgent and Katie rushed back in, phone in hand.

"Dad, Colonel Merritt's been calling. Says it's important and you're not answering."

After another swallow of coffee, I responded. "It can wait 'til I finish my breakfast."

"Seriously?"

"Seriously." Smearing a napkin across my mouth, I garbled, "A man shouldn't make decisions on an empty stomach."

She sighed, half smiling despite herself. "You're hopeless."

"Runs in the family, remember?"

I shoved the last bite in my mouth, finished my brew, and stood. I slid a couple of tens out of my wallet and set them on the table but Mona swooped in before I could head for my jacket and set the check down.

"Twenty bucks on an eight-dollar meal . . . buying forgiveness, Mercer?"

"Hazard pay for listening to me."

"Next time bring Natasha. She'll have my 'OPEN' sign fixed before the coffee's brewed."

Outside the fog had lifted. Morning sunlight had finally caught the chrome on the dually and blinded me for a second. Katie kept pace with my long legs, heels ticking on wet pavement.

She kissed my cheek. "People to see, things to do. Think about the lot, okay?"

"Yeah, yeah."

"I mean it, Dad. It's sitting there."

I smiled. "So am I."

She rolled her eyes, laughed, and headed for that old truck of hers, being kept alive with Saturday tools and stubbornness since she was sixteen. I watched her go, climbed into my truck and let the idle settle into a low, steady growl as I reached for the phone on the dash.

The line clicked once, then carried that old gravel voice like it had rolled out of a sandstorm. "Buck. Been a long time."

"Colonel Merritt." I leaned back in the seat. "I figured you'd retired by now. Or been arrested."

Merritt chuckled a dry, worn sound. "They keep trying to retire me. I don't take the hint." "Yeah," I said. "Still got the same charm too."

There was a pause on the line, long enough to matter.

"Heard about Maggie," Merritt said quietly. "Didn't know how to call without soundin' like a damn Hallmark card."

I nodded, though Merritt couldn't see it. "Appreciate it, Colonel. She tried to keep me in line until her parting breath. Like my Aunt Joy told her—no one else would have me."

"She was a good woman," Merritt said. "Kept you alive through more than one campaign."

"More than one breakfast too."

The silence that followed wasn't awkward. It was familiar. The kind that comes between men who've already said everything once before. Finally, Merritt's tone shifted, steel replacing the gravel.

"All right, down to business. You ever run north of the Canadian border?"

"Once or twice. Why?"

"I've got four loads of classified hardware sitting in Cape Canaveral. They belong up near St. John's, Newfoundland. I need them there inside ten days."

I let out a short laugh. "You always were an optimist."

"I'm serious, Mercer. I spoke to Katie and already cleared it on your end, and your name is on the movement order. Carrier of record: Mercer Hauling & Recovery."

That made me sit up. "How the hell do you know it's on my end?"

"Because I put it there. You still got your crew?"

"Most of 'em," I said. "The rest I can find."

"Then find 'em. You're wheels up in forty-eight hours."

"Negative," I said flatly. "You'll have us in four days, not two. These aren't yard jockeys I'm calling. I need my A-team: Ron, Ducky, and Chad for the haul, Harley and Billy Bob for the piloting. The works. Half of 'em are scattered on jobs, and you know how long it takes to pull permits for a run that crosses that much ground."

"Mercer," Merritt said, voice tightening, "you never needed an excuse before."

"You know damn well you can't rush permits or customs," I said. "We do it right or we don't do it at all. Different world. Take it or leave it."

A pause, then that low rumble of approval only an old commander could give.

"You haven't changed."

"Neither have you," I said. "Still trying to run the world with a clipboard and bad coffee."

Merritt chuckled. "Four days, then. But when you roll, I want comms up and tracking live."

"Copy that."

"Good man," he said. "And Buck?"

"Yeah?"

"Good to hear your voice again."

"Same, Colonel."

The line went dead with a click that sounded too final for comfort.

I sat there for a moment, staring out as the last of the fog curled off the highway. Somewhere under the hum of the idling truck, I felt the old rhythm start up again. I thought I'd buried that with Maggie.

I thought of Bret Wallace, my right hand. The one man who could fix anything short of a broken promise. We met fifteen years back, the night his bowling alley caught fire. I was rolling home from a late run when I saw smoke curling over Main Street and pulled in. Roof gone. Neon sign half melted. Bret standing in the strobes of the fire trucks with ash in his hair, looking like somebody yanked the floor out from under him.

I walked up, handed him a jug of water, and said, "Hell of a night to quit smokin'."

He laughed once. The kind that hurts. "Guess I'll need a new career."

Next morning I showed up with a thermos and a shovel to help clean up and look for smoldering spots. "Startin' fresh," I told him. "Come help me with these trucks. Ain't much, but it's honest."

We've been at it ever since—he's the brain and I'm the brawn. Bret keeps everything running smoothly from home base unless I need him mobile with his parts-store-on-wheels for a big run. Two men held together by grit, bad jokes, and an unwritten code: if one of us breaks down, the other doesn't leave him on the shoulder.

I scrolled my contacts and tapped his name. He answered mid-yawn. "You better have my morning fix if you're callin' this early."

"You'll want more than coffee," I said. "Colonel Merritt called."

That woke him up fast. "Merritt? What's he done now?"

"Four loads of classified freight sitting in Cape Canaveral. Destination St. John's, Newfoundland. Ten-day window."

"Classified?" Bret said. "You always did find the quiet jobs."

"Yeah, well, we're rolling in four days. Same deal as before—permits, escorts, border paperwork. I told Merritt I'd need the A-team."

"I'm in," Bret said without hesitation. "Trailer's still sittin' at your place, right?"

"Right where you left it. Bring the dually, we'll start checking gear and calling the rest."

He laughed that low morning rumble that said he was already grabbing his boots. "Make a fresh pot, boss. Sounds like we're headed north again."

"Copy that," I said, and hung up.

For all the years we'd worked side by side, I never stopped trusting Bret's hands or his word. If I called at daylight, he showed by sunrise. Some friendships don't need speeches; they're built in grease and miles.

I thought next of Ron Calhoun. Nobody knew what the man had done before trucking and he liked it that way. He'd mention "long nights overseas" and "temporary duty stations" but if you asked for details, he'd grin and say, "You ever try to explain classified paperwork to a dispatcher?"

Once, I'd seen a folded flag and three passports in his glove box and decided not to ask. Whatever he'd done, it left him calm where other men cracked, the kind of steady that comes from surviving something you don't talk about.

I hit his number. It rang four times before the chaos started in the background. A woman barked, "Ronald Calhoun! You left the hose runnin' again!" Then another voice, younger: "Dad, I need a hundred for textbooks before noon!"

Ron sighed like a man losing a battle on two fronts. "Mercer, please tell me you're callin' to kidnap me."

"Depends how far you want to go."

"Far enough they can't find me 'til Christmas."

"You'll get your wish. Four loads, Cape Canaveral to Newfoundland. Merritt's behind it."

Ron whistled low. "You and that colonel. Every time you two talk, I end up sleep-deprived and half-frozen."

"Four days to the Cape. Same crew as before. You in?"

"I'm outta excuses and my boots already found my feet," he said. "Give me twelve hours to pack and kiss the wife goodbye. She yells every time I chase one of your fool runs; might as well earn it."

From the background came, "Earn what?!"

"Nothing, sweetheart!" he yelled back, then lowered his voice. "See you at sunrise."

The line clicked dead and I smiled. For all his mystery and quiet skill, Ron Calhoun still couldn't hide from domestic artillery fire. Whatever black-ops badge he once wore, these days his hardest mission was surviving Tuesday morning at home.

Then there was Ducky Carver.

I met him years ago when he was driving for a two-truck outfit out of Tulsa. His boss was the kind who paid late, cut corners, and called it "experience." Ducky was green and loyal to a fault, running junk equipment and hauling whatever fit on his deck. We'd talked on the phone back then. Me trying to steer him toward better work, him stubborn as a fence post.

"Can't leave, Buck," he'd say. "Gave the man my word."

Didn't matter that the man shorted his checks and sent him out overweight with bald tires. Ducky stayed until the day the outfit folded and his bossman vanished without warning.

That night he called me, voice flat. "Guess I'm out of a job."

"No, you're not," I told him. "You work for me now. Be in Mount Pleasant by morning."

He showed up with a duffel bag and a box of tools. Worked like he was trying to repay the world for giving him another shot. When I retired, I handed him one of my old trucks and the step-deck that matched it. Told him he'd earned it, not for skill, but for keeping his word when it would've been easier to walk away.

Now, years later, I found his number and hit send. The line picked up to wind gusts and the hollow thunk of someone smacking a vending machine.

"Pops? You picked a fine time to interrupt breakfast. Machine took my dollar and the chips are sitting there staring at me."

"Still arguing with snacks?" I asked.

"Yeah. So far they're winning. What's up?"

"Big one, four loads, Cape Canaveral to Newfoundland. Ten days."

He whistled. "You serious?"

"Dead. We will meet at my place in the morning. Bring the Kenworth, full gear, extra tarps, and your sense of humor."

"Guess my vacation's canceled."

"Didn't know you took one."

"Didn't either," Ducky said, laughing. "See you at sunrise."

When the call ended, I could see him in my mind standing beside that old W900L—coffee in one hand, pride in the other. Same kid who once stayed loyal to a bad boss because he'd promised he would. Some men are built from steel. Ducky Carver's built from his word.

Next was Chad Raines, though most folks around Baytown call him Preacher. Army Ranger, mechanic, and full-time man of God. He can drive anything with wheels and quote scripture while double-clutching through Houston traffic. When Merritt's name came up last time, Chad said, "If that man asked me to haul sand to the moon, I'd ask which truck do you want me in?"

He'd come home from the service quiet, like a man learning how to live in peace. Bought an old church that had lost its congregation, started fixing it board by board, and occasionally preached on Sundays to whoever wandered in—truckers, farmers, and kids who like free donuts. The rest of the week he hauled freight for me. Never missed a load, never missed a prayer.

I dialed his number. He picked up on the third ring over the sound of hammering.

"Mercer," he said, a little out of breath. "You caught me between preaching and patching the church roof. Thing's got more holes than last Sunday's attendance."

"Still moonlighting as a roofer?"

"Only on God's house. What's up?"

"Four loads out of Cape Canaveral. Classified. Ten-day window. Merritt's name is on it."

Nail gun popped once. Then: "Didn't think I'd hear that name again. What's the plan?"

"Four days to the Cape. Bret's in. Ron and Ducky too. Same crew, same rules."

"You'll have me," he said. "I'll finish patching this roof and tell the deacons to cover for me."

"Bring your Kenworth, your step-deck, and your Bible," I told him. "You're driving, and I've got a feeling we'll need a man of God on this one."

He laughed. "Truck's fueled, trailer's ready, Bible's on the dash."

"Sunrise at the yard."

"Copy that, Pops. Hang on a second."

I heard his boots scuff, then his voice dropped a notch. "Lord," he said, "You know the road better than we do. You know what's waiting between here and wherever this ends. I'm asking you to put your hand on Pops and every rig he calls for this job. Give us clear minds and steady hands. Keep evil out of our path and bring us home when the work is done. In Jesus' name, amen."

"Amen."

"Now I'll see you at sunrise."

The line went quiet except for wind through the rafters. I pictured him standing there, hammer in hand, sunlight spilling through broken boards. A soldier turned preacher, fixing what's left and still thanking God for it. If faith could haul freight, Chad Raines would've been first across the border.

By the time I scrolled to Harley Vance, the phone showed nearly noon. I hadn't talked to her or Billy Bob in a while so I had no idea where they were running these days. But with those two running pilot cars, they were never parked for long.

Harley runs lead no-nonsense, nerves like steel, and a voice that can clear traffic faster than a trooper with his lights on. She cut her teeth running wreckers through hurricane debris down in Biloxi. Tough woman. Tougher than most roads deserve.

Billy Bob Granger is her shadow and her opposite. Tail gunner since the day I met him. Born in Shreveport, raised on barbecue and bad ideas, he bounced around half the South before figuring out the only place he belongs is behind a CB mic. Loud, funny, and reckless on weekends, but I've never seen him lose a load or a friend. I always said if Harley was the steering wheel, Billy Bob was the brakes—squeaky, loud, and damned reliable when you needed them.

I hit dial. Harley answered on the third ring, her Bluetooth crackling under highway noise.

"Talk to me, Mercer. You callin' to bless our day or ruin it?"

"Depends who's drivin'."

"Then I better get back-up on the line," she said. "Hold up while I drag Billy Bob into this."

I listened to a couple of beeps and a short pause. "Mercer, you still there?" Harley came back.

"Still here. Billy Bob, you on?"

"Unfortunately," a second voice drawled. "You have both of us, Pops. We're halfway across Florida haulin' a fiberglass mouse house to Orlando. Looks like Disney needs a new backyard."

"So you're headed east," I said.

"Two days out, unless the usual idiots with cameras or minivans act up," Harley said. "You got something cooking?"

"Big one," I told her. "Four sealed loads, Cape Canaveral to Newfoundland. Delivery in about ten days and I need my best escorts."

A beat. Billy Bob whistled low. "Well, hell. We going north of the border? Hope Mickey don't mind."

Harley's tone tightened—not fear, focus. "Same crew?"

"Same crew," I said. "Bret, Ron, Ducky, Chad. We roll in four days. I want you two at the Cape ahead of us eyes on the site, see what you can lock down, link up with Merritt's people. When we hit Florida, you're the bookends. Lead and tail. Keep the world off our sheet metal."

Billy Bob snorted. "So basically, we're the welcome committee and the bouncer."

"Yeah," I said. "Just without the balloons."

"Copy that," Harley said. "We'll dump this carnival junk at Disney and head east. You'll have your lead and chase parked at the Cape by Thursday night."

"Try not to spook the Air Force on the way in."

Harley laughed once, short and sharp. "If they get jumpy, we'll smile."

"Or she'll yell," Billy Bob added. "Works better than warning lights half the time."

"Still got that big amber light on your dash?" I asked.

"Bright, loud, and judgmental," Billy Bob said. "Same as always."

"Good," I told him. "You'll need it."

"Roger that, Pops," Harley said. "We'll clear things up front and watch your tail."

The line buzzed a moment before Billy Bob added, "Tell Mona we said hi and to keep the coffee hot. Sounds like you're bringin' a circus."

"Copy," I said. "See you at the Cape."

When the call ended, I leaned back and watched a line of trucks slide by on the highway. Harley and Billy Bob had been with me on some of the worst hauls of my life—bridge collapses, tornado runs, and one snowstorm so bad the rigs froze solid. They never complained, never quit, and always laughed louder than the storm.

If Bret was my right hand, Ron my cool head, Ducky my heart, and Chad my conscience, then Harley and Billy Bob were my eyes. Like an owl, Harley's pilot car on point out front, Billy Bob's pilot car guarding the tail, keeping the world off our back. The kind of people you don't have to call twice.

Calls done, the phone was quiet again. I sat there for a minute, watching the midday warmth ghost off the pavement and trucks drift past like memories with mirrors. Every one of those names on my screen was more than a driver. They were the kind God builds for storms—different shapes, same steel. Bret with steady hands. Ron with that soldier calm. Ducky with a heart too loyal for his own good. Chad with his prayers and busted knuckles. Harley and Billy Bob raising hell at both ends of the line. I've hauled freight with a lot of folks, but only a few I'd trust with my life. These are them. I figure somewhere along the line the good Lord looked down and decided a bunch of misfits needed each other more than we needed sense. Seems like every time the world gets heavy, He steers us back into the same lane.

I thumbed the ignition and realized the old girl was still idling. How long had I been sitting here? I borrowed a line I'd heard Chad say half to himself, half to heaven: "Lord, even if we can't be perfect, keep us safe while we're rolling."

The Rusty Fork's lot was thinned out. The breakfast crowd long gone, a few pickups idled under the noon sun, and the smell of burgers drifted out of the kitchen vent. I'd been sitting there since Katie left me with orders to call the Colonel, piecing together a job big enough to wake the dead and maybe me along with it. I rubbed my scruffy jaw and scrolled to Katie's number. She answered on the second ring, voice bright and busy.

"Hey, Dad. Calling to report you ate something fried for lunch?"

"Worse," I said. "We got a job."

She groaned softly. "Let me guess… Merritt."

"So he talked to you."

"Yeah," she said. "About an hour ago. Said he wanted to 'confirm availability,' which is code for 'your dad's about to be gone for a while.' What he didn't tell me was the destination."

"The Merritt kind," I said. "Four loads. Cape Canaveral to Newfoundland. Classified freight. Ten days."

There was a shuffle, then Katie said, "I'm putting you on speaker."

A click. Then Natasha's voice, faint but sharp: "Did he say Newfoundland? Katie and I were going through invoices. Merritt didn't mention Canada."

"Well," I told them, "You two might want to wrap up what you're doing. We roll in four days. I want you both at the house in the morning with Bret. We need to plan this trip."

"Oh, we'll be there," Katie said. "But before we get buried in your trip you remember that yard we talked about selling? The one you keep calling a project even though nothing's been alive there since Mom's garden died?"

I groaned. "You two been conspiring?"

Natasha laughed. "We call it financial triage. If you're hauling for Merritt again, we need every dollar of working capital we can find."

"It's fine," I said. "I'll pull from savings if I have to."

"No, you won't," Katie shot back. "This run'll pay off big enough, but we still need cash up front for permits, fuel, escorts. The whole mess. That yard is sitting there—let's use it. You're the one who taught us to think like operators, not wishful thinkers."

Sunlight flashed off a passing feed truck as I stared through the windshield, jaw tight. "It's Maggie's land," I said quietly.

They both went quiet a moment before Natasha spoke, softer now. "She'd want it put to work, Pops."

I let the dually idle through the silence before answering. "Bring the paperwork in the morning. I'll look it over."

Katie's voice warmed. "We will. Seven a.m. Coffee in hand."

"Make it strong," I said. "Looks like I'll need it."

"Love you, Dad."

"Love you too, kids."

I ended the call, set the phone back in the cradle, and looked through the café windows. Mona had swapped the specials board for the lunch crowd—barbecue sandwiches today. The neon sign flickered in the sun, and the highway hummed soft and steady beyond town. I let the diesel settle into its easy rhythm and eased out of the lot. The road home shimmered in the heat, mirages dancing over the black top. As I turned up the long gravel drive, the tool trailer sat waiting behind the fence, gleaming faintly in the midday sun. I parked in front of the house, killed the engine, and sat for a breath. Gus barked once from the porch, tail thumping like he already knew.

"All right, Maggie," I said under my breath, smiling. "One more run."

Journal Entry 1

Day zero and I'm already tired of the phone.

Sat in Rusty Fork's parking lot while Merritt dropped his little ten-day bomb on me. Spent the rest of the afternoon with a dead-cold coffee and a phone that wouldn't quit.

Called Bret first, then Ron, Ducky, and Chad. Harley and Billy Bob said yes before I finished asking. Chad prayed over the run like he'd been waiting on it.

Katie had that tone that's half business, half worry. Natasha backed her up on the numbers. They're better at this part than I ever was. Tomorrow they'll be at the house with Bret and a stack of paperwork I've been avoiding.

Trucks are still scattered wherever the last load left them. Tonight, nothing moves. That's fine. Day zero matters.

Cast the line and set the hook. Make the promise: bring them out, bring them back.

Tomorrow, we start earning it.

—Pops

Chapter 2

THE CREW AND THE PROMISE

Morning came slow over the yard as steam lifted off the gravel from last night's rain. A crow perched on the shop roof, sounding like a squeaky hinge that needed oil. I sat at the kitchen table looking out the window, warming my hands on a steaming mug of coffee, the kind that could strip chrome.

Gus wandered under the table, tail thumping once. He'd been around since Maggie was alive, a gangly pup who chewed through one of her garden hoses and looked proud about it. I can still see her chasing him with a towel, laughing and yelling, "You're lucky I like you, fur-brain!" Now the old hound's muzzle was silver and when he sighed it sounded like a tired truck setting its brakes.

The kitchen smelled of burnt toast and memory. The radio on the counter murmured through static until I found the farm report.

"This is your Tuesday, February twelfth, Farm Bureau update. Freeze warnings through the Northeast, gust advisories up the Florida and Carolina coasts, and soy prices holding steady."

I nodded to nobody in particular. February always did sound like trouble.

The table was a battlefield of mail, half-folded maps, and one blue folder labeled Yard Sale—Final Documents. Katie must've dropped it off quiet enough after I'd gone to bed, she hadn't even woken Gus. I flipped it open expecting closing papers and found more than that. Tucked behind the deed packet was a printed email stamped across the top:

···✦✦◆✦✦···

MOVEMENT PACKAGE: "IRON REACH / FROST-LINE" (FOUR UNITS) – ROUTE Florida (FL) → Maine (ME) → Newfoundland (NL)

From: Col. Merritt

Attachments: route.pdf   permits.zip   manifests.pdf

Team:

You are tasked to transport four sealed units of crated military equipment.

Do not open; seals will be in place upon arrival at the Cape. All units will be tarped prior to your arrival, and the tarps must remain intact and fully secured for the duration of transport due to the sensitive nature of freight. Bring extra tarps in case of damage during transit. Maintain full security coverage.

All units are considered oversize and overweight, requiring the following:

- Two pilot cars assigned to the convoy for the full route.
- Continuous police coordination through every jurisdiction as required by state permit.

- Travel limited to daylight hours unless otherwise authorized.
- No visual access to interior contents, sensitive material, military eyes only.
- Maintain two-truck spacing during escorted movement.
- Communications (comms): Primary: Natasha Cole (Ops) will maintain live routing updates; Bret Wallace will serve as comms backup and field liaison.
- Destination: Port aux Basques ferry → forward movement to Frostline Forward Operating Site (FOS FROSTLINE) per attached routing.

Questions or deviations to be directed to my office prior to change.

—Col. Merritt

·· ✦ ✦ ✦ ✦ ··

I set the page down and rubbed my thumb over the corner. Whatever this job was, it wasn't simple freight. Sizeable, sealed, and secret. That meant heavy, real heavy, and it meant I'd better start thinking about what gear we'd need to move it.

I ran the job in my head. I'd be driving my old W900L and pulling my tri-axle removable gooseneck trailer—RGN—named for the specialized hitch on the front. To explain, the hitch, or gooseneck, stays connected to the semi-truck and detaches from the trailer leaving the trailer deck sitting on the ground like a ramp. It's got about twenty-nine feet of load space on the bottom with another short section at the rear that slopes up. Wheeled loads can be driven right onto the deck while other oversized pieces are usually lowered on by crane. Once everything is secured, the semi, with the neck attached, would back up, hook it, lock the pins, and lift the front until it's level again. Rolling height's about eighteen inches off the pavement, kept low intentionally so over-height loads clear the underside of bridges.

I took another sip of my morning jolt and watched the steam twist. The kind of gear we'd need said plenty about the kind of job Merritt was calling in.

Headlights swept across the blinds. A door slammed outside. Three voices: Katie's, Bret's, and Nat's drifted up the walk, half-arguing, half-laughing. Bret had parked his Ram 3500 dually on the other side of the fence so he could hook up to the tool trailer. The trailer doors were painted with the Mercer Ops logo, and inside was everything from air lines and alternators to coffee filters and hope. It wasn't fancy, but it was the heartbeat that kept the rest of us moving when things broke. A rack of antennas ran across the dually's roof: comms, GPS, and one he swore could talk to Mars. Natasha always took care of computer operations from headquarters—state permits, fuel, escorts, federal, state, or local regulations—but once we were on the road Bret handled communications, routing, and any trouble a computer couldn't fix. Around here, he was our insurance policy with a socket set.

Gus barked once, announcing them.

Katie led the charge, ponytail catching sunlight. "Dad!" she hollered from the porch. "You decent or still pretending retirement means boxer shorts and a bathrobe?"

"Retirement means whatever keeps the neighbors nervous," I said, opening the door.

Bret carried a folder thick enough to stop a bullet. Natasha balanced two steaming cups of joe in one hand and her ever-present tablet in the other. She'd been that way since she was sixteen—steady, precise, too sharp for her own good sometimes. Back then, she was the kid who spent more nights on our couch than at her own house. Maggie found her one night sitting on the bleachers after a high school football game, trying not to cry. By morning she was brushing her teeth with one of Katie's spares and pretending it was temporary. It never was.

"Morning, Pops," she said now, handing me a cup. "You look like a man about to do something fiscally irresponsible."

I smiled. "Guess it runs in the family."

We gathered around the kitchen table where Maggie and I used to pay bills and pray the numbers liked each other.

Katie slid the deed paperwork forward. "All right. The buyer wired the deposit. This makes it official—you're selling the old lot."

I stared at the page. The word "transfer" looked too final. "You sure about this, Katie-girl?"

"It's my name on the deed, remember?" she said gently. "Mom put it in my trust years ago. You forgot because you were too busy fixing trucks and ignoring doctors."

I snorted. "And apparently teaching you how to sneak around like a cat burglar."

Katie grinned. "You were asleep. Didn't want to wake you or Gus."

"You could've left a note."

"Would've ruined the suspense."

The silence that followed was thick but kind. Gus shifted under the table, tail brushing our boots. Bret cleared his throat. "That lot's been more rust than income for years. It's time."

Natasha nodded. "The sale covers fuel and oversize permits, you know. The states' way of saying they'll let you drag something bigger than usual down their road as long as you follow their rules."

Although legal loads top out around eight-and-a-half feet wide and eighty thousand pounds total, the oversize/overweight loads we usually haul laugh at both those numbers. Before we roll, every state we enter must sign off telling us what route to take, when we can move, and what we'd better avoid.

She flipped her tablet around, a smirk tugging at her lip. "Oh, Merritt called again. Wanted to make sure we got the email about the mess we'll be hauling to the frozen tundra."

I chuckled. "Yeah, he's still writing like he's billing the alphabet."

"Pretty much," Nat said.

I looked up at her—the face that had gone from teenage trouble to the calm center of every storm I've had since. "You know, Mattie and I never did figure out how to thank you for coming back."

Nat blinked, thrown off for a second. "For what?"

"For all of it. You could've stayed gone. You had that big engineering job, a parking space, bonuses and coffee machines that talked. But you came home anyway, sat down at that folding table with a half-dead laptop and built Mercer Ops from scratch."

She shrugged. "I was burned out on boardrooms, and permits don't lie to you."

Katie laughed. "That's debatable."

I sipped my coffee. "You two made this place work again. Your mama'd be proud."

Katie leaned her elbows on the table. "This isn't just about closing a chapter, Dad. It's about funding the next one."

I traced a ring stain on the table. "Your mama loved that yard. Said the weeds made it look alive."

Natasha smiled. "She also said you couldn't organize a tool-box if your life depended on it."

We all laughed and the tension cracked like ice in spring.

When the papers were signed, I leaned back and looked out toward the shop. "I remember when we bought that land. She planted wildflowers along the fence and said, 'Someday this'll be worth something more than money.' Guess she was right."

Katie touched my hand. "It always has been."

We packed up the folders and walked out to the yard together. Morning had turned bright. Bret and Nat headed for their vehicles, still debating permit software updates.

Katie lingered, watching me scratch Gus's ear. "Try not to make this run harder than it has to be," she said. "And don't forget, Nat stays here. Someone's gotta make sure you don't end up on the nightly news."

I grinned. "Wouldn't be the first time."

By noon the yard was filled with diesel and reunion.

First came Ron, easing his Peterbilt through the gate like a man driving a memory. His '87 Pete 379 still turned heads, six hundred horses, Cat engine under the hood, about eighteen hundred fifty pounds of torque, and a tri-axle lowboy behind it built to carry sins and steel in equal measure. Old paint, clean lines, and enough motor to climb a wall if it's paved right. Ron doesn't talk much, but that truck sure does.

Chad rolled in behind him, chrome flashing in the sun, his tri-axle step-deck following close and square. The '99 W900L looked ready to pick a fight with the wind. Six hundred horse-power, also eighteen hundred fifty pounds of torque, and turned up as far as she'll go. She doesn't pass many fuel stops, but she'll pass everything else when he's in the mood. Behind it, the step-deck rides low and tight with chains hanging off the back like Mr. T's jewelry.

Ducky showed last—late, loud, and grinning, pulling in with his '05 W900L and pulling that ratty old tri-axle step-deck that somehow clears every scale on charm. You could read the load plan looking at his trailer.

A step-deck has two levels. At the front is a short upper section about eight feet long and five feet off the ground, then a three-foot drop to the forty-five-foot lower deck and riding about three feet off the pavement. That drop is similar to an RGN in that it lets us carry taller loads without smacking the underside of bridges, but loaded from the back with ramps. There are three axles to spread the weight evenly so the DOT boys at the scale house don't start complaining. For comparison, when you're out driving on the interstate, a flatbed is one long, straight platform, riding about five feet off the asphalt and carrying standard height, open deck freight.

They parked, stretched, and gathered by the shop door. I stood in the center with a clipboard I didn't need, but it made me look official.

"All right, folks," I said. "Here's the deal. We've got a classified haul leaving at dawn three days from now. Colonel Merritt's people want it quiet and fast. Bret's handling permits. Nat stays here managing comms and routing. Ron, you're lead. Chad, you're in the rear. Ducky, you're my wing man. We pick up Billy Bob and Harley at the Cape."

Ducky whistled. "Classified, huh? Last time we heard that word, we ended up threading a storm with a generator strapped to the deck."

Ron folded his arms, "And Pops still said yes."

The air went still for a second, then somebody let out a breath they didn't know they were holding, and we all laughed because if we didn't laugh now, the worry would start too early.

Bret flipped a page. "We'll run I-30 east out of Mount Pleasant, then US 59 around Texarkana, I-49 south to I-220 and I-20 into Jackson. From there, US 49 south to US 98 east, catch I-10 across Mobile, then I-295 and I-95 down to the Cape. Two-day run. Overnight in Mobile at the Oasis, near the Alabama line. About five hundred twenty miles the first day, five-fifty the next."

Nat pointed at her tablet. "I'll be tracking you from here. If anything goes sideways, call before you start improvising."

"We always do," Chad assured.

Ducky smirked. "What if the satellite's watching?"

"Smile," she said. "At least Merritt will know which idiot to yell at first."

As the laughter settled, Ron looked toward the old diner sign down the highway. "You think we'll hit Granny D's before we cross into Florida?"

"Wouldn't miss it," I said. "Granny D's still got her CB tuned to channel nineteen. She'll know we're coming."

Chad nodded. "That woman's pie got me through rough times."

Ducky grinned. "She's got a slice for every occasion."

"Only if you tip good," I said.

Time to go. The sound of engines filled the yard again, one by one, those big diesels waking up, stacks breathing black. Gus barked once, circling the trucks like he was blessing them. Katie stood by the gate, arms folded, hiding her worry.

I climbed into the W900, settled into the seat, and turned the key. The starter grumbled once, then that big Cummins engine caught with a deep cough and a slow, rolling idle that filled the cab like a heartbeat. Gauges flickered awake, needles stretching after sleep. The radio clicked alive with a whisper of static, then a DJ's voice easing through a steel-guitar intro. I turned it down to a hum, just enough to feel the day coming awake.

I eased her into gear. Ron pulled out first, his old Pete settling into the lane like it had done a thousand times. I followed his taillights, Ducky fell in behind me, and Chad brought up the rear. Bret swung out last, tool trailer rattling.

"Try not to break anything important!" Katie hollered. "And that includes yourselves!"

Ducky leaned out his window and yelled back, "No guarantees!"

Katie shook her head, smiling despite herself. Gus barked once as we rolled past the fence, like he was seeing us off.

By Texarkana the fog had burned off, and the road opened wide. Ducky came on the radio: "Running empty, this might be the last time we see seventy-five all week."

Ron laughed. "Then let's open them up."

We hit I-49 south. The pavement opened and a tailwind pushed us toward Shreveport. The trucks ran light with no loads to hold us back. Chrome flashing, pipes barking, we blew by a couple of reefers like they were up on blocks.

"Y'all forget something back there?" one of them called over nineteen.

"Yeah," Ducky shot back. "Your girlfriend!"

Laughter rolled through the speakers.

Outside Shreveport, traffic funneled into a work zone, barrels, cones, and a guy in a hard hat staring at his phone like he was running air traffic control.

Bret called from the dually: "Left lane ends quick. Ease out of it."

We crawled past orange barrels that looked like they'd been through a war. A bull hauler came charging up the open lane, chrome lit up like a carnival, horn bellowing as he threaded the gap.

Ron whistled. "There goes the smell of money."

"Man's got a schedule and a trailer full of steak," I said.

"Bet they all think we're sightseeing," Chad added.

"Copy that," Ducky said. "But sightseeing at seventy-five mph."

Once clear of Monroe, LA, we opened them back up rolling fast and smooth. I-20 straightened out ahead—that endless gray ribbon running toward Jackson.

"Smokey at the one-five-nine eastbound," came a voice from a flatbed up ahead.

"Copy that," Ron said. "He's got his eyes on the radar, not his coffee."

We dropped a couple miles per hour, played nice through that stretch, and watched him in the mirror until his car disappeared.

By Jackson, MS, it was early afternoon and we had blown through a half tank of fuel. Bret called it.

"Petro Truckstop off the next exit then take a left. Fuel up, refill thermoses if you got 'em, and pretend to check tires."

We pulled in, hoods glinting under the canopy lights. The fuel island was stacked with rigs, dry vans, reefers, a grain hopper, and one car hauler trying to look patient. I walked the length of the truck and trailer checking tires and lights, kicked a few tires to prove I cared, and leaned on the fender while Bret topped off the dually. Ducky wandered in for coffee and came back with a cinnamon roll the size of a hubcap. "Snack of champions," he said.

"Or diabetics," Chad muttered.

The radio stayed lively when we rolled back out thirty minutes later. A flatbed behind us keyed up: "Y'all running late for something?"

"Nah. Just showing the kids what horsepower looks like."

"Copy that," he laughed. "If I don't see you again, y'all be safe."

We merged onto US 49 south, pine trees flashing past in green waves. Sunlight bounced off mirrors and chrome, and for the first time in a long while the world felt wide open.

By the time we caught US 98 east towards Mobile, the sun was sliding low and the sky turned pink behind the mirrors. We rolled past the state line under a billboard that said, "Welcome to Alabama—Home of Sweet Tea and Speed Traps."

Ron keyed up. "You think they mean that second part?"

Bret laughed. "They mean it."

We eased out of it just enough to look innocent.

Long past sundown, we chugged to a stop at the Oasis Café outside Mobile. The air was thick with sea salt and the place glowed like a ship—neon buzzing, pumps blinking like tired eyes. A big sign promised REAL FOOD, CLEAN SHOWERS, AND QUESTIONABLE COFFEE.

Inside, the diner was half-empty but alive. Booths of drivers trading lies, a jukebox humming something half-country, half-static. The air smelled of bacon fat, onion rings, and the kind of hope that only exists at midnight on the road. Every meal, and I mean EVERY meal is served in a metal pie tin. Yup, you heard right—whether it's pork chops and mashed potatoes with gravy, a taco salad, or a piece of pie, you're eating out of a pie tin and that's how Granny D wanted it. No risk of breaking, no replacement costs, nothing fancy.

The flat screen over the counter flickered with a Weather Channel segment:

"Good evening! Here's your Tuesday, February twelfth travel update," the anchor said. "A cold front is pushing across the Mississippi Valley bringing fog and light rain from Shreveport through Mobile. Expect gusty crosswinds on I-10 later tonight and sticky conditions due to the rain on elevated bridges."

Granny D, back by the grill, swung around to face the TV. "It's 'SLICK conditions,' honey, not 'sticky.' Somebody send that man back to grade school!"

Granny D's daughter, Maria, snorted. "Mom, you've been correcting the Weather Channel for years."

"And they still haven't learned," she said, snapping her towel.

"Well, if it ain't Pops Mercer," Maria called, spotting me at the door. "Thought you finally parked for good."

"Retired," I said. "In theory."

Maria shook her head. "You were born with diesel in your blood, Pops. Only thing you're retired from is admitting it."

Still back in the kitchen, that familiar voice barked again, "Tell Ducky to wipe his boots before he tracks mud on my clean floor!"

Ducky froze mid-step. "How does she always know?"

Granny D emerged holding a pie tin. "Because Sugar, God gave me eyes, ears, and security cameras. Now sit your behind down before I correct your posture and your grammar."

He grinned. "Ain't nothin' wrong with my . . ."

"Isn't," she cut in sharply, flipping the pie tin onto the counter. "Isn't anything wrong. Lord help your poor English teacher."

The place erupted in laughter as we slid into a booth, chrome trim worn smooth by a thousand rough hands. Maria slid empty mugs onto the table, seemingly able to make them stop in front of each of us and started filling them with mud while Granny D made her rounds, her towel draped over one shoulder like a badge. We all ordered piles of food like we hadn't eaten all week: chicken fried steak and eggs, bacon double cheeseburger with tater tots, fried catfish with fries and hushpuppies, and two more heart attacks on a plate that I can't remember.

Behind the counter hung an old photo of Papa T, grinning in a faded Notre Dame cap, arm around a younger Maria. He'd been a godly man with the kind of charm that could sell ice water to Eskimos and make them thank him for it. A few years back, the good Lord called him home. Maria left her tech job, stock options, fancy coffee drinks that cost more than fuel and came back to help her mama keep this place alive for the truckers. You could see their personal touches in every inch of the café: Granny D had Papa T's cap nailed above the register and Maria's new espresso machine somehow still smelled like cinnamon.

Granny D caught me looking at the picture. "He'd be proud, you know."

"Of the café?" I asked.

"Of you hard-headed boys still out here chasing the horizon. I remember when Maggie used to make you sit right there while she paid the bill. Said if she didn't, you'd end up buying coffee for the entire highway."

I smiled. "Sounds about right."

Her eyes softened for half a breath before she snapped the towel again. Having cleared away our dinner tins, she set down plates of pie and rested a hand on my shoulder.

"Now eat this pie before I decide you don't deserve it."

Ducky pointed at her. "That right there's why I missed this place."

"But I didn't miss your mouth," she shot back. "Eat."

We shoved pie into our faces until the metal plates were mostly silver again. Ron told a story about hauling a bulldozer into a hurricane zone, and Granny D interrupted twice—once to fix his verb tense and once to hand him a napkin.

When I reached for the check, she smacked my hand lightly. "You boys bring me back a good story instead. Preferably one that doesn't end in jail."

I smiled. "No promises."

As we headed for the door, she called after us, "Weather's got teeth tonight. Don't let it bite you."

Out in the lot, the rigs slept; chrome glowing in the neon spill. I leaned against my fender, listening to the tick of cooling metal and the faint laughter from inside the diner. Tomorrow the road would start calling names again. For tonight it whispered, "Rest while you can."

Journal Entry 2

Day one always starts louder than it should.

Engines barked to life, coughing out the last of their rest.

The crew rolled in one by one, some half awake, some already grinning like fools who forgot what they signed up for.

Bret had the tablet glowing, Ron was already checking straps that didn't need checking, and Ducky managed to spill coffee on a clean shirt before we hit the highway.

Felt good seeing it all again—same faces, same habits, same noise.

By midmorning we were pointed east, empty decks and full hearts, sunlight bouncing off mirrors like it remembered our names.

Jackson by dark. Fuel, jokes, pie on the mind.

Granny D fed us like she always does, with pie big enough to make a man rethink retirement.

First miles behind us, a thousand waiting ahead.

Not a bad start.

—Pops

Chapter 3

BETWEEN COFFEE AND COASTLINE

Bret had us circle up in the Oasis lot before the sun even yawned. Clipboard in one hand and caffeine in the other, his look meant somebody was about to get told how the world works. Rigs idled behind us in a loose half-moon, air drying off stacks in pale breaths. You could hear the soft hiss of valves and the tick of warm metal as the night let go.

"Quick safety brief," he said. "We're empty to the Cape, so don't drive like you're hauling thousands of pounds and don't drive like you're trying to impress anybody either. Empty trailers can get pushed around by high winds. Stopping is even worse. Settle down before somebody does something dumb and we derail this trip before we even get loaded."

He pointed with the clipboard as he called the order. "Running order is Pops up front, then Ron, Ducky, Chad, and I'll take the rear. If anybody sneezes wrong, I'm the one mopping up the mess."

He patted his dually. "I've got airbags, alternator, belts, hoses, filters, lines and fittings, spare markers and tires, twenty jugs of oil, tarps, straps, a big breaker bar, and a toolbox that would make Harbor Freight blush. That's good considering how you boys treat equipment—like it's a rental with good insurance. Let's get some chow."

After Granny D regaled our hearts with laughable stories we've heard a hundred times and filled our bellies with eggs, bacon, sausage, biscuits and gravy, and toast with homemade apple butter, we piled back into our rigs. Ducky's step-deck gave its usual shake when he hit the throttle, a little rattle rolling down the frame.

"That rattle adds character," he said.

Bret didn't blink. "DOT doesn't grade on personality. Fix it. Make sure your coffee lid's tight—let's not be wearing it today."

Engines came awake in the cold, one by one. Granny D stood in the diner doorway holding that pot of go-go juice like a scepter. "Keep it between the ditches!"

"Best we can," I said as I eased the Kenworth toward the exit.

Mirrors wet with condensation, glass clean, gauges steady. The lot lights fell away in the side glass as the line formed behind me—Ron, Ducky, Chad, Bret—five rigs breathing in the early morning darkness and ready to go earn their keep. The morning was still mostly night, but the road was waiting.

We were soon east of Mobile. The city long behind us, highway stretching flat and gray all the way to forever. Our empty trailers bounced making every joint in the road sound like applause. You could feel it through the seat—steel humming, tires whispering. The hood floating a little freer. The air smelled like the promise of rain.

Ron came over the radio first. "Set your cruise and stay awake. I-10's ours till the world ends."

Bret answered, "Great, now it knows where to find us."

Five empties, feeling good. Chrome bright, stacks barking, mirrors throwing sunlight. We weren't heavy, so we rolled quick—five grown men acting like kids who got out early for recess.

Traffic stayed light until we caught a line of box trucks running nose-to-tail.

"Slow truck traffic ahead," I said.

Ducky laughed. "I'll show 'em what horsepower looks like."

"Hold your horses, cowboy," Bret warned. "This ain't the Daytona Five Hundred."

One by one we eased around the line—blinkers on, checking mirrors. A tourist in a silver SUV tried to squeeze between Ron and Ducky halfway through.

Ron muttered, "He's got rental-car confidence."

Ducky said, "Bet he thinks 'CB' stands for Cruise Button."

Bret came back dry as toast. "Keep it polite, boys. They've got kids, and you've got insurance rates."

A camper van drifted across the white line.

Chad keyed up. "That camper is sponsored by Dramamine."

"Don't laugh," Ron said. "They're probably livestreaming how free they feel right before they sideswipe a barrel."

"Freedom's dangerous," Bret said. "Stay clear. We'll pass when he remembers which lane he's supposed to be in."

When we finally hit a stretch of open asphalt, Ducky mashed his throttle. The empty step-deck barked hard, turbo spooling up.

"Ease up!" Bret barked.

Ducky groaned, "You ruin all my fun."

"Manners are cheaper than a tow bill," Bret said.

The CB stayed alive—old stories, new jabs, no silence. Somebody brought up the worst diners they'd eaten in while someone else bragged about out-braking a trooper on a downgrade. Nothing heroic. The kind of talk that fills those long miles.

A hawk glided low over the median, head tilted like it'd never seen a line of trucks before. I wondered how many convoys it had seen crawl across this same slab of asphalt. Probably shook its head the same way Bret did every time Ducky opened his mouth.

By the time the Escambia Bay Bridge came up, the clouds were heavy over the Gulf and the wind started leaning on the trailers. Still, we were in good spirits. Five rigs running empty, mist starting to speckle the glass, engines humming in perfect rhythm.

Bret's voice cut through the laughter. "All right, settle it down. We're empty and the pavement's gonna get slick. Keep your spacing and let's pull it back about five mph. Last thing I need is one of you sliding into someone's YouTube video."

Ron snorted. "Copy that, Safety Mom."

"Call me what you want," Bret said.

We all eased back together, convoy settling into a calmer rhythm. The laughter softer now but still there. Five friends running empty, still chasing the line between fun and smart, and the rain deciding what to do next. By Pensacola, the mist had turned to honest rain, big drops slapping the hood and crawling down the glass in crooked lines. The road got slick fast, and the smell of wet asphalt mixed with diesel. Construction cones closed the right lane, funneling us into a crawl behind a fleet of trucks.

"Every time I hit Pensacola, somebody's rebuilding the same mile of road," I said.

"Job security," Ron answered.

A pair of white company trucks ran ahead, side-by-side, playing a game of my lane, your lane. One had his blinker on for five miles; the other was drafting a dump truck close enough to check his load. I figuratively puffed my chest pretending I might actually pull over and get jiggy with these two.

"Hey eastbound with the green logo. Pick a lane before I pick it for you."

No answer.

"Bet he's on the phone with dispatch asking for permission to complete the pass," Ducky said.

"Or how to do it," Bret added.

The CB cracked with laughter.

We slowed through the work zone, orange barrels leaning in the wind and puddles shining with oil rainbows. An excavator sat half-sunk in the mud, its operator staring out blankly.

Once clear, I dropped back to sixty and eased around a line of slower rigs—flatbeds stacked with pipe, a reefer bleeding cold vapor into the rain, a box truck with "Fresh Produce" on the side that looked like it hadn't seen a farm since the Reagan years.

Chad came over the radio. "Pops, you passing that reefer?"

"Yeah," I said. "He's losing speed faster than a politician in church."

We settled into a rhythm passing one rig, falling in behind another, every windshield wiper thumping out its own beat.

Bret's voice broke in. "Watch out boys. Wind's picking up. Trailers are starting to wag their tails."

I turned down the CB and flipped on the old AM/FM for a minute. Some DJ out of Pensacola was doing a weather update between Conway Twitty songs. "Rain all the way to Tallahassee," he said. "Stay home if you can."

"Too late for that," I muttered.

The next song rolled in—steel guitar, slow and familiar. I turned it up just enough to drown the wiper squeak. Fat drops of rain splattered loud against the windshield.

Gus's leash hung on the handle of the passenger door where I'd left it back at the yard, and for a second I thought about Maggie and all the times she sat beside me with that same music rolling low.

"Pops, you alive up there?" Ron asked.

"Still breathing," I said. "Just remembering when country sounded like heartbreak instead of karaoke."

"Now you're showing your age," Ducky said.

"Watch your spacing. That RV's weaving like he's drunk," I said.

A Winnebago drifted across the right line and back. The driver was staring at his phone like it held the map to heaven.

Bret keyed up. "Copy that. If he drifts again, let him have the shoulder."

Rain thickened, windshield wipers losing the race.

"Anybody listening to books on tape?" Chad asked. "My radio sounds like it's under water."

Ron said, "Ducky tried one once but said the guy's voice put him to sleep."

Ducky replied, "That was a self-help book. I don't need help."

"Clearly," Bret said. "Stick to comic books."

I grinned. "That explains his driving."

We all laughed again. The kind that comes easy even when the weather doesn't.

By Crestview, traffic stacked up behind a pair of semis crawling uphill, rain hammering steady. A pickup with kayaks in the bed went flying past on the shoulder like it was late for a funeral. Bret sighed. "Natural selection in progress."

"Hope he packed a snorkel," Ron said.

Past DeFuniak Springs, the rain turned heavy enough to blur the horizon. Wipers beat time like a metronome losing patience. We slowed to fifty-five, keeping tight enough to see each other's markers but loose enough not to share bumpers. A cattle hauler blew by doing eighty, spray hitting so hard it sounded like gravel on the hood.

"That guy's in a hurry to get to the next weigh station," Ron chided.

"Or he's washing the cows," Bret laughed.

"Maybe both," I said. "Bet those cows smell better than he does."

The CB popped again. Ducky hummed a few bars of some song none of us could place.

"Please stop," Chad begged.

"Don't stifle art," Ducky crowed.

"Call it what you want," I moaned. "It's still off-key."

Bret laughed quietly. "And they wonder why I drink black coffee by the gallon."

Between the clouds, sunlight cut through in thin stripes, lighting the wet asphalt ahead like silver ribbons. For a few minutes the rain eased, just enough for the tires to stop throwing walls of spray. "Looks like the worst of the storm is sliding north," Ron commented hopefully.

"Don't jinx it," Bret replied. "These clouds hear everything."

We rolled toward Marianna, five rigs on one long ribbon of wet road. The radios hummed, laughter still flickering in the static. We weren't ahead of anything; we were chasing the storm, rain thickening by the mile.

Near Tallahassee the rain picked up again, heavy enough to erase the horizon. Wipers worked overtime, the glass shimmering with sheets of water and the blurred glow of taillights. Traffic bunched up behind blinking arrows and orange cones protecting equipment stretched across the median like steel skeletons.

A set of company doubles ahead kept bouncing on every joint in the road, with each hit spraying a rooster tail of water high enough to wash a billboard.

"Why are those doubles out here in this weather? Those trailers are dancing all over the place. Remind me, how many brains do they issue per fleet?" I asked.

"One per terminal, and that's shared," Bret laughed.

The line crawled for nearly an hour—trucks stacked nose-to-tail, brake lights glowing red through the mist. My left leg was starting to cramp from the clutch work.

"Somebody call the weather hotline and tell 'em we're canceling Florida," Ducky whined.

"No refunds," Chad replied. "You bought the ticket."

Finally, the lanes opened. The rain turned into a gray mist just enough to coat

everything. The wipers thumped slower, and we picked up to a lazy sixty. I thumbed the CB.

"All right, boys, breathe again. Let's get our spacing back. We're still chasing that storm, but no reason to let it think it's winning."

"Then it's doomed," Chad taunted.

The laughter rolled again, bouncing down the channel with the same rhythm as the tires.

Somewhere near Midway, static crept across channel nineteen—faint, scratchy, and familiar.

"Well, I'll be damned," a voice said. "That you, Pops Mercer?"

I smiled before I keyed up. "Stubby Ray, you still alive?"

"Mostly. Saw that old Kenworth of yours going east. Figured the circus was back in town."

Ron cut in. "You still owe me twenty from that poker game in '09!"

"Statute of limitations wiped that out," Stubby retorted. "You boys are always headin' toward trouble."

I yawned. "Just stretching our legs."

"Uh-huh. Last time you said that half of Louisiana lost power and a bridge inspector quit."

"That was a good week," Bret said.

Another voice slid in, in a gravel-thick, slow drawl. "If that's Mercer and Calhoun, tell 'em Tennessee Mike says they still owe me coffee."

"Mike, I thought you retired," Ron probed.

"Retired twice. I still ain't learned what that means."

Stubby came back, signal fading with the rain. "Well, you boys behave yourselves… keep the greasy side down and tell Ducky he still can't back a trailer straight."

Then static.

"Stubby's radio sounds like it's talking through a wet sock," Ducky mused.

"Better than your singing," Bret grumbled.

"That's called soul," Ducky retorted.

"That's called noise pollution," Chad moaned.

We laughed, all of us, the sound rolling east through the mist like marbles in a tin can.

A few miles of quiet followed the hum of tires and the low drone of the CB.

Then another voice came through, low and warm: "Breaker one-nine… tell me I didn't hear Mercer and Calhoun again. You boys still tearing up my state?"

Ron perked up. "That you, Sarge?"

"Retired Sergeant now, thank you kindly," came the voice. "Mostly fishin' these days. Still got the photo of you four parked across both lanes on I-10."

"That was years ago and it was Ducky's fault," I said, pointing my finger at nothing.

"Was not! You said to follow you!" Ducky protested.

"He did," Sarge replied. "Right through the cones, past the scale, and straight through my patience."

The radio cracked with laughter again.

"Y'all stay outta my county this time," Sarge pleaded. "I don't get hazard pay for nostalgia."

"Copy that," I said. "We'll wave as we pass your exit."

"Do that and keep that wheel straight, old man."

His radio faded, replaced by the steady hum of the highway and Bret's dry mutter: "I still say we should've framed that ticket."

The rain thinned out past Madison, leaving streaks of sunlight across the asphalt. Steam lifted from the road like ghosts leaving a dance floor. The gauges were steady; the cab smelled like coffee, wet rubber, and two days without a shower. We'd burned up most of the day rolling east and chasing that wall of weather. Ahead, the signs started reading Lake City—Forty Miles.

I keyed up. "All right, boys. We'll fuel at TA Jacksonville South before the Cape. Keep rolling and try not to make any new friends with badges."

"Copy that," Bret confirmed. "Not my kind of social life anyway."

"Yeah," Ducky added. "Too much paperwork."

Ron came back laughing. "That's what you said after the weigh station."

"Exactly," Ducky said. "Lesson learned."

Out the windshield, the clouds broke just enough to show a strip of blue on the horizon, slick and shining like a promise. We rolled toward it, still chasing the storm. By the time the signs said Lake City—Ten Miles, the light in the sky faded to that flat silver you only get before dark rain. The wipers squeaked on dry glass, then slapped hard again when the next squall hit.

Bret came on the radio. "All right, gentlemen, next fuel stop's TA Jacksonville South—Exit 329. Top off, check lights, and pretend we're adults. Cape's waiting."

Ron chuckled, "Copy that. Ten bucks says Ducky misses the turn."

"I heard that," Ducky countered. "I've been there more times than you've been married."

"Exactly my concern," Bret teased.

I smiled. "Settle down, ladies. We'll get there."

Traffic got heavier as we hit the outskirts of Jacksonville—cars darting like minnows, brake lights blinking at random, and that special brand of Florida crazy that comes out when the pavement shines. A minivan cut across two lanes to catch an exit that wasn't even open.

"Somebody tell that guy GPS isn't a suggestion box," Chad advised.

"Bet he's chasing half-price churros," Ducky replied.

"Half-priced brain cells," Bret muttered.

We finally got to our exit, slowing as we rolled down the ramp with the smell of diesel and wet asphalt greeting us like home. The TA canopy glowed blue and white through the drizzle, puddles reflecting the lights like broken glass.

I swung wide and took pump three. Ron eased up beside me, Ducky and Chad behind him and Bret at the back of the line in his one-ton dually hauling our parts store. Five rigs, noses out, rain tapping on aluminum.

The tanks clicked full one by one and the pumps clicked off into the sound of the rain. Bret walked along the line of trucks, quick checks on tires and lights, boots splashing through the puddles. Nobody said much.

I climbed into the seat, wiped the glass clear, and fired up the Kenworth. She settled back into that deep steady thrum that felt like home. CB crackled—Ron checking in first, then Ducky, Chad, and finally Bret. "Ready to go?"

"All right," I directed, "the Cape's about a hundred-fifty miles."

"Copy," Bret answered. "Let's roll south."

We pulled back onto I-95. The rigs fell into line like horses in a parade. The rain hadn't quit but had softened to a fine mist blowing sideways across the lanes. Headlights stretched out ahead of us, yellow streaks on wet pavement. Every few miles a semi passed the other way, spray ghosting in the dark.

The highway curved south through St. Augustine. Ron keyed up, voice calm and tired. "Feels like we're driving through a dream."

"More like a nightmare," I said.

"Same difference," he replied.

Bret came on a few minutes later. "Harley's already at the Cape. Says gate security's expecting us. She's got our paperwork ready, so no clown shows at the gate."

"Copy that," I declared. "We'll play nice."

"That'll be a first," Ducky muttered.

We hit Cocoa Beach around 10:30 p.m. Wind gusting off the ocean, rocking the trailers just enough to remind you they were empty and light on their feet. I caught the smell of salt. The Cape always smelled like that, even from miles away.

Harley broke in over the CB, voice clear even through the static. "Hey guys, this is Harley. You'll take Exit 205A, left at the light onto State Highway 528 East. Stay single file once you get to the main gate. They've opened West Yard B-2 for staging. Watch your turns coming in. It's tight and has jersey walls on both sides."

"Copy that," I assured. "See you soon."

The green sign flashed through the rain: 205A Cape Canaveral / 528 East. I eased off the throttle, blinkers on with the guys following off the highway nose-to-tail. The ramp curved upwards, water streaming down the concrete.

With the green light we made our left turns single file, then accelerated toward the main gate about fifteen miles ahead.

Twenty minutes later, the guard gate came into view, warning lights blinking. Security lights glowed on tall poles at the entrance, white as day. Two officers stepped out, rain slickers shining in the lights. Bret moved to the front and handled the hand-off; they waved us through one at a time, checking IDs under the canopy.

Beyond the fence the road widened into a staging lot. The place smelled like wet gravel and jet fuel. The rain eased down to a drizzle as we swung in slow, each rig following the next through the puddles. I parked at the head of the line, set the brakes, and let the engine idle back to a lazy rumble. Ron pulled in behind me, Ducky after him followed by Chad. Bret brought up the rear. Harley and Billy Bob idled their pilot vehicles near the gate, lights flashing soft amber against the trailers.

I keyed the mic. "All right, boys, we'll shut down here 'til morning."

"Copy that," a tired Ron replied.

"Can we call it a night or are we going to do calisthenics now?" Ducky asked.

"Only exercise you're getting is walking to the restroom," Bret joked.

"Good. I'm built for short distances," Ducky replied.

Engines clicked off one by one and the yard went still. The sounds that followed were pure Cape. Wind through the fences, distant hum of turbines, a low metallic ring from somewhere down near the launch pads.

I sat for a minute, hand resting on the shifter, watching the rain trace lines down the glass. The yard lights threw long shadows across the wet ground. Out there in the dark beyond the fence, tomorrow's load waited, whatever it was.

Bret walked past my door, clipboard under his arm. "Get some sleep. Six a.m. safety check. The colonel will meet us at oh-seven-hundred."

"Night, Bret."

"Night, Pops. Try not to dream about paperwork."

He grinned, boots splashing through the puddles as he walked toward his truck. I turned off my headlights. The yard smelled like steel and salt, and something electric hung in the air, holding its breath. Tomorrow we'd find out why.

The yard had gone quiet except for wind on sheet metal and the hum of the perimeter lights. Then headlights came from the west gate, green six-by-sixes rolling in behind a low-boom crane. Tires splashed across the puddles, soldiers jumping down before the trucks even stopped. A captain in a rain slicker hit the ground first, clipboard already open, voice sharp over the wind.

"Mercer?"

"That's us," I said.

"You're loading tonight," he barked. "They moved the window forward. Command wants these units tied down before oh-one hundred."

Bret, who had parked next to me, overheard the captain and groaned low enough for only the CB to hear. "Of course they do."

The captain swung an arm toward the fence. "Mount up and reposition along the east fence line. Keep spacing tight. Lights on and for God's sake, watch for personnel."

"Copy. Everyone, fire up and move," Bret bellered. "Follow my tracks, twenty-foot gaps."

My bleary-eyed crew crawled back into their driver's seats and engines roared back to life. Before the last rig was even in place, the crane operator started swinging his boom, holding a huge crate hanging on for dear life. Rain hammered the trailer decks hard enough to sting.

Bret's voice came fast and sharp. "Wind's shifting, tell that operator to stop. Now!"

Too late.

The gust hit broadside. The suspended crate twisted like it was a sail, cables shrieking against the pulleys. The crate swung wide and slammed into Ducky's step-deck with a crack that sounded like cannon fire. Metal flexed. Sparks jumped.

"SHIT!" Ducky yelled. The impact shoved his truck half a lane sideways, tires skidding on the wet concrete.

"Everyone stay where you are and duck!" Bret barked.

The crate swung again, slower this time, screeching across the trailer before it stopped.

Bret was already there, boots splashing through a puddle deep enough to hide a truck in. He leaned between the truck and the trailer. "The airline snapped, and the pigtail was sheared in half!"

The captain stomped closer, shouting over the wind. "We can't stop now!"

"The hell we can't," Bret fired back. "You drop another crate and somebody's going to get killed tonight!"

MPs (military police) ran over from the gate, radios crackling. "Stop all movement!"

The crane operator froze in his cab, eyes wide, rain bouncing off the windshield. Nobody wanted to breathe but someone finally dragged a generator off a truck, yanked the cords, and strung lights across the puddled concrete. The first bulb flickered, then the whole set buzzed to life, painting everything in a yellow haze.

"Back it up two feet, Pops," Bret called. "They want clearance between you and the crane."

"Copy," I said, easing the truck in reverse. The tires splashed as they rolled through standing water.

The rain came hard again, blowing sideways in the wind. That's when I saw the black power cable lying across the pavement, half submerged and vanishing under the puddles. I didn't have time to stop before the right drive tire ran over it.

The world flashed white.

A pop like a gunshot, blue light under the tires, then half the floodlights blinked out. For a heartbeat the whole Cape went black, nothing but lightning to light the cranes.

"Power's out!" someone yelled.

"Kill the generator!"

"What the hell happened?"

Reaching for the mic, I yelled. "Nobody move! Stay put until they cut power to that line! Repeat, do not move!"

"Copy," Bret confirmed, voice tight and steady. "Ducky, freeze. You're sitting near live wires."

"Trust me," Ducky said. "I'm welded to the seat."

MPs sprinted through the dark with flashlights, beams cutting through the rain. The smell hit next: burnt rubber, ozone, and hot wiring. Someone threw the switch on the generator; it coughed once and died, smoke curling into the rain.

For a few seconds the only sound was my rapid breathing, then the backup unit coughed to life on the far side of the lot, throwing weak yellow light across the scene. Bret stood beside Ducky's trailer, coat plastered to his back, clipboard long gone. "Nobody's hurt," he said finally, loud enough for everyone to hear. "But power's down and the trailer is damaged. We're done for tonight."

The captain didn't argue this time. He stared at the mess, jaw locked, rain dripping off the bill of his hat. Bret keyed up again. "Everyone, we are done for the night. Lights off, engines off. We're shutting this circus down."

One by one the engines went quiet until all you could hear was wind and rain spraying the trucks. The yard steamed like a giant radiator cooling off. Bret climbed up on Ducky's trailer, leaned close to check the torn lines, then slapped the trailer twice. "We'll fix it at first light. Tonight, we sleep in the wreckage."

Ron's voice came soft over the CB. "Hell of a start, Pops."

"Yeah," I said. "And this is the warm-up act."

Lightning flickered over the distant towers, the reflection dancing across wet glass and chrome. Every flash made the whole yard look frozen mid-disaster: cables tangled, cranes idle, soldiers scampering in the rain. We'd left the diner around daylight, dry and rested. Now we were soaked, half-blind, and already behind schedule.

Wind slammed the side of the trailer, rattling the chains in the headache rack. I reached for the mic but stopped. Nothing left to say. Outside, Bret moved between the trucks, tapping on doors, checking on everyone. He was soaked straight through and still doing his job.

I leaned back in the seat, listening to the rain hammer the roof and the engines tick as they cooled.

Journal Entry 3

Long day running empty and wet from Mobile all the way to the Cape.

Trailers danced in the wind half the morning.

Traffic was the usual circus, box trucks drifting, RVs weaving, a cattle hauler who thought he was late for a rodeo.

Crew stayed sharp. Radio stayed alive.

Fuel at TA Jacksonville South, lights checked, and everything pointed toward the Cape.

Thought we'd shut down early. I should've known better.

Staging turned into a mess fast.

Crane crew rushed the lift, wind caught the crate, and it swung straight into Ducky's step-deck.

Snapped his airline and sheared his pigtail clean in half.

Before that even sunk in, I rolled over a power cable hidden under the puddles—big flash, half the yard went dark.

Smell of burnt rubber and ozone.

Bret took control like he always does. Shut everything down.

Nobody hurt, but the trailer's bent and we're behind before we've even loaded.

Storm still working the fences.

Feels like the Cape itself is waiting to see if we're worth the trouble.

Tomorrow starts early.

—Pops

Chapter 4

NORTHBOUND

The world outside was gray and humid when I opened the door. Rain had quit sometime in the night, leaving the air heavy and the ground shining like black glass. The smell of wet concrete and hot diesel drifted up from the idling light towers. It was 0530 by the dash clock. Too early! Bret was already out there, moving between trucks, clipboard in hand and steam rising off his coat.

"Airline and pigtail are replaced," he said when I stepped down. "Safety cleared us to finish loading once the colonel has had his look."

Nobody needed to say it. We were starting the day cleaning up last night's wreck. The yard was a swamp. Boots slogged through the mud and everyone moved slow and quiet.

Daylight came up slow and seagulls argued somewhere past the fence, proof the ocean was still close even if you couldn't see it. Out toward the gate, the MPs stood under dripping hoods and the rumor of a black Suburban heading toward us was finally turning real in the gray.

"Colonel Merritt," Bret nodded at the vehicle, not looking up from his clipboard. "Inbound from command with final orders."

I nodded, sipping my morning jolt.

The yard looked different in daylight. It was not chaos anymore but a mess we had to deal with. Soldiers walked the lines, checking chocks and binders. Ducky crouched by his trailer, wiping grease off his gloves like it could undo the night.

Engines started one by one, exhaust curling into the damp. Compressors chittered, then settled when the air finally equalized. We weren't moving yet, just warming the trucks after a long, wet night. The low-air buzzers screamed their morning protest until the needles climbed and the governors kicked off.

The Suburban arrived at the gate, tires splashing through puddles while MPs straightened the way you do when rank is about to walk by. Colonel Merritt climbed out, hat pulled low, coat unbuttoned, and eyes that said he hadn't slept since the rain started. He stopped beside my door, eyeballing the dent in the side of Ducky's trailer, the patched cable, and the line of rigs still glistening wet.

"You boys sure know how to make an entrance."

"Not in the plan," I said.

"Neither was the storm." He looked past me at the cranes staging the last crates, tarps folded back and ready for us. "These loads go north under DoD rules. You do not break those seals, you do not peek, you do not guess. Move them, deliver them, and keep your mouths shut while you do it."

"Yes sir," Bret answered before I could.

Merritt turned to me. "You've done this dance before, Buck. You know what happens when curiosity outranks discipline."

I nodded. "Usually involves paperwork and yelling."

He almost smiled. "Then save us both the paperwork."

He handed me a folder wrapped in plastic. Habit took over. I checked the top line for the CBL number and today's date before I even breathed. "Route sheets and emergency contacts. Call the number on top if anything breaks. Do not improvise."

"Yes sir."

He scanned the lineup one more time. The men, the trucks, the mud-splashed tires. Almost to himself he muttered, "Every time I see you, it's either raining or on fire." Then he climbed back into the Suburban, door thudding shut.

When his taillights cleared the gate, the cranes woke the yard again. Everyone was moving quicker now. One crate after another found its cradle, chains clattering, binders singing their metal note. By 0830 the last pin dropped. The last signature hit the clipboard, and we were officially loaded again.

"Coffee before we roll?" Ducky asked.

"Convoy BR 27, Mercer Ops," Natasha piped in. "Routes have been loaded onto your tablets. Permits verified Florida to Georgia to the Carolinas. From the Cape you'll run I-95 north to I-295 north, then back to 95 up to the Georgia line. I-95's work zones are tight so watch the lane restrictions through St. Johns and Kingsland. Military transponders and tracking are live. Copy?"

Bret keyed up. "Copy, Ops. Four trucks and one support. Permits loaded and lane restrictions noted."

"Weather shows scattered cells on your line, nothing heavy," she reported. "Roll when the MPs cut you loose. And try not to break anything before Georgia."

Tired laughter rolled across the radios.

"Copy that, Nat," I replied. "We'll behave."

"Sure you will. Ops out."

We idled toward the gate in order: me, Ron, Ducky, Chad, and Bret chasing. Sitting outside, Billy Bob called the lanes clear at the gate, and Harley took the street for us. The MPs raised the arm, saluted, and we eased back onto State Highway 528 like ghosts leaving a graveyard. The sky still hung low, a dull pewter dome, but at least it was not throwing lightning bolts anymore.

There's a stretch, usually early in the day, when the road lets you catch your breath. The trucks settle in and the radios are mostly quiet. I like that time. It tricks you into thinking the job is easy for a minute.

The rain returned in spits, tapping the windshield like second thoughts. The smell of salt faded, replaced by pine. Traffic got heavier around Daytona with the usual mid-morning mix of commuters and folks who didn't know where they were going.

The quiet didn't last long.

"Pops, I'm losing air pressure," Ron said. "Secondary is dropping. Compressor is keeping up but working hard."

"Copy that," I answered. "Harley, find us somewhere safe to get off."

"Saw a sign a minute ago. There's a weigh station ahead," Harley said. "I'll take the ramp and make sure it's empty and check for potholes and puddles so nobody is swimming."

"Back door closing it down," Billy Bob said, blocking traffic so no one joined our little emergency parade. We eased the line off the interstate and onto the ramp behind Harley, strobes painting the wet concrete. In the weigh station parking lot, everyone jumped out of their trucks.

Ron dropped to the ground and slid under his trailer. Running his hand along the rails, he quickly detected the problem. "Airbag is rubbing the frame. Bag is nicked."

"I don't have a spare bag for a trailer," Bret called back. "Cap the airline and ride with it until tonight."

"Copy," Ron said. "Bring me a plug."

Bret jogged for his airline kit. Ducky, flashlight in hand, held the light steady, beaming on the fitting where the compressor clawed to keep up and the dryer kicked again.

"Cracking it," Ron warned. He backed the fitting a quarter turn, and the leak went from a hiss to full pour. Bret was already there, shoving the replacement cap into Ron's hand. He seated it, spun it tight, and the sound collapsed to nothing. They waited two beats in the rain. No whisper, no bubble. Ron palmed the cap once more, satisfied. "Holding."

Harley summarized the events. "Mercer Ops, this is Harley. We're down ten minutes for air leak at old vacant weigh station northbound. One airbag disabled."

Natasha's voice came back, smooth and steady. "Copy, Harley. Routing note added. Weather is still calling for light rain north of you. Call when you're mobile."

We were mid-fix when blue lights touched the mirrors. A county trooper rolled in behind Billy Bob's car, took one look at a line of oversize loads, and decided the day needed supervision.

He walked up careful, counting trucks like a man doing math that didn't add up. His eyes flicked to the permit packet clipped to my visor and relaxed a notch. "Afternoon. DOT safety check. You folks okay?"

"Temporary stop," I said. "Airline rubbed through on the RGN. We're fixing it so we're not rolling on unsafe equipment."

He nodded, professional. "Good. We've had some illegal oversize runs through here."

While on the phone with our DoD contact, Bret handed over the paperwork stack like a man donating blood. The trooper's eyes hit the DoD seal and he paused. "If these are tamper evident, I'm supposed to verify contents."

Bret's earpiece chirped: "This is Captain Haines, Defense Transportation Command. Trooper, do not breach those seals! Confirm plate numbers and count only. This convoy is under live tracking."

The trooper's radio crackled before he could reply. "Trooper, be advised those plates are flagged federal. Tracking active." You could hear who was in charge by the tone.

The trooper straightened, spoke into his mic, got his confirmation, and the tension bled out of his shoulders. He turned back to me, still doing his job. "For my report, if this were unsafe, I would be required to inspect."

"Copy that."

He looked past me down the line, impressed despite himself. "You boys take up some highway."

"We rent by the mile," I said.

Behind me, Ducky piped up, "Go ahead and open them. We're curious too."

Harley clapped a hand over his mouth. "He's kidding. He's done now."

The trooper smiled, but you could tell he wasn't thrilled. "Get that line capped and roll when it's safe. I'll follow you to the next exit."

By the time he finished his report, Ron had confirmed the bad line was capped and the remaining bags were sharing the weight. It wasn't pretty, but the trailer sat right enough for the time being.

"Rolling," Harley called.

"Rolling," Billy Bob echoed.

The trooper blocked the right lane. We rolled the shoulder for speed, then slid in as one piece. We kept north. The pines thinned out and it finally felt like we had some room again.

The afternoon gave way to a colder, sharper light, and the miles started to count the way only miles do, steady and relentless.

Billy Bob's drawl came through. "Got a minivan drafting for fuel mileage. I'm gonna educate him."

Harley said, "Keep them back a bit further."

Billy Bob answered, "Yes ma'am, will do."

We laughed. The kind of tired laughing you only hear on the CB.

We cleared Jacksonville in the gray and slid into Georgia as the sun leaned west. Harley's lead lights shimmered on wet pavement, carving a yellow path through mist.

By late afternoon we were cutting into the Pooler and Port Wentworth exits, a place heavy haulers love because the lots are big and the parts houses know their faces.

Harley scouted the lot first. "Plenty of room on the east fence side. Bring it in slow." Tires popped gravel and the Jake burped once as we settled into the row.

Billy Bob said, "Locals gawking. Somebody's filming. Hope we get royalties."

We parked in a row along the curb and feeling safe, headed inside where it was dry.

The truckstop diner was the usual kind; bright lights, tired people, bacon on the grill.

Harley and Billy Bob joined the table still in their reflective vests, rain streaked down to their boots. Harley's phone buzzed. Her contact in Pooler had texted a selfie with the replacement airbag on the counter.

"That's proof of life," she said, sliding the phone toward Ron. That kind of tiny mercy keeps men civil.

A muted TV over the counter rolled through local headlines, rain moving up the coast, traffic alerts near Savannah, and a quick shot of military transports crossing some base gate two states away. Nobody at the counter cared, but we all caught each other's eyes at the same second and then went back to eating.

We ate, joked, and let the day's dumb edges soften. Ducky tried to pantomime Ron's airbag fix technique and Ron shot him down with a glare that could weld. Halfway through dessert, Bret's phone buzzed like a wasp. He squinted at a text, then took the call. The knowing in his eyes said it was not another vendor.

"Colonel's office," he said. "New instructions." I wiped my hands and took the phone. The voice on the other end was careful and exact.

"Convoy BR 27, you are cleared north via I-95. Proceed to Fort Liberty for inspection on arrival, target 0900 local, inspection window open until 1600. If you arrive after 1600, hold outside the gate and report in. After inspection, continue north using I-95 to I-287 to I-87 to I-84 bypass to rejoin I-95 at Bangor and proceed to Houlton crossing into Canada. We are monitoring your schedule. Let's try to reduce surprises."

I let that sit. Fort Liberty in the morning, window until 1600? "We'll be lucky to hit Florence before 0900," I said. Bret started recalculating routes on the tablet.

Harley tapped her mug. "Part'll be in by eight tonight. No heroics required."

Billy Bob added, "Heroics are for daylight and better weather."

The air was damp and cool when we stepped out of the diner but the rain had stopped. Neon buzzed overhead, painting the puddles pink and green. A few trucks idled by the fuel island, marker lights glowing like tired eyes.

Bret stretched, rubbing his neck. "All right, I'll go grab the parts from Harley's contact."

Ducky pointed toward the far fence. "There's an odd fellow parked over there. Old Ford, late model, looks female, like she's been living out of that truck for a while."

I followed his nod. A red pickup sat crooked by the fence, tailgate down, toolbox half open. A tarp was stretched over the bed, weighed down with straps. The driver, a woman maybe mid-to-late-thirties, stood beside it talking to a mechanic from the tire shop. Ball cap low, long braid down one shoulder, jacket that looked more ex-military than store bought. She wasn't smiling, but she didn't seem lost either. She carried herself like she knew her way around trouble.

"Traveler," Ron said. "Knows her way around a wrench."

"Probably waiting on parts," Bret guessed. "Smart. Staying near the light."

"Not from around here," Ducky added. "Plates say Texas."

I watched her a second longer. Something about the way she squared her shoulders stuck with me. Then Harley's voice cut through. "Come on, old man. Stare any longer and she's gonna start charging you rent."

We laughed and headed back toward the rigs, puddles shining under the lot lights.

Night settled in fast. Back in the rigs, we rolled over to the fuel island, topped our tanks, and lined up back at our place on the curb. We checked lights and tightened straps until our thumbs complained and Bret, having returned from his errand, helped Ron replace the busted airbag. A state trooper rolled by once to give us the nod, not official, neighborly.

We sat outside afterward, coffee cooling fast in the damp air. Neon painted the rigs in bad colors and the lot hummed with small conversations: Ron muttering about torque values, Bret cursing at permits, Natasha smoothing a new printout somewhere hundreds of miles away but still part of the noise in our ears.

"The colonel is watching," I whispered into the dark. "Satellites and all that."

"Then we'll be boring," Chad whispered back.

"Boring is underrated," Ron added.

I took one last slow walk down the line. The lot lights washed over wet chrome while heat rolled up off the stacks. The air smelled of damp, diesel, and fried onions from the diner vents. The kind of perfume truckers wear to bed.

Every rig sat right, chains tight, flags popping in the breeze, banners wet and glistening. Ducky's step-deck looked sore but serviceable. Bret's dually squatted under its load of parts like a mule that knew tomorrow already hurt. I leaned against the fender and still felt the road in my bones. Somewhere up there the colonel probably saw our dots moving on his screen and figured we were just another convoy pulling a job. For us every mile was earned.

I climbed into the sleeper, boots still wet, and let the engine idle low under me. It struck me how quiet it gets once the radios go silent. Peace, for the moment. One more day down, weather, traffic, and all the usual headaches. Nothing heroic, work done the way it ought to be.

"Not a bad day," I said to nobody. "Just loud and long and expensive."

Journal Entry 4

Started the morning in Cape mud with everything still soaked from last night. Colonel came through, handed off the CBL papers and reminded us not to get clever. We finished loading and pointed the trucks north.

Traffic stacked up around Daytona. Ron lost air on his trailer and we ducked into an old weigh station and capped the airline in the rain. Ten minutes flat. Harley kept the ramp safe and Billy Bob blocked the back door like he was born for it. Trooper showed up and tried to check the crates until Defense Command straightened him out.

Rolled into Georgia before dark. Parts waiting in Pooler. Replaced the bad airbag and tightened everything down. Saw a woman working out of a red pickup by the fence. Looked like she'd been living on the road for a while. Didn't get her name but Harley accused me of staring too long.

Shut the trucks down under neon lights. Boots still wet. Everyone tired but solid. Not a perfect day, but we kept it moving.

—Pops

Chapter 5

INSPECTION DAY

The alarm hit 0430 like somebody kicking the bunk. I rolled out stiff as an old leaf spring and just as creaky. The cab smelled like yesterday's brew. Outside, the lot was a mess of taillights and idling trucks ready to hit the highway, with Harley already staged at the exit as lead pilot and Billy Bob behind Bret as tail-end.

Cold drizzle went straight down my collar the second I stepped out. Rain again. I walked the line anyway, checked straps and lights, listened for leaks, thumped tires that sounded about like you'd expect at that hour, and made sure the kingpin lock was seated. Somewhere in the dark, Ducky sneezed loud enough to rattle his own mirrors.

Back in the seat, I fired up my truck. The heater coughed a few times before it decided to work and pushed lukewarm air at my knees. Gauges came up slowly. I did a tug test and said a small prayer over the air system.

Bret came on the radio, too awake for that hour. "Sound off when you're ready," he said.

"Good to go, physically," I said. "Mentally, check back after coffee."

"Ready," Ron said. "But my rain gear ain't."

"Ready," Ducky said. "Boots are floating, but I'm alive."

"Set," Chad said. "Still not sure why we like this job."

"Tool truck's ready," Bret said. "Sarcasm department's open."

Natasha came on the radio from Texas. "No curfews before Richmond. Expect inspection at Fort Liberty on arrival. Make sure no one breaks those seals."

Harley keyed up. "I'm up and ready, barely. Billy Bob, you vertical?"

"Upright and complaining," Billy Bob said from the rear.

"Good enough," she said. "All right, boys, ease them out nice and smooth. Billy Bob, keep the rear clear for the turn. Let's get this circus moving before somebody changes their mind."

I eased the clutch out and rolled with the line of trucks. Ron up front, me behind him, then Ducky and Chad. Bret's tool truck sat behind them. Harley led, and Billy Bob covered the rear. That early in the morning, Georgia or not, we were seven half-frozen drivers heading north.

The sky was nothing but dark clouds stacked low. The kind that meant trouble. We had talked about today's inspection the night before. Nobody was excited.

"Inspection day ruins a good morning every time," Ducky said.

"Last one cost me my lunch and my patience," Harley said.

"Only thing worse than MPs with clipboards is MPs with nothing to do," Ron said.

"Perfect," Bret said. "Idle hands and official forms. What could go wrong?"

"Keep rolling," I said. "We'll win them over with our charm."

The rain started as little taps on the glass, then settled in steady and heavy. Wipers slapped back and forth. Headlights smeared across the wet highway. From up in the cab, I watched the weather close in. Signs disappeared early. Trees faded. Everything tunneled down to gray. "If it gets any worse, I'm turning on sonar," Harley said.

"Keep your lights on and give each other room," Natasha instructed from afar. "DOT cameras are showing maybe a quarter mile of visibility up there."

"If one more pickup cuts me off, I'm putting them in the ditch," Billy Bob said from the rear.

"Big talk," I said, but it didn't take long for Billy Bob's words to be manifest by a driver heading in the other direction. A silver sedan came flying up, throwing water everywhere. The driver never slowed down. He hit a stretch of standing water, broke loose, spun twice, and slid straight into the median. Mud and grass blasted over the guardrail and his windshield.

"One less fool on the road," Bret said. "Keep rolling."

"Copy," I said, even though my blood pressure didn't like it.

"Darwin Award, southbound," Ducky chuckled.

"Make it lifetime achievement," Ron added.

"Don't even think about stopping," Harley said. "I am not explaining that in this weather."

The rain came harder right then, pounding the roof so loud it drowned everything else out. The defroster fell behind and the wipers started chattering on the glass.

"If this is how it starts, I don't want to see the rest of it," I groaned.

"You'll live," Bret said. "Maybe."

Static and tired laughter filled the cabs, the kind you hear when everybody knows the day is going to be long and there is nothing to do but ride it out.

"Lord, if You're handing out blessings today," Chad prayed, "start with wipers that work and drivers who believe in physics. And if that's too much, just keep us safe and out of the ditch."

"Preach it, brother," Harley said.

By the time Fort Liberty's gate showed through the mist, we had been in steady rain for an hour. My wipers squeaked on every pass and my mirrors showed nothing but spray and faint lights behind me.

"Back it down, guys," Harley said. "We're approaching the gate."

Concrete barriers stood out wet and slick. K-9s waited to walk the line of trucks, handlers fought the rain and the dogs. Everything was the same dull color—trucks, uniforms, pavement. Harley eased up to the checkpoint first, wipers slapping. The young MP stepped out and waved her over. "Ma'am, your decal's unreadable," he said.

"I've got a digital copy. Will that work?" Harley asked.

He thumbed his radio, listened to someone on the other end, then nodded. "Stand by."

A short wait, some back and forth on his side, and finally he waved her on. "Confirmed. Proceed to inspection area."

"Copy. Apparently I smell too civilian for you," Harley said, responding to a K-9 whose nose had wandered into her open window.

"Those dogs are about to climb in," Bret cautioned.

"If they try to eat my fries, I'm suing," she said.

"Those fries are older than the dogs," Ron laughed.

"Still good," she answered.

Harley rolled forward and the line crept with her. I followed her through the barrier, idling toward the shack. Rain hammered the roof, visibility down to a smear.

That's when the loudspeaker cracked on. "Convoy, move to the inspection area."

"Copy," I said, rolling forward.

Ducky pulled up behind me, climbed out and jogged up to hand off his paperwork, but he forgot one thing. He never set his brakes. The Kenworth hissed, then eased forward, one foot, then two.

"Ducky! Brakes!" Bret yelled.

Too late. The truck bumped the back of a black SUV parked by the shack. Not hard, but loud enough to sound like trouble. For a second everyone froze. Then it got loud.

Doors flew open. Two suits jumped out, shouting over the rain. "You rammed a government vehicle!" one of them yelled.

"Nobody rammed anything here," I said. "The truck rolled forward a foot." I dropped down onto the pavement. Water went over my boots.

"What the hell is going on back there?" Harley called.

"If this gets any dumber, I'm calling a lawyer," Ron said.

"You look familiar," the second suit said to Ducky. "You're the guy from Fort Hood last month, right?"

"Only hood I've been near was on a Peterbilt," Ducky smirked.

"Face the truck," Suit One snapped. "Hands where I can see them!"

Another SUV rolled up, lights bouncing off the wet pavement. An MP truck squeezed in. Bret tried to step between them and almost got clipped. "Everybody calm down!" he hollered. "You're arresting the only man in North Carolina who still irons his safety gear."

They marched Ducky toward a hangar, boots splashing. Inside, it smelled like old paint and sweat. Forklifts drove past stacks of crates marked DO NOT TOUCH. They pushed Ducky into a little gray office with a metal desk that looked older than both of us.

"You hit a government vehicle on federal property," Suit One said.

"Then that government SUV finally did something today," Ducky answered.

Suit One pulled up the Fort Hood video, watched a few seconds, and his shoulders dropped. "This isn't him," he muttered.

"You sure?" Suit Two asked.

"Unless the guy we're after lost thirty pounds and grew hair," Suit One shook his head. "You're good. Try not to autograph any more federal vehicles."

"Send the bill to gravity," Ducky said.

They pushed a towel across the desk to Ducky. "Sorry, driver," one of them said.

Ducky got one more crack off as they walked him back to his vehicle. "I'm sure the other guy's uglier." He slogged through the mud and climbed back into his truck. As soon as his door shut, Harley hit him on the radio.

"Next time, set the brakes, hero," she scolded.

"Next time, they can park their parade farther from the action," he said.

I was halfway back to my truck when an MP with a clipboard stepped out of the shack and walked right into me. Papers went everywhere! We both hit the mud. Bret ran in to help but hit the same slick spot and joined us, wallowing in the muck on the ground. A Major stepped out like he was walking onto a stage, dry and pressed.

"Outstanding," he said. "Coordination between military and civilian personnel, an unqualified success." Nobody said a word. "Carry on," he said. "I've seen enough."

The rain kept working on the yard until it turned into knee-deep mud. Forklifts spun their tires. Paperwork got wet, and mud caked on boots. A fire truck rolled up for a spill that turned out to be dirty rainwater with a little coolant in it. Somebody tried to shut the hangar door. It jammed halfway down and stayed there.

Somewhere in that noise, dogs, radios, and shouting, I thought about another convoy in another country. Same type of rain. Same hurry up and wait. Back then it was rifles instead of clipboards. Same kind of mess, different uniforms.

By 1100 they finally cut us loose. I climbed back into my seat, soaked clean through and my toes were cold and wet. I keyed the mic.

"Everybody good?" I asked.

"Still upright," Harley said. "That's the best you're getting."

"My socks are squishing in my boots," Ducky said. "They're done for."

"My knees hate me," Ron groaned. "Rest of me agrees."

"Add me to that list," Chad said. "Feels like we did a full shift standing in the mud."

"Quit whining and check your mirrors," Bret said. "We're leaving."

"Clear at the back," Billy Bob said. "Let's roll before somebody tries to write a sequel."

"Copy that," Harley said. "Same order we came in. Keep it tight through the gate."

I eased out behind Harley and the line followed, tires throwing mud while the MPs watched us leave like they were glad the storm was somebody else's problem now.

Back on the highway, the rain had settled to a light mist. Nerves died down but not quite that fast. Everyone drove quieter. Mirrors got checked more. Even the wipers sounded tired.

As Fort Liberty dropped out of the mirrors, chatter picked up again.

"Next stop better have donuts," Harley said.

"Long as it's not a police station," Ducky laughed.

"Or a base," Ron added.

The rain faded to haze. The road in front of us still shined but at least it wasn't trying to drown us. Later, the clouds finally tore open in spots. Sunlight came through in pale strips. The highway steamed and shimmered as the water burned off.

About two hours up the road, a sign for the TA at Stony Creek showed up and looked like a decent place to quit fighting the day. I keyed the mic. "TA Stony Creek up ahead," I said. "Fuel and a breather. Anybody got a better idea?"

"Fuel, food, and bathrooms that aren't condemned," Harley said. "I'm in."

"Copy that," Bret said. "We're overdue for soap."

The lot was not built for a show like ours. Small spaces, tight turns, reefers and vans parked everywhere. We did what we always do and lined up nose-out along the fence where there was just enough curb to hold four trucks with room to pull out.

Bret walked the line with his flashlight and clipboard, tapping straps and binders and checking chains. "Roll at zero-five-thirty," he said. "I want the Carson weigh station behind us before daylight."

"That five thirty a.m.?" Ducky asked.

"Yup."

"Even the chickens aren't awake then," Ducky said. "They're still negotiating with God."

Laughter rolled across the channel.

Harley and Billy Bob headed across the service road toward the Hampton Inn, their pilot cars parked where they could roll early.

"If the showers and the coffee are hot, I might cry," Harley chirped tiredly.

"And if the bed's warm, I might marry it," Billy Bob replied.

"You can stand in line for a room like everybody else," she told him as she pushed through the doors.

Natasha checked back in. "Pops, DOT confirmed escorts will meet you south of DC, Exit 166A, Springfield, 0900 with four Virginia state patrol units. They will hand you off to four Maryland state patrol units at the Maryland state line."

"Copy that," I said. "Tell them we'll be expecting coffee and donuts."

"You'll need it," she said. "Weather front's lifting north of Richmond. You'll have clear skies in the morning up to DC. Don't be late. They hate waiting."

"Wouldn't dream of it," I said.

The trucks settled as we shut them down. Our APU generators clicked on automatically to warm our sleepers. The smell of diesel hung over the lot. I leaned back on the bunk with my boots on the floor and the radio turned low.

Fort Liberty kept replaying in my head. Dogs, mud, radios all keyed up at once. I've seen worse. Convoys that couldn't find their own checkpoint, customs that turned six hours into two days and soldiers arguing over MREs like they were steak dinners. Liberty was tame compared to that. This felt more like a field exercise somebody turned into a bad comedy, and at least nobody pointed guns at us. Just pens and clipboards. Tomorrow we would swing around DC and Baltimore. I had run that loop before. Sirens, work zones, and sudden lane changes that burn more patience than diesel.

"Maybe this time we'll catch a break," I said. The radio crackled but didn't answer. Couldn't blame it. Tomorrow we would roll before daylight again, hoping for clear lanes, no surprises, and escort units that showed up on time. But hope is cheap, and we use a lot of it.

For now, the lot was still. Out there the storm was moving east. Inside, the slow tick of cooling metal pulled me toward sleep and the small hope that the next leg might behave.

Journal Entry 5

Rained most of the morning. Not a hard storm, just steady and annoying. We rolled through the gate at Fort Liberty already wet and running behind. MPs looked half-awake. K-9s were ready to work. Two black SUVs sat off to the side with people inside who did not look like they smiled much.

Harley handled the permits like a pro, even with three dogs trying to climb in her window. She never blinked.

Ducky forgot his brakes and bumped one of the SUVs just enough to make those federal types sitting in them lose their minds. Bret stepped in and smoothed it over before it turned into something worse.

By the time they cleared us, the yard looked like a mud pit. Chains clattered. Boots sank. Somebody set off a fire alarm in the hangar. A Major walked out dry as a bone and called the whole mess an unqualified success.

We laughed harder than the joke deserved. Mostly we were glad nobody ended up in cuffs.

We rolled out with the rain chasing us instead of sitting on top of us. Spirits were better than they had any right to be.

Tonight we're at Stony Creek. Fuel tanks and bellies full. Trucks lined nose-out along the fence, shut down and cooling off. APU's humming.

Tomorrow we are rolling early again. If we can beat the weather and stay on the right side of the escorts, we'll call it a win.

Long day. Good crew. No injuries. No breakdowns.

That's about all a man can ask for.

—Pops

Chapter 6

ZERO-FIVE-THIRTY AND COUNTING

The alarm hit like a terrible idea. Four-thirty felt more like punishment than planning. Fog hugged the lot and everything was wet and cold.

I killed the bunk light, slid into clean socks and my now-dry boots, and stepped down into the cold. First things first, pre-trip. Hood up: oil level where it should be, coolant on the mark, no fresh drips under the pan. Belt looks right, no cords showing. I shut the hood and went straight to hoses and glad-hands, seals clean, no cuts. Air lines clear of the catwalk. Pigtail seated. Walked to the end of the trailer: RGN neck pins seated, lines and pigtail to the neck clipped and not rubbing. At the end, I turned and walked up the other side: chains and binders tight, edge protectors still in place, no slack in the tarp straps. Banner and flags where they belong, clean and readable. Quick tap of each tire with the hammer, solid thud, no flats. Checked the marker lights and taillights. All lit.

Across the row, Ron was doing the same dance with his RGN. Ducky and Chad were working their step-decks, checking loads and chains so nothing would turn into confetti at sixty mph. Harley idled up front with the light bar on low. Billy

Bob was angled at the exit, coffee in hand and watching the mirrors for early idiots.

After I hurriedly filled my thermos with liquid life, I climbed back in and cranked the W900. Let her idle up and build air. Needles climbed slow in the damp. 110psi… 120… air dryer gave a clean purge. I set the trailer brake, dropped it in gear for a quick tug test, then back to neutral. Gauges steady. Heater finally found its manners.

"Radio check, everybody," Bret came on, voice always too awake for this time of morning.

Harley: "Up."

"Pops—up."

"Ron—up."

"Ducky—up."

"Chad—up."

"Bret—up."

"Billy Bob—up, rear pilot."

Bret read the routing like a grocery list. "I-95 north. Virginia State Police link-up Exit 166A by 0900. Hold lane two when they grab us. Speed is fifty-five through the push. Maryland picks us up at the line. Scales may be asleep but don't bet rent on it. Grab your leftover donuts and heat up your breakfast burritos. It's one of those days. Questions?"

Nobody had any. We'd all seen this movie.

"All right," Bret said, "order for the record: Harley lead, then Pops, Ron, Ducky, Chad, Bret with the tool trailer, and Billy Bob rear pilot. Spacing two hundred feet until we're formed up, more if the fog keeps coming in. Confirm ready."

"Pops ready."

"Ron ready."

"Ducky ready."

"Chad ready."

"Ready," Bret said.

"Rear ready," Billy Bob added.

"Copy all," Harley said. "Rolling, on me."

I eased off the brake, rolled to the stop line, and checked the mirrors: four trucks, two pilots, Bret's tool trailer, everybody where they belonged. Harley called, "Roll out." Me, Ron, Ducky, Chad and Bret, with Billy Bob bringing up the rear. By the time we hit the on-ramp, formation was set and the fog was just another thing we were driving through.

"Carson's up in ten miles," Bret reminded. "Pray for mercy."

Ducky muttered something about holy water and caffeine.

"If they're open," I said, "we'll at least get a good story."

The glow of the scale house appeared in the distance, then mercy answered—CLOSED—in bright orange letters. A miracle in neon. Billy Bob said, "Well I'll be, there is a God and he loves truckers."

Harley came back, "Copy that. Let's not give Him a reason to change His mind."

We rolled past the empty scales, engines humming nice and low. Richmond's skyline showed faint in the dawn with horizon the color of cold steel, but the day felt like it might give us a chance. Fredericksburg came and went in a blur of taillights.

Natasha checked in from Texas, voice crisp as static. "Convoy, status check?"

"Up and caffeinated," I said.

"Good. Patrol staging at Exit 166A, four Virginia units. ETA?"

"Thirty out."

Traffic thickened north of Stafford, commuters weaving between trailers like moths around porch lights. Harley called out lane merges; Billy Bob ran interference at the rear, flashing amber at anyone brave or stupid enough to squeeze in. At 0858, Bret's voice came over the radio. "Eyes up. Exit 166A in two miles. State Patrol's waiting."

Four white cruisers sat on the shoulder, blue strobes painting the fog. One stepped forward, hand up, radio to his mouth. "Convoy leader, you're with us from here to the Potomac. Hold lane two, maintain fifty-five or whatever we can get away with. We'll make room. Welcome to DC."

"Copy that, officer. Appreciate the help."

"You got it, boys. Let's make some noise." Two of the troopers pulled ahead of Harley, one in each lane. The other two slid in behind Bret and Billy Bob, one blocking the right lane, the other in the left. Sirens and light bars carved a path through the building city traffic.

I checked my mirrors, four trucks nose-to-tail, Bret behind Chad, pilots and patrol cars bracketing us front and rear. "All right," I said into the mic, steady. "Let's go earn our keep."

The Beltway went sideways in a heartbeat. Ramps spit out cars. Delivery vans leapt lanes like rules were optional. The lead trooper hammered his siren in short, angry bursts and the road peeled back an inch at a time.

Harley called out, "Left two, left two, now. Pops, hold the center line. Ron, keep your tail inside the paint."

Chad came back, "Copy, holding center line."

"Copy, Harley," Ron replied.

Billy Bob interjected, "Pops, I've got two idiots at your right. I'm blocking one, shooing the other." A black SUV slipped up at our two o'clock, windows dark. Another ran the shoulder.

Harley: "Unmarked units, two of 'em."

Trooper: "We see them. Do not stop. Keep rolling."

We rolled. Everything bunched up fast as we entered the bustling city. Splitting the lanes with our over-width loads, we rode lanes one and two on the left, and lanes three and four on the right. Ron and I held the center line; the step-decks tucked inside; pilots shot the gaps with inches to spare—I was gritting my teeth! A minivan panic-braked and clipped the back corner of my trailer. Paint traded, nothing more, but it rang through the frame like a tuning fork.

Bret: "Trailer strike, right rear!"

Trooper: "Do not stop. Maintain formation. City cops will get them at the ramp." I let out a breath I didn't know I'd been holding and kept the wheel steady.

The air changed. Not exactly wind but a rise in pressure and a low thump—thump—thump. Suddenly, two black bird helicopters were shadowing us, seemingly coming from nowhere. No markings. No hurry. They paced us for a long mile.

Ron: "Well… that's new."

Ducky: "If this turns into a movie, I want better lighting."

Bret muttered, "Probably DHS drills. Still creepy."

We cleared the Potomac with the cruisers still holding the ramps shut and the craziness of DC traffic was behind us at last. It took the better part of an hour to claw our way around that town. Nobody cheered, but everyone sighed a breath of relief.

For a mile or two, the rhythm reminded me of Kuwait. The same engine drone, same heat behind the eyes. Only difference was the skyline and the paperwork.

"If DC was a blender," Harley said, "then Baltimore's the garbage disposal. I-695 westbound in thirty-five. Eyes up, mouths shut."

"Copy," Bret said. "Drink your courage."

At the state line, the Virginia troopers peeled off to the shoulder, gave a final flash of their blues, and turned back. Maryland units slid in, black and gold, calm as winter. They didn't waste any time. Siren, hand, stare. Lanes parted.

Baltimore hit like a door frame in the dark. Three lanes weren't enough. The city shoved back with buses, dump trucks, and people who used their horn like a legal document. The helicopters returned, lower this time, rotor wash tugging at tarps. Three unmarked SUVs worked the shoulders.

Harley: "Bridge! Move left and ride the center. You're drifting, bring it back."

Chad: "Got it."

Billy Bob: "Rear's good. Two heroes tried to draft us; I told 'em no with my bumper."

A motorcycle screamed up the white line, throttle pinned, mirror to mirror. Bret yelled, "Hold your lanes! Let him go!" He clipped a cone, wobbled, and recovered. One of the black SUV's lunged, caught him near the shoulder, doors popped, and two men in black—government assist I'm guessing—stepped out to have a chat with the driver.

Trooper: "If the scale's open, you're not stopping. Keep moving!"

Halfway round the loop the scale house blinked at the I-695/I-95 interchange, the OPEN sign glowing and trucks stacked up on the ramps and shoulder. We held our line as the troopers ran us past the whole mess in lane two. No one said a word.

Ducky whooped, "Twice blessed!"

Ron: "Say it quieter, Duck! Don't tempt fate."

A delivery truck tried to cut our line and found a Maryland cruiser instead. Siren. Hand. Shame. The cop never broke stride.

We started seeing scattered debris on the shoulders: a broken pallet, what looked like the remains of a couch, someone's ice chest, and a ruptured trash bag that had vomited its contents. A soda can bounced off Chad's door and rattled away like it was never even there.

Bret: "Everybody watch out for all the junk."

Harley: "If it were a beer, this would be a different conversation."

We hit a sudden slowdown and the convoy tightened up with everyone braking at once. Air hissed, chains strained, and then it smoothed. The helicopters peeled east toward the harbor and one of the SUVs drifted away down an off ramp, the barely perceptible figure staring at us through dark glass as he slid away.

"All right," Harley said, softer now. "Forty minutes to the state line. Keep it smooth and boring."

Bret: "Copy. No sightseeing, no naps."

Ducky: "Define nap."

Ron: "Define sightseeing."

The Maryland cruisers stayed with us; their blue lights washed down to a steady glow now. The CB went quiet except for static and breathing. For the first time all day the world sounded normal. We climbed the bridge over the Susquehanna and the river flashed below.

Natasha came back on frequency, businesslike and warm. "Convoy, you're looking good. MSP releases you at the Delaware line. The Petro at Wilmington's expecting you."

"Copy that, Texas," I said. "Tell 'em to start the percolator."

She paused then added, lighter, "And Pops… I'm packing a bag."

"Say again?"

"I've got permits done for the next legs. I'm driving north. Don't worry—I'll stay out of your mirrors. Two days if I behave. Less if I don't."

Bret: "Texas, you going sightseeing?"

"Never been to Canada," she said. "Ferry sounds fun."

Harley laughed. "Hope you brought warm socks!"

"Copy. Drive safe," I said, and felt the grin I didn't mean to have.

Traffic loosened. Shoulders widened. Everything felt steady again. The MSP lead keyed up as the green DELAWARE line sign slid past at 1:22 p.m. "Convoy, you're clear of Maryland jurisdiction. Petro Wilmington twenty miles ahead. Hell of a run today."

Bret said, "Appreciate it, sir. We'll try not to make the six o'clock news."

"Do us all a favor," he said, and the cruisers peeled away with a brief salute.

"That was a fun half a day," Ducky crowed. "We drove a whopping 230 miles!" Laughter and sighs of relief mingled across the airwaves.

Traffic eased up after the cruisers broke off. We stretched the line back out, got some breathing room, and let the speed settle at fifty-five. Nobody said much. Twenty miles felt like a cool-down lap after a roller derby race. By the time the Petro signs came up, my pulse was back where it belonged and I could feel my shoulders again.

We rolled into the Petro lot with the pilot cars and Bret easing in behind us, engines ticking down, air bleeding off like tired lungs. The blacktop shimmered under a thin lazy sun and the smell of diesel and work hung in the air. Nobody even talked about food yet; first stop was the pumps. We lined up, and every man moved like his boots weighed twenty pounds. Bret pointed at the island. "Top off, additive in both tanks. It's gonna get colder the farther north we go."

I twisted off the fuel caps, let the pumps hum, and dumped two jugs of anti-gel into each tank. Diesel splashed on my glove; the smell of work. Beside me, Ron thumped a tire and frowned. "You might want to look at that outer right tire," he said.

I crouched down. The right rear had a clean slice through the sidewall, probably from when that car clipped the trailer. "Damn." I keyed my mic. "Bret, I've got a wounded tire, right rear trailer. Gonna need a service call."

Ducky finished topping off and started his walk-around. "Well, ain't this a love note from above," he marveled, holding up a chain link stretched half-white from stress. "One more mile and it would've popped like a wishbone!" He pulled a spare out of the headache rack, swapped it out, and tossed the bad one into the scrap bucket.

Across the lot, Harley's pilot car, a jeep, sat angled weird. Billy Bob was under the front end with a flashlight. "You got a leak or a rattle?" Bret asked, walking over.

"Neither," Harley replied. "Lost a light bar mount and the wiring got yanked by all the junk in the road. Blinky lights shorted out when we hit the bridge."

Bret crouched down, traced the line, and grunted. "We can fix that here. Billy, grab the crimpers and heat-shrink." Ten minutes later the blinky lights blinked steady again, wires re-taped, mount bolted. "Good enough to finish the trip, I hope," Bret said.

By the time the pumps clicked off, the service truck rolled up for my tire. The mechanic was a kid with cold hands and a long handshake. Ducky surrendered the spare tire from his headache rack and the kid swapped the trailer tire fast, torqued the lugs, and gave a nod. "Looks like you've had a morning."

"Baltimore tried to kill us," I said.

"Then you earned this break." He took off after I paid him his blood money of five hundred fifty dollars, and the lot went quiet again except for the hiss of cooling engines and trucks coming and going on the highway. Everyone smelled like fuel and exhaustion.

We parked in an empty row and killed what was left of the noise.

Harley parked first and stretched like she'd survived a bar fight. "All right, minor miracles handled. Nobody ever speak of Baltimore again," she said, stretching. "We still eating? I hope so because I am starving!"

"Coffee first," Ducky said. "Then I'll consider solids."

The Petro café sat behind a rack of chrome mudflaps and keychains that never sold. Inside, the air was a mix of fryer grease, burnt toast, and bean juice that could jumpstart a heart. A small TV over the counter played a weather report, snow bands pushing east from Ohio, maybe hitting Pennsylvania by morning. The waitress caught me watching. "You boys headed that way?"

"Unfortunately," I sighed.

She poured coffee into a mug until it trembled at the top. "Then you're gonna need more of this."

The radio behind her mumbled classic-rock songs between static bursts. Bret sat down with a sigh that could've cracked glass. Ducky poked at a menu like it owed him money. Harley scrolled her phone for pilot updates while Billy Bob stirred sugar into what looked more like motor oil than brew. Ron pointed at the TV when a quick flash of traffic cam showed snow on I-81. "There's our preview."

"Yeah," I complained. "We're always two counties behind the bad news."

Plates came fast: burgers, eggs, anything hot and tasty enough to fill the void. Nobody said much until the second round of coffee, when Ducky finally leaned back and grinned. "If this place had recliners, I'd never leave."

"Don't tempt me," Harley confessed. "They'd have to tow me out."

Ducky: "Amen. Now where's the bar?"

Ron: "If there isn't one, I'll build it."

Bret: "Fuel, fixes, food, and showers. Give it an hour before we ruin all our good decisions."

We paid the check and stepped back out into the daylight. The air felt colder after the warmth of the café. Here for the night, meet-up with Pennsylvania Troopers in the morning.

All of us happier with full bellies, we headed for the truck stop showers hoping for good water pressure and plenty of heat. Bret, Harley, and Billy Bob cut across the lot toward a little motel by the driveway to grab rooms. Pilots don't sleep in their trucks unless they're stuck.

After my shower, I sat on the step of the W900, boots on the gravel, watching heat mirages wobble above the lanes. My hands were still shaking from the tight grip I'd had on the steering wheel all morning. Means we made it through. Fort Liberty, DC, Baltimore, and every other ounce of madness Maryland could throw at us was in the rear view mirror. "Tomorrow— Philadelphia," I said to no one. New city, new rules, same chaos waiting to be earned.

For tonight, we let the chatter and B.S. come easy. Some would settle for a cuppa joe; somebody would find something stronger. The engines cooled, straps relaxed, and the lot fell back into its usual noise.

Journal Entry 6

Rolled out in the dark with fog on the lot and a knot in my gut.

Virginia troopers picked us up at Exit 166A, two up front and two behind, Harley and Billy Bob tucked between them.

DC turned into a knife fight in traffic, bad merges, tight lanes, one light tap on the trailer and a lot of white knuckles.

Two black helicopters paced us for a few miles; nobody felt like joking after that.

Virginia peeled off at the river and Maryland slid in, same pattern, same sirens, steady hands.

Baltimore did its best to break the line, motorcycle up the white line, unmarked SUVs on the shoulders, scale open and troopers waving us past the whole mess.

Made Petro Wilmington early afternoon. Fuel first, then repairs: one cut trailer tire, one stretched chain, one cranky light bar.

Service truck earned his five-fifty, Ducky dug a spare out of the headache rack, Bret made the blinky lights blink again.

We ate, showered, and shut it down while there was still daylight on the lot.

Crew tired but steady. Trucks tucked in. Tomorrow belongs to Philadelphia.

—Pops

Chapter 7

CITY OF BROTHERLY SHOVE

We left the Petro late enough to make the sun mad. Ducky, who slept through Harley pounding on his cab like a lot lizard looking for company, stumbled out wrapped in a blanket. Bret was already pacing with his mug of rocket fuel, muttering over a clipboard like it had personally offended him. "0730 departure?" He asked.

"No," I said. "0800. Let the men pretend we're civilized."

Ducky rubbed his eyes. "That's a whole extra hour for caffeine! Bless you, Pops."

Harley said, "Don't get used to it."

Natasha's voice crackled in just as the engines started warming. "Morning, everybody. Pennsylvania State Police staging at the Delaware line at 0830. Philly units join you at Exit Six, 0900. You are cleared straight through on I-95. Should be easy."

I winced. "Those are dangerous words."

She laughed. "Weather is clear, traffic light. What could possibly go wrong?"

Click.

We rolled north on I-95, past warehouses and billboards, tires whispering over fresh pavement. Sun finally came through the haze. At the Delaware line, four white PA cruisers waited, strobes flashing off the guardrail. The lead trooper leaned out his window, half-grin, half-warning. "Morning, gentlemen. Welcome to Pennsylvania, where the food is great but the roads are not. Hold lane two and we will carry you to Exit Six."

For a while it felt like maybe, maybe the day would behave. Traffic opened up ahead of the troopers, and Harley guided the rhythm. "Move left. Tighten the gap. You're drifting wide." Billy Bob brought up the rear, amber lights flashing steady as a heartbeat.

The radio snapped again. "Convoy lead, Philly police here. You on channel nineteen?"

Harley answered first, like she should. "Copy, Philly, we hear you."

I followed. "We are with you on nineteen."

"Update for the convoy," the officer said. "I-95 northbound is closed ahead due to a civil protest. Diverting you to I-476 north, then US 1. Philly PD coordinating."

I exhaled, irritated. "What's the protest?"

"Cheesesteaks," he said, perfectly straight. "Vegans versus carnivores. Whole thing went sideways before breakfast."

"You're kidding," Ducky said.

"Nope."

"Only in Philly," Harley said. "Everybody has an opinion about cheesesteak. Most of them are loud."

We hit the bypass, blue lights lit up the trees as we rolled, and soon we started seeing people on the overpasses waving hand-painted cardboard signs: EQUAL CHEESE FOR ALL and MAKE PHILLY VEGAN AGAIN.

"We're being detoured by a food fight," Harley said.

"Only in America," Bret said, then immediately shifted back to business. "All units hold twenty-five through the tight city streets. Eyes ahead. Ignore the circus."

Just before the US 1 ramp, Billy Bob came in low. "Uh, boss. You have a tail. Pickup, maybe a half ton, rust on the fenders."

"Describe it."

"Old Ford. Tarp in on the bed. Windows down. Driver has a cap and shades. Kinda small."

"Probably curious."

"Maybe," Billy Bob said. "Knows how to keep the right distance."

We dropped onto the city streets and the convoy turned into a show none of us asked for. Philly smelled like steak and green peppers. Protesters were stepping off the sidewalks and waving signs, chanting about meat equality, and one guy in a cow suit danced dangerously close to Ducky's fender.

A block later someone threw tofu. It splattered on the hood like a sad snowball.

"First blood, Pops. I'm a casualty," Ducky joked.

"You'll live," Harley said. "Do not swerve. He's filming."

The troopers blocked intersections, waving us through lights that had given up on logic. Cars stopped, people stared, and kids cheered. It was city chaos, loud and steady. Every mirror reflected blue, red, and endless camera flashes.

That little pickup stayed behind the last escort, never closer than a few car lengths. Once, when we slowed way down, I saw the driver's arm resting on the window, a slender wrist, silver bracelet catching the light. Definitely not some random old man—looks female.

We clawed our way north on Route 1, passing strip malls and half shuttered diners. Harley kept us alive. "Tight left. Van cutting in. Hold the center. Brake. Brake!"

Up front, the lead trooper feathered his siren in short, angry yelps. The lanes didn't clear but cars eased out of our way one at a time. Some protester with a megaphone yelled something about corporate meat logistics. "Buddy, you don't even know how right you are," Ron muttered.

By the time traffic eased up again the city was behind us, but the damage was done. Our schedule was shot. So were our nerves.

The trooper keyed up again. "There's an accident on the bridge into Jersey. Two lanes open, debris along the left lane. It'll be slow going through there."

Harley answered before I could. "Copy. Left lane is a mess. Split the shoulder and right lane and watch for all the crap in the road." We slowed down to a crawl and followed the troopers to the end of the bridge. They stopped us in a line with flashers on and the traffic squeezing past on the left.

Harley and Billy Bob jumped out at the foot of the bridge, tape measures in hand as they checked the distance between the accident and the right guard rail. "I got fifteen three here," Harley called. "You'll only have inches to spare."

"We'll take every inch we can get," Bret said.

We rolled forward one by one with traffic now backed up and waiting behind us. The little pickup came too, still hanging back, headlights low, unbothered by the police presence. One of the PA troopers glanced at it, frowned, and let it pass. "Whoever she is," he murmured, "she has guts."

Halfway across, the bridge trembled under our combined weight. That's when it hit me. I was right back in the desert.

A convoy of five-ton trucks rolling through Kuwait City. Air tasting of metal and heat. Engines drumming, rifles slung across our laps. MPs were waving us through intersections that stank of dust and trash. Locals stood around on the sidewalks, children were waving flags made from plastic grocery bags.

Back then the air shimmered with danger. The sound underneath was the same deep, steady thunder.

Twenty years gone, and I was still holding that same wheel with tight knuckles. The only difference was the scenery and the uniforms. Back then the fear was from incoming fire. Now it was impatient commuters and a protest over sandwich meat.

The CB snapped me out of it. "Bridge is clear. Bring it on up, Pops," Harley called.

"Copy," I said, my throat dry. The desert fell away. The Delaware River was below, blue lights flashing around me, and work to do.

On the Jersey side, four NJ cruisers waited with lights already going.

"Welcome to the Garden State," a trooper said. "We'll take you to the Turnpike split. Keep it tight and legal. The media is watching."

"Of course they are," Bret grumbled.

We rolled again, moving slow under a sky that kept changing; the little, red pickup tucked behind the last trooper, keeping that same respectable distance. Ducky pointed it out twice. Ron caught it once. "Not a gawker," he said. "Drives like she belongs."

Rain started light, then steady, tapping the cab roof like fingers on a table. By 1:15 p.m. we had cleared Trenton. The pickup was still shadowing us. Once it drew near enough for me to see the silhouette. Slim shoulders, ponytail under a ballcap. I blinked, and traffic swallowed her again.

Natasha checked in. "Pops, what's your status?"

"North of Trenton."

"Copy that. I'm in Virginia. Going to make up time tonight—will likely catch up sometime tomorrow."

"Be safe and keep the rubber side down."

"Always do."

The Jersey troopers handed us off at the northern check-point like passing a relay baton.

"New York units are waiting two miles up," one of them said.

"Appreciate it," I said. "You boys earned your pay today."

The lead trooper chuckled. "So did you. Drive safe, Captain."

That word hit harder than he meant. It had been a long time since anyone called me that.

Chapter 8

NORTHBOUND PUSH

The "Welcome to New York" sign slid past at 1:28 p.m. Just as the Jersey trooper said, four New York State police were waiting at mile marker two, picked us up, and the highway leaned north into the hills. Clouds stacked low and heavy, holding snow in them somewhere but not ready to drop it. The convoy settled into a steady rhythm on I-87—four trucks, two pilots, and Bret's white Ram riding behind Ron like a shepherd keeping strays in line.

Three car lengths behind Chad's step-deck, that same beat-up, red Ford kept its distance. Never crowding. Never gone.

"Anybody get that tag yet?" Harley asked.

"Texas plates," Billy Bob replied from the rear pilot truck. "Driver sits low. Cap pulled down. Could be press. Could be lost."

"Or both," Ducky said.

Traffic thinned out. The road climbed through bare trees and rock cuts, nothing complicated but enough to keep your eyes honest. Somewhere near mile marker ten, Ron keyed up with that slow drifting tone he gets when the past steps out in front of him. "You ever think the ground's the only thing that keeps us honest?"

None of us answered. Everyone knew that tone.

Ron keyed up again, with that "you are not going to believe this" voice. "Back when I was twenty-four, my brother talked me into dusting beans for him. Says it's easy. 'Just fly low and don't hit anything.'" He snorted. "His old AgCat was held together with spit and baling wire. Seat didn't even lock into position."

Bret groaned. "This better end with you on the ground."

"First pass goes fine," Ron said. "Second pass, not so much. Throttle sticks wide open. That plane jumps like it saw the devil and pins me to the seat; then the seat skids back and I can't even reach the pedals!"

Ducky cut in. "How low were you?"

"Low enough to count the beans in the field," Ron replied. "I'm shaving the tops off the crop when I see a fence coming up fast."

Harley came on. "Tell me you pulled up!"

"Barely. Main wheels cleared that fence by maybe a hair's breadth and my brother's on the ground waving his arms like he's guiding planes at O'Hare." He let out a breath. "Then the tailwheel tags the fence and kicks me sideways. I slam down into the bean field, take out a few more plants, bounce up a couple more times before I get her stopped." He paused. "My brother comes running up and asks if I SPILLED MY DRINK like we didn't just almost redecorate half the county with my body parts!"

A couple of gasps and a few muffled chuckles settled across the line.

"That's the day I learned two things," Ron finished. "One, planes do not care about fear. Two, I belong on the ground, not in the air."

Nobody had anything to add. The road hummed, steady and cold.

At 2:10 p.m. blue strobes climbed through my mirrors. "Convoy lead, New York State Police," a voice came over the radio. "We're checking a vehicle tailing your column. Stand by."

"Copy," I said.

A cruiser slid in behind the old Ford. The pickup eased onto the shoulder without fuss, like the driver had done it a thousand times. Ten minutes later: "Convoy lead, vehicle clear. No threat. Allowing it to rejoin behind your rear pilot."

"Copy." The Ford merged back in behind Billy Bob at the same respectful distance.

"Told you it was a woman," Harley said. "Y'all owe me five bucks." Nobody argued.

The highway opened enough for her to ease closer. She held her lane smoother than half the commuters out there. For a second I caught a glimpse—that slender wrist, sun-tinted brown hair sticking out the back of the ball cap—then traffic swallowed her again.

At 3:10 p.m. the long climb north of Suffern started working on everyone. Wind pushed at the trailers. Flurries tapped the windshield but did not stick.

Billy Bob came on, low and steady. "Pops, that red Ford behind me blew a cloud of black smoke. She's losing speed and heading for the shoulder."

"Copy," I said. "Peel off and check on her. We cannot stop the trucks here. Catch us at Newburgh."

"On it." He eased out of formation, made a U-turn, and tucked in behind the Ford with his flashers on. A minute later the radio cracked again. "Pops. This Ford is done. No oil—it's all on the road. Probably spun a bearing to boot. Driver says she's fine, cold and frustrated. She's with me and we're headed to Newburgh."

"Copy. Trucks will keep rolling. See you there."

Snow thickened off and on, never serious but steady enough to remind us what state we were in. By 4:30 p.m. the sky had turned an angry color of gray. Road signs for Newburgh started showing up like mile markers.

I held it steady and let the engine work. Somewhere in the middle of this drone Maggie drifted back into my mind. She was humming off-key in the passenger seat, boots on the dash, fixing my spelling on invoices with a pen she kept losing and finding. I still have the napkin she wrote on once: fuel, coffee, remind Buck to breathe. I keep it in my logbook.

I touched it once and kept rolling.

At 5:38 p.m. the decades-old fuel stop at Newburgh came up on the right with that gravel-covered lot every heavy hauler between Albany and Jersey has parked in at least once.

The fluorescent island glowed through the settling dusk. We'd been rolling hard since the Petro and the trucks needed more than fuel. Eyes and hands needed to assess every seal, every chain, every critical point. Fort Liberty had seen too many hands near our loads, too much chaos, too many chances for someone to get curious.

I keyed the mic. "All right, full stop. After you fuel, I want walkarounds on everything before we shut down for the night. That crowd in Fort Liberty was a little too close for comfort. Let's make sure nothing wandered off."

"Copy," Bret answered. "I'll start at the front, work back."

We filed into the small fuel island one at a time. Ron, Ducky, Chad, me. Bret brought up the rear in the dually, already scanning before his wheels stopped rolling. Harley and Billy Bob parked the pilot trucks on the outer edge of the lot, engines idling, amber lights still flashing a slow, steady pulse.

The fuel pump clicked off. I topped the main tank, then the auxiliary, checking the numbers out of habit. Behind me, Ron was waiting patiently, his head stuck under his RGN with a flashlight, checking the undercarriage for anything that might have worked loose.

Ducky stretched beside his step-deck, popping his back. "You think somebody messed with our loads at Liberty?"

"Don't know," I said. "But if they did, I'd rather find it now than at the border."

I walked the length of my RGN, checking tie-downs, edge protectors, the tension on every binder. Everything looked right. Chains snug, tarps tight, flags still bright despite the miles. Then I reached the starboard cargo, middle seal. It was intact. Serial number matched the manifest. Wire unbroken.

But something felt wrong.

I crouched low, angling my flashlight across the housing. Fresh scratches. Clean metal showing through the paint, running vertical along the seal mount. Not deep, but deliberate. The kind of marks that do not happen by accident.

"Bret," I called over the radio. "Starboard cargo, middle seal. You need to see this."

His boots crunched across the gravel thirty seconds later. He crouched beside me, ran his gloved finger near the marks without touching them, tilting his head to catch the light.

"Forklift marks go horizontal," he said out loud to himself. "These are vertical. Like someone tried to pry the housing to see if they could crack the seal without breaking the wire."

Ron appeared from around the corner, moving quiet as always. He studied the scratches, then the seal itself, then the paint around the edges. His face stayed neutral, but his eyes narrowed. "Whoever did this knew what they were doing," Ron said. "They were testing. Checking if it was possible."

"Possible to what?" Ducky asked, beam from his flashlight swinging toward us.

"To get inside without leaving evidence," Ron said.

The wind cut across the lot, cold and sharp. Traffic hummed on the interstate. Normal sounds, but everything felt different now. The fuel pumps. The idling rigs. The distant hiss of air brakes, all of it suddenly felt too exposed. "Do we call it in?" Bret asked.

I looked at the seal. Intact, but wrong.

Chad joined us, hands in his pockets, steam curling from his breath. "What are we looking at?"

"Somebody tried to open this," I said. "Didn't succeed. But they tried." The silence lasted three beats. Long enough for the weight of it to settle.

"We calling Merritt?" Chad asked.

I stood up, brushing grit off my knee, feeling the ache in my lower back from too many hours in the seat. "We document it. Photos, time, location. We send it to Nat, encrypted. She forwards it to Merritt. We keep rolling."

"And if whoever did this is watching?" Ron asked quietly.

"Then they already know we're carrying something worth the risk," I said. "Stopping won't change that. Might make it worse." I keyed the handheld. "Nat, you there?"

Her voice came back immediately, sharp and clear. "Copy, Pops."

"We're sending you photos. Eyes only for Merritt. Mark it urgent but not emergency. We need guidance, but we're not stopping unless he says stop."

A pause. Then: "Understood. Sending you a secure upload link now."

Bret's phone buzzed. He opened the encrypted app, positioned his camera, and took the photos from six angles. Clinical. Professional. Wide shots, close-ups, details of the scratches against the paint. The kind of documentation that holds up in court or covers your ass when things go sideways.

The upload bar crawled across his phone screen. Thirty percent. Fifty. Seventy-five. When it finished, he pocketed the device and looked at me. "Done," he said. "Uploaded."

We stood there a moment longer, six people trying to read meaning into scratches on painted steel. The wind picked up, rattling a loose tarp on someone else's trailer two lanes over. A semi rolled past on the highway and a Jake Brake barked in the distance as it rolled down a grade.

The lot filled with the usual noise, air brakes sighing, engines holding steady, chains rattling. Snowflakes started sticking to chrome and tarps. Four trucks settled into their parking slots. The air smelled like diesel and a long day earned. I left the W900 idling. It was too cold to shut anything down.

Billy Bob pulled in beside Harley's truck with a tired woman stepping out behind him, her jacket tight, duffel bag thrown over her shoulder. She thanked him, steady and polite. Harley tapped her on the arm and walked her toward the motel across the lot. Nobody asked questions. Everyone had been stranded somewhere once.

Drivers peeled off toward their bunks or to the motel. Tonight was microwave dinner. Bret checked the clipboard, muttered something, and climbed back into the Ram. I walked the line of trucks, checked straps and chains out of habit. Everything was fine. Habit still won the day.

Snow fell thick and soft, muffling the lot. I stood in the shadow of the cab with a cup of coffee cooling in my hand. "Feels like the road's about to earn its keep," I muttered into the brisk air. I climbed into the truck, shut the door, and let the quiet settle in the cab.

···◆◆◆···

Three o'clock in the morning, Stewart Airport Super 8: A pair of headlights cut through the snow. Natasha's van rolled in slow, tired, stubborn. She'd been driving since dawn the day before, permits, customs packets, and empty coffee cups stacked on the passenger seat.

She killed the engine and leaned back, eyes heavy.

Maggie's words came out of nowhere: "You don't have to be blood to be family. You just have to show up."

Natasha smiled, worn out but still herself. "Still showing up, Mags." She pulled her jacket over her shoulders and let exhaustion take over. Snow whispered against the glass. The lot settled into silence. Up the hill, four trucks idled under a sky that was getting worse.

Morning, and trouble were on their way.

···◆◆◆···

Journal Entry 7

Hit Philly with a bad feeling and proved right.

I-95 closed for a protest, signs and tofu flying. Troopers guided us onto the bypass and up Route 1.

Harley talked us through the tight stuff, Billy Bob kept the back door clear, and the locals treated us like a parade they did not order.

Bridge into Jersey was half blocked from a wreck. Harley and Billy Bob measured, troopers walked us through slow, inches to spare.

Jersey wind met us at the line, New York drizzle tried to finish the job. Police escorts handed us off at state lines as expected.

Some beat-up red Ford started shadowing the convoy. Troopers checked it, said no threat, let it ride behind Billy Bob.

Ron passed the time with his crop duster story and reminded us all why we like to keep our feet on the ground.

Long pull north of Suffern took the fight out of that Ford. Billy watched it blow smoke and die on the shoulder.

We kept the line moving while he peeled off, scooped up the driver, and brought her on to Newburgh.

Noticed there'd been an attempt at mischief on the load. Everyone suddenly peeled open their extra set of eyeballs in the back of their heads.

End of this run: trucks parked where they should be, storm building, one more round of miles waiting on the other side of the snow.

—Pops

Chapter 9

ROAD IN THE SNOW

The lot at Newburgh was still dark at zero-four-thirty. Engines idled steady, same as they had all night, coughing white breath into the cold air. The smell was of diesel and coffee heating on a camp stove. Plows idled along the fence line, blades down, waiting for orders. A salt truck rumbled past throwing that pre-storm brine that turns your boots sticky.

Over at the motel, Bret had the tailgate of his dually dropped, maps and tablets spread out. Natasha climbed out of her cargo van, headset still around her neck, eyes glassy from no sleep.

"Listen up," she said, voice rough. "We roll at 0530. CT State Police are meeting us at Danbury. They will run us across Connecticut and hand us off at the Massachusetts line. We stop once for fuel at Sturbridge. If the weather tanks, expect them to push the pace. That's it. Do not wake me unless somebody dies."

Bret nodded. "Copy. Get some rack time. Umm… who's gonna drive your vehicle?"

Natasha crawled back into the van bunk and was lights out before her boots hit the floor mat, seeming not to care.

Harley and Billy Bob came over from the motel next door. Between them walked a woman with a Marine sea bag and a steaming travel mug. Harley called out, "Morning, boys. Picked up a stray at the Motor Court. Figured I'd bring her to the party."

The woman smiled, road-worn but steady. "Rebecca Lane, freelance reporter. Thanks for the lift, and for not asking how the motel coffee is."

Bret pulled into the lot having left the motel and raised an eyebrow. "You're the one that's been shadowing us?"

"Yeah. Been following you since the Carolinas. Figured it might be a good story. My pickup finally quit south of here." She took a sip of coffee, eyes drifting across the rigs. "I was heading to St. John's. My dad is a retired Navy rescue swimmer and he's sick. Figured I would ride north, see him, maybe get a story."

Ducky leaned on his trailer fender. "So, your old man is one of those guys that jumps out of helicopters?"

"When the Marines forget how to swim, yeah," she said.

Laughter rolled across the lot. Ducky grinned and pointed at her duffel. "You sure you're a Marine? You talk too nice."

She didn't blink. "Well if I'm not yelling, I can hit harder."

More laughter. Even Ron cracked a smile.

Rebecca nodded toward the van in the motel parking lot. "Your girl looks done. I can take the wheel till she wakes up."

Bret hesitated. "We need to clear that with DoD."

"I spent eight years in the Marine motor pool," she said. "I have filled out enough paperwork to rebuild the Pentagon."

Bret sighed. "Fine. You can drive. Just keep up."

At zero-five-thirty, Harley rolled out first, roof lights flashing through the snow haze. Engines rose together, low and steady. Natasha's cargo van, now driven by Rebecca, fell in behind Bret and in front of Billy Bob. The convoy nosed east onto I-84, tires crunching the greasy film that hides under first snow. Many days, there's only time for the food you brought with you.

Out the windshield, we saw plows parked at rest areas, troopers dealing with spun-out commuters who thought all-season tires were magic.

Harley's voice crackled. "The grade near Waterbury is slick. Drop a gear and follow my ruts."

"Copy," Ron said.

Ducky added, "Some sedan tested the guardrail. Insurance adjustment in progress."

Rebecca came on, calm and collected. "Ops van good to go. Natasha is out cold. Hopefully she'll stay that way for a while."

By the time dawn fought through the overcast, we rolled into the Danbury rest area. Two state cruisers sat nose-out by the ramp, blue lights bouncing off the snow.

"Mercer convoy, you're with us," the lead trooper called over the radio. "We will run you across the state. Need to check your line of trucks before we get rolling."

The engines idled. Exhaust drifted sideways in the wind. Troopers walked the line of trucks, flashlights sweeping under the trailers, counting tires and checking tag numbers against the permits.

"Looks good," one said. "Scales are open, but we aren't stopping. You'll run with us straight to the Massachusetts border." He slapped the paperwork closed. "Weather's turning. We'll make time the best that we can."

Bret radioed, "All right, time to roll."

For the next couple hours, Connecticut went by in a blur. We saw snowplows idling at the on-ramps, salt trucks shadowing us, police cruisers leap-frogging traffic so the trucks could stay tight. Snow thickened around Hartford. Slush spattered the mirrors. Every few miles another four-wheeler sat twisted in a ditch.

Rebecca handled the van like she'd been with us for years, even throttle, clean spacing, hands steady. She drove like she understood what happened when you got it wrong.

Late morning brought the TA Sturbridge fuel stop. The cruisers staged at the exit while we topped off, diesel fumes, wet boots, and that warm blast when the café door opened.

Rebecca sat beside me at the counter as we waited for our to-go meals. "Your guys always this cheerful in bad weather?"

"Cheerful keeps you awake," I said.

She smirked. "Guess that explains the jokes."

Back outside, the escorts were already staging again.

On the ramp, the CT cruisers peeled right. Harley keyed up. "CT units clear. MA units standing by."

Two Massachusetts State Police SUVs waited under the overpass. They pulled ahead of Harley, lights sweeping across the flurries.

"Mercer convoy," the lead trooper said. "We'll take you through Worcester, then hand you off at the New Hampshire line. Maintain fifty where possible."

"Copy," Bret said.

Snow floated sideways in the wind as we climbed toward Worcester.

Halfway through town, Harley called, "MA dispatch says one of our RGN permits did not transmit. They want a confirmation."

"Whose?" Bret asked.

"Ron's."

The troopers staged us on the shoulder of the on-ramp. Bret and a sleepy Natasha dug through the laptop while Rebecca sent the digital copy to the officer's tablet.

Ten minutes later, he returned. "Server glitch. You're all set."

"Copy," Bret said. "Rolling."

North of I-495, the sky lightened and the snow turned to scattered flurries. At the New Hampshire border the cruisers peeled away, lights flashing a quick farewell.

Natasha keyed up, her voice clearer now. "Heads up. New Hampshire doesn't require state escorts. It's us and the pilots until Maine. State Police will meet us near Augusta."

Roads through southern New Hampshire were a patchwork of wet asphalt and packed snow. Tire spray fogged the mirrors.

Ron called one out. "Blue Camry at the forty-two. Driver looks fine. Pride is totaled."

Billy Bob jumped in. "I've seen worse. Remember I-40 in Oklahoma? Ice thicker than a politician's promise."

"Yeah," I said. "At least this storm is staying vertical."

Rebecca added, "Dash sensors say thirty-two even. One degree colder and things get sporty."

North of Augusta, snow started building again. Harley called back, "Maine units on the ramp, half mile ahead. Behave."

At fourteen-forty-five, we eased onto the wide apron near the state-line inspection station. Two Maine State Police cruisers idled there, salt crusted on the hoods.

The lead officer stepped out. "Afternoon, Mercer convoy. Dispatch wants a quick check. You made good time, only thirty minutes late."

Bret climbed down. "Copy."

"Radar shows a nasty weather band forming between Bangor and Houlton," the officer said. "We can proceed, but if visibility drops under a quarter mile, we shut you down wherever we can. Keep radios up." He returned to his cruiser and the convoy rolled north.

Snow came in fine, sharp flakes that stung the glass. Billy Bob said, "Every storm has a sound, Pops. This one hums like it's waiting on us to screw up."

"Yeah," I answered, watching Rebecca's silhouette in the van's mirror. "So am I."

Troopers updated us every few miles. "Visibility holding. Bangor clear."

Ron added, "Left lane slick past the eighty-three mile marker."

Chad followed with, "Let's do a prayer before dark. Lord, keep the tires true, our wits sharp, and keep the angels bored. Amen."

Past Bangor the traffic thinned, only rigs and plows now.

·· + + ◆ + +··

Rebecca and Natasha talked quietly in the van. "Your dad is sick?" Natasha asked.

"He has heart trouble," Rebecca said. "And I ran out of excuses not to go."

"Seems like reason enough."

·· + + ◆ + +··

By nineteen-forty-five, blue lights pulled us into the wide apron of the Rider Big Stop short of the Canadian border.

The troopers idled near the pumps. "You made it," the older one said. "Dispatch says you are clear to park here. Weather is turning. If it gets worse, you'll be here awhile."

"Understood," Bret said.

Engines idled heavily. Rebecca and Natasha climbed out, stretching stiff legs. Chad and Ron checked straps under the fuel island lights. Harley and Billy Bob parked nose-out near the far edge.

The café across the lot glowed warm. Inside, heat hit like a furnace door opening. Burgers, fries, and burnt coffee filled the air.

Ducky pointed at the muted TV. "Snow advisories south of Scranton. Factory fire near Harrisburg. Weather guy says the next forty-eight hours will test travelers' patience. That's weather talk for 'you're not going to like tomorrow.'"

The waitress, gray ponytail swinging, filled mugs without asking. "Kitchen closes in twenty. Order quick."

"Chicken fried steak," Bret said.

Rebecca and Natasha sat by the window. Rebecca thawed her hands on her mug. "Truck stop cafés all smell the same."

Nat shrugged. "Smells like every truck stop since the eighties."

Billy Bob lifted his mug. "Holy ground. When you survive a day like today, you eat whatever they will give you."

"To surviving," Harley added.

Later, as I climbed back into the cab, the phone buzzed. "Hey, kid," I said.

"You parked?"

"Parked at the border. On time."

"Mom would be proud you're still on schedule."

"Maybe. We will see what tomorrow does."

"Who's the new driver?"

"Rebecca Lane. Marine mechanic. Drives like she's part of this convoy."

Katie laughed. "Sounds like your kind of trouble."

"Not like that," I said. "Just reminds me good people still exist."

"Talk to her," Katie said. "Mom always said you needed someone who gets the road."

"Maybe after the storm."

"Call me tomorrow."

"Love you, kid."

"Love you too, Dad."

The lot glowed orange under the lights. Snow drifted around the parked rigs. Rebecca and Natasha sipped coffee in the van. Billy Bob snored in his pilot truck—there would be no motels tonight. Ron stood by his load staring north like he could already see the ferry.

I wrote the day's log.

Journal Entry 8

Long day into a colder night.

We left Newburgh before daylight and chased snow all the way to Maine. Engines barked at the cold, tires felt wooden, coffee was rough, but it did its job and kept us moving.

Natasha looked half-dead and still ran a briefing like a drill sergeant with a hangover. Our new joiner from the broke-down Ford, Rebecca, took the van and drove like she had always been one of us, with steady hands, quiet confidence.

Connecticut gave us slick grades and short tempers. Massachusetts loaned us a rookie trooper, but he kept it shiny side up. By the time the Maine line showed, the snow was working sideways.

The Big Stop café smelled like grease and exhaustion. Billy Bob called it Holy Ground. He's not wrong. We ate, laughed louder than the food deserved, and drank coffee strong enough to make your eye twitch.

Katie called after. Said Maggie would have been proud I am still on time. Told me to talk to Rebecca. Maybe I will—after the storm.

Engines humming, snow building, crew worn out but steady.

We made the line. That's enough for one day.

—Pops

Chapter 10

WHITEOUT AT THE LINE

Wind hammered the cab like sand against sheet metal. The truck idled low and steady. I cracked the door and cold slapped my face hard enough to sting my teeth. The lot lights turned the snow into a glowing wall, blowing sideways in the wind. On a good gust you might get five feet of visibility.

Engines were still running up and down our row. The same ones that kept us from freezing last night. Ron's exhaust stacks plumed sideways. Chad stood in the drift by his bumper, collar up. Overnight we'd hung winter fronts, thick vinyl poly covers that button across the grille like a truck's winter coat. They've got a center flap you open or close to meter airflow, enough to keep the radiator hot, keep the engine from icing, and keep the cab heaters blowing warm air. Ours were stiff from lack of use and snapped in the wind until we got them buttoned down. The kind of job you do with numb fingers and a lot of cussing, then brag in the morning like it was nothing.

The CB hissed. "Border's shut till further notice," Bret said, voice flat from lack of sleep. "Troopers say plows can't see the lines on Highway 1 or I-95. Everybody stay put."

"Copy," I confirmed. "We're not playing heroes today."

Ducky keyed up, words buried in static. "Good day for indoor hobbies we don't have."

I made a pass down the line, boots punching through crunchy ice. Checked lights, wiped ice off the gladhands, listened to engines. The cold had a sound, thin metal ticking, nylon straps drumming in the wind, distant plow blades throwing sparks you could feel but not see. Across the road, an ambulance rolled past slowly, red lights smeared to pink by the snow.

By zero-five-thirty the café had its lights on. We went in like survivors. The warmth hit like opening an oven. Bacon and hashbrowns already on the grill and coffee that could jump-start a dead battery. The cook wore a knit hat pulled to his eyebrows.

The waitress, same gray ponytail as last night, set mugs in front of us before we even found seats. "We're open till the coffee runs out," she said. "Or the roof caves in, whichever comes first."

The door blew open again. Bret came in out of the weather, shaking snow off his coat; Rebecca and Natasha right behind him, cheeks raw from the walk. Nat set down her tablet and a stack of manila folders like coasters.

"Manifests are ready," she announced. "Permits on the tablets, conditions read, route approved when it opens."

"Good," I agreed. "Let it snow. We won't be the ones holding everyone up today."

The waitress topped us off without asking. "You boys headed into Canada?"

"As soon as they'll let us," Rebecca said.

"Stay inside. We're slow," the waitress assured. "This weather isn't fit for moose."

We settled into that comfortable hush truckers get when the world isn't loud enough for them. The scanner by the register chattered: fire call on US 1, two vehicles off in the ditch, patrol requesting a second plow. Somewhere outside, a fire truck went by, sirens blaring and chains clacking.

Harley and Billy Bob stayed put in their pilot cars out in the lot, engines idling, heaters running, parking lights glowing faint through the white. Harley kept her Jeep nosed into the wind, wipers beating time, a legal pad on the dash with plate numbers and notes only she could decipher. Every few minutes she rolled forward or back a foot, checking that nothing had drifted tight against the bumpers, freezing her in place. Billy Bob did the opposite, windows fogged, country station low, one boot up on the dash while he watched the mirrors for anyone foolish enough to try and move. He and Harley swapped an occasional story over the CB.

The TV over the counter cut from a smiling host to a red banner and a storm map that was a mess of blue and white. No sound needed; the pictures did the talking. With headlights half-buried, a string of semis jackknifed across the median like bent paperclips. One trailer had peeled open, cargo scattered and half swallowed by drifts. A stainless milk tanker lay on its side, pale mist leaking from a busted line, torn to rags by the wind. No flares today, only LED beacons strobing low in the snow, their pulse smeared sideways.

The camera jumped to a trooper shouting into the storm, snow pasted to his mustache. His voice was lost to static but his arms weren't—chopping the air, a gesture that said stop to anything with wheels. Two wreckers worked on a rig that had folded up on itself, nose kissing the trailer and the frame twisted wrong. A firefighter crawled belly-down under the bumper while another held a blanket against the wind like a wall.

The scanner spelled it out: jackknifes, cars in the ditch, LifeFlight grounded.

Someone at the counter said, "That's the Bangor side," and the whole café went still. Spoons hung in mid air. Coffee went cold while we watched.

I felt the table breathe out all at once. I've made calls in weather like that. You never forget the voice on the other end.

Ron said it low. "That's why you shut down."

"Clock don't matter if you don't make it," Chad added, eyes on the screen.

I nodded. "Road's not the enemy till you make it one."

Bret rubbed his hands together, breaking the spell. "All right," he halfway grinned. "We're planted till they dig us out. Might as well tell lies and call it training."

Ducky leaned back, charging his battery. "Ron's got the most gray. Start us off, professor."

Ron slid in across from me still thawing his hands on his cup. "I went through a whiteout in Vail my rookie year," he muttered, his voice wafting through the steam. "Sat three hours behind a jackknifed truck. Learned the difference between shutting down and getting stuck that day." He smiled a little. The kind that doesn't reach the eyes. "That was twenty-seven years ago. I was running team with my wife, Carla. We thought we'd see the country before we settled down. First six months were postcard perfect, sunsets, truck stop steaks, every rest area felt like a date night."

He ran his thumb along the cup's rim. "Then came winter in Wyoming. We hit black ice outside Rock Springs, jackknifed the trailer, tore up the fender, and spent the night waiting on a wrecker in negative ten. She never said a word, sat there holding the dog. After that, she said maybe the road wasn't her dream after all."

No one said anything. Even Ducky looked down.

Ron took a long sip. "My girls were little when I started running solo, back when we lived in that ranch house with the broken porch light. I'd leave before dawn so they wouldn't cry and stand in their doorway to be with them just a few more moments. They'd be asleep, stuffed animals everywhere, hair all tangled, soft breathing. I used to whisper a promise: Daddy will be home soon. Sometimes it was true."

He looked at the white blur outside. "I missed my eldest's first school play. They dressed her up like a sunflower. Carla taped a picture of her on the fridge holding that yellow paper petal crown. I stared at it for days. Told myself it was one time. Then it happened again the next year."

He shook his head gently. "But I taught them both how to back a trailer behind the barn. They'd argue about who got to steer and who got to spot. I still have the shaky phone video of it, two giggling girls fighting over who hit the cone. Carla says I'm in the background beaming like an idiot."

He paused, voice low. "They still text me good morning when I'm rolling. They don't have to, they just do. I think they're making sure I'm still out here somewhere."

The table went quiet again, heavier this time.

Rebecca looked across at him. "Sounds like you did the best you could."

Ron shrugged. "You hope it adds up someday."

Ducky cleared his throat. "Hell, Ron, you're makin' me feel like I should call my ex and apologize."

Ron cracked half a smile. "Don't. She's probably happier thinking you're still lost at sea."

The laughter came quick. The kind you grab onto before things get too real.

Nat had been quiet through it, hands wrapped around her mug, eyes moving from face to face like she was logging every story. She hides it well, but long nights show up in the way she blinks, slow and deliberate. I caught her glancing at the door once, not because she wanted to leave, but like she was counting how many rigs sat out there with our name on the side and how many families would expect them back. She carries all that in her head and still remembers who takes cream and who likes it black.

Chad let the chuckles fade before he spoke. "My kid built a volcano for a school project last week," he said quietly. "Texted me a picture. Dunno if it'll still be there when I get back."

He rubbed his palms together like he was trying to keep the memory warm. "He's eight. Smart as a whip. Last time I was home, he asked why I drive so far and come back so tired. Hard thing to answer when you're dead on your feet."

He stared into the steam. "He leaves the porch light on when he knows I'm due back. Started doing that on his own. Says it 'helps airplanes and daddies find home.' I told him I'm not an airplane. He said, 'Yeah, but your truck is loud enough to count.'"

A couple smiles flickered around the table.

"When he was five," Chad said, "I taught him how to change the lightbulbs in that old church I bought. Roof leaks like a sieve, windows fog if you breathe too close. He held the flashlight while I fixed the wiring. His hands were shaking because he was cold, but he wouldn't give up. Afterward he told me that church was 'ours.' Haven't forgotten that."

He looked out the window again. "I don't get to preach in it much yet—mostly cool, sunny Sundays. Some things deserve a little care." The wind hammered the glass; nobody looked away from him.

Rebecca smiled gently. "You'll make it home before that volcano cools off."

"I hope so," Chad said. "That glue wasn't great."

Ducky slapped his hand down on the table. "All right, before we all start cryin' in our hashbrowns, y'all ever heard about the time I borrowed a cigarette boat in Miami?"

Bret groaned. "No, and we're not going to."

"Oh, you're gonna," Ducky said, leaning in like it was gospel. "So there I was—young,

handsome, brave, and dumb."

Ron didn't blink. "Two outta four checks out."

"Anyway," Ducky went on, "this beautiful machine's sittin' at the dock, white paint shining like sin, twin Mercs whispering, 'Take me, D.' Couple buddies say, 'Let's go see Cuba!' I tell 'em,

'Boys, I can barely see the end of the pier.' Did that stop us? Nope. We borrow the

boat—technically more of an unauthorized extended test drive—and blast out of the harbor like

James Bond with bad judgment. Ten miles offshore— BLAM! We hit a reef like a pothole from

God. Boat went down faster than my credit score!"

The table cracked up. Ducky kept going.

"So we're swimming in with a couple of life jackets that popped out of the water after the boat went down, waves tossing us like socks in a dryer. A couple hours later we hit the beach—sunburned, exhausted, smellin' like gas and seaweed. And there she is—Lola. Red dress, smile like vacation pay. I figure I earned a little romance after nearly drowning."

"Bad call," Harley laughed over the radio from the lot.

"Oh, it gets better," Ducky said. "We go to dinner. She orders lobster, I order steak. We talk, we laugh, sparks flying.

Then the band starts up. She jumps up saying, 'This is my favorite song!'—sings every word perfectly. Only problem—she's got a lower range than me."

Even Rebecca choked on her coffee.

"Turns out," Ducky said, slapping the table again, "Lola is Larry! Big Larry. Shoulders like a Kenworth hood. But you know what? I bought her—him—dessert anyway. Cheesecake. 'Cause I'm a gentleman, and I was still breathing, which, at that point, was a win."

He sat back, smug. "Moral of the story: don't borrow boats, check your charts, and pay attention to the key your date is singing in."

Ron raised his cup. "To Larry."

Ducky clinked mugs. "To Larry—the one that got away."

We were grinning again, all of us, and that's when Bret surprised us. He didn't clear his throat or tap his cup. He started talking, eyes on the table.

"When I first came to work for Pops," Bret said, "I handled dispatch weekends and nights. Figured it was safer than running a bar at midnight. I was wrong."

He rubbed his thumb along the ceramic handle. "We had a young guy running nights. Twenty-three, maybe. Still wrote his logs like a fifth grader. Called in from Amarillo asking if we could bump his next delivery window because he was tired. I told him to grab a nap at the truck stop and check back in an hour."

Bret breathed slow, steady.

"Another carrier called twenty minutes later. Said they saw a Mercer trailer in the median. I didn't even know the driver's name by heart yet. Still learning the roster. Had to read it off a clipboard when I called his emergency contact." He shook his head once, jaw tight. "That was the first time I ever heard what a mother sounds like when her world ends."

He tapped the table with a knuckle.

"And that's why I run safety instead of driving full time. Why I count chains when you're not looking; why I ride your asses about logs and brakes and stupid little details. Making those 2 a.m. calls. The ones that start with, 'Is this next of kin?' You make one of those and it changes how you see the job. Every trip turns into math, weight, distance, fatigue. Folks think I'm uptight but I know how good men disappear fast. If I can keep one person from ending up as a name on a clipboard, it's worth it, and if I can keep you eight people safe AND make the delivery, I will have done my job well." Bret looked up at the ceiling.

The fryer splattered in the back like rain hitting hot steel.

Rebecca reached across and rested her hand on Bret's forearm. "That's not paperwork," she said softly. "That's leadership."

Bret nodded once, eyes down now. "Yeah. Well. Doesn't make it easier."

"My father used to say leadership is getting everyone home in one piece."

Bret nodded again. "Smart man."

We let the quiet settle again. Good quiet. The kind that comes after somebody says something true.

First time Bret rolled into my yard he still smelled like fryer grease and bowling alley beer, nervous as a long-tailed cat in a room full of rocking chairs. I handed him a clipboard and a fuel card and told him not to lose either. A month later he was sleeping on the couch in the parts room between shifts so he wouldn't miss a call. Somewhere between those nights and that Amarillo wreck he went from employee to somebody I trusted with my keys and my life.

I took a breath and found myself talking before I meant to. "Maggie used to leave notes in my lunchbox," I said. "Little ones. Sometimes stupid. Sometimes sweet. One time she wrote, 'Come home safe. You still owe me a dance.'"

Rebecca looked at me, eyes soft.

"Katie found those notes in a shoebox last year," I said. "Read every one of 'em." I shook my head once. "Some things hit late."

Nobody said a word, but everyone was listening.

Ducky finally broke the heaviness by slapping the table. "All right. Enough feelings. Someone hand me a fork before I start hugging people."

Laughter rolled around the booth, grateful, messy, needed. And the storm kept howling outside like it didn't care one bit about any of it.

The CB in Bret's coat pocket crackled. "…plow convoy eastbound One… visibility less than a quarter mile…"

Static, then a dispatcher from somewhere south: "Route One closed between Houlton and Monticello. Crews staging till daylight."

Bret thumbed the volume down and set the mic aside. "There goes our morning commute. We're planted till they dig us out."

Outside, snow churned under the lot lights and piled high against the windows. Somewhere in the distance a Jake Brake groaned and got swallowed by the wind.

Rebecca looked around the table. "So this is what you all do when the world stops moving?"

"Pretty much," Bret said. "Drink bad coffee and call it a meeting."

Ducky raised his cup. "Best staff meeting I've ever had."

The CB popped again, Harley's voice. "Mercer Ops, Harley. Visibility zero at the east entrance. Drifts up to the bumper on the state plow."

Natasha picked up her handheld. "Clear copy, Harley. Hold what you've got. DOT's staging trucks in the rest area till morning."

Harley laughed, "Holding. Billy Bob just opened his door and the wind tried to repossess it."

A beat later: "Mercer Ops, Billy Bob. Confirm the porta potty from the construction site across the street is crossing the lot at speed. Advice?"

Bret sighed. "Copy, Billy Bob. Do not pursue the porta potty."

"Copy. It's winning anyway."

The table busted out laughing again.

Rebecca glanced toward the window. "Harley sounds calm for someone sitting in a blizzard."

Ron nodded. "Calm is her default setting. Been running pilot since before some of us were legal to drive. Lost her brother in a wreck outside Kansas City. Swore if she couldn't stop fate, she'd at least light the way. That's why she's out front."

"And Billy Bob?" Rebecca asked.

"Part driver, part chaos," Ducky said.

Ron chuckled. "He's from Oklahoma. Claims he delivered fence posts during a funnel cloud. Tied himself to the trailer like a rodeo saint."

"Did it work?" she asked.

"He lived," I said. "So technically, yes."

The room settled again. The wind drummed steady on the glass. The waitress turned up the oldies station; steel guitar leaked through static.

Rebecca's eyes went around the booth, taking stock, Ron staring into his coffee with Wyoming buried somewhere behind his eyes and Chad scrolling photos, his thumb lingering on an eight-year-old with a cardboard volcano. Bret jotting notes even though the trucks weren't moving, Ducky humming a tune that didn't exist, and Nat tapping away on her tablet, half-asleep and still working.

The radio crackled again. "Mercer Ops, Harley. Plow crew reports secondary lot is full. They're stacking folks at the overflow by the scales. Wind's gaining speed."

"Copy," Nat said. "We're tucked in. Call if you need bodies."

"Copy," Harley replied. "We're good."

Snow rattled the windows hard and we all whipped around to see if it would break through. The cook flipped the CLOSED sign halfway and went right back to the grill. It started to feel less like a truck stop and more like a lifeboat. Guys who would normally park by themselves and eat in silence had drifted closer together, pulled in by the noise and the warmth and the promise that they would be safe from the storm for a while.

Nat shuffled her notes every time the scanner crackled, bumping our roll time forward in pencil, then forward again. Rebecca had her notebook out now too, pen moving in short bursts, but she kept stopping to look up, to read faces, like she knew this might be the only day she ever saw all of us sitting still.

We kept talking because that's what you do when the road's shut and time won't move. Ron's voice turned low explaining how to read a drifting lane by the shadow of the poles. Bret told a story about a rookie who thought steer tires were optional and learned about gravity the expensive way. Chad admitted he keeps a crayon drawing stuffed in the visor, rocket ship, stick figure dad, big smile. Ducky swore those drawings would improve fuel mileage. Nat slid Bret a list: chains inventory, battery checks, morning order, ferry window.

"Mercer Ops, Billy Bob." The radio again. "Heads up, ambulance stuck at the south exit. Fire crew on scene. They'll need the lane clear if anyone's rolling in the next hour."

"Copy," Bret said. "We're shut down till Customs opens tomorrow, but we'll keep the lane clear on our side."

"Copy."

By early afternoon the coffee had us warm enough to forget how bad it was outside. The storm hadn't eased; it was getting worse, snow blowing harder, wind finding new seams in the door. The generator coughed, then caught. The lights blinked and stayed.

The waitress set a fresh pot at our table like communion and pointed a thumb at the storage room. "Cots in there if you need 'em. Blankets too, just in case. We'll be here all night too."

"Appreciate it," I said.

Rebecca leaned closer. "You ever stop moving?"

"Storms do it," I said. "Maggie did, too. She made me slow down and smell the flowers." I nudged my cup. "Katie keeps me honest now. Didn't give herself a choice when her mom passed. Nat..." I smiled. "You know Nat from the passenger seat. Lemme tell you how that started."

I told her about the county line gas station and the trash bag, and the dead phone. I told her about Maggie's sandwich and a promise, and the one about two teenage girls in one bathroom. The coffee can with someday written on it, corporate Dallas, glass offices, and free lattes. I told her about the late-night call. The shop lights rewired, permits that don't lie.

Rebecca listened, eyes soft. "She sounds like family."

"She is," I said. "Blood's the receipt. Family's what you keep paying into overtime."

Silence settled in a good way. Outside, the storm threw a construction barrel across the lot. Inside, it was staying warm for the moment; the old song on the radio lost a verse to static and found it again.

The waitress stepped out with another pot. "Fellas, if you're topping off anyway… our generator's getting thirsty. We burned through the spare cans. If you could bring a couple back full, I'll keep the lights on and the grill hot."

"Done," I said, standing up. "We're due to check the rigs." I called it. "All right, rotate to the pumps. One at a time. If you can't see the island, stop and wait for a guide. Ducky, grab the café's cans by the back door. Chad, you're the mule."

"Copy," Bret said, zipping up.

"Yessir," Ducky said. "Humanitarian mission."

Support vehicles first, then the trucks. We moved them like chess pieces. The wind tried to push me backward. Drifts at the island were knee-deep and rising. The hose stiff as a broom handle. Bret moved from truck to truck with both hands up, guiding drivers onto the island with the whiteout closing around us. Ron's gloves froze stiff and Chad's truck smoked like a freight train till it pushed the damp out of the pipes. Diesel pumped slow. A splash hit my sleeve and froze there.

Ducky and Chad slid past with two red five-gallon cans apiece, heads down, boots chuffing. "Special delivery," Ducky puffed. "Five-star dining runs on number two diesel."

"Don't you dare spill that," the waitress called from the cracked service door, hair whipped by the gust. "You'll be soaking it up with a biscuit."

"Yes ma'am," Chad grinned, and set the cans inside by the humming unit. He thumbed the cap, added a shot of anti-gel, and swirled it like he'd done it a hundred times. "That should keep her from coughing at shift change."

We kept the rotation crawling at the fuel island, one rig in and one rig out, Bret's silhouette in the storm guiding each driver on and off the island. Ron checked fuel necks and knocked ice off filler caps. I watched the numbers climb and told myself fuel was warmth and range and options.

When our little circus wrapped, I walked the line. "Additive in?"

Thumbs went up.

"Two bottles per tank," Ron said. "What do you take us for, rookies?"

Everyone laughed. Ducky pointed. "You are a rookie, Ron."

I twisted off my own caps, let the pump hum, and poured two bottles of anti-gel into each tank, expensive as diamonds and worth it, if only for peace of mind. The smell bit sharp enough to make my eyes water, but it meant tomorrow we'd roll instead of fighting gelled fuel.

Ducky pulled through the fuel island with a mustache full of ice and said he was moving to Florida. Nobody believed him.

We filled every tank to the top and gave the neck rings a quick wipe so they'd open in the morning. Bret hauled the last café can to the back door and the waitress met him with a stack of to-go boxes and a look that said debt paid in pancakes and bacon. The generator settled into a steady hum.

"Much obliged," she said. "I'll keep the coffee alive in here."

"Fair trade," Bret said.

We all huddled under the café awning pretending it was warmer there, as the pumps disappeared behind another curtain of white and the lot felt a little less mean knowing it'd stay lit for the night with the cook and the coffee queen hunkered down in there riding out the storm same as us.

Customs came back over the radio just before 5 p.m.

"Operations suspended 'til ten hundred tomorrow," Bret relayed.

You could hear the groan without a sound.

Collars up, we trudged back to our cabs. The drift by my truck was mid-thigh now, packed like mashed potatoes. The ops van sat buried under a snow mound. The pilot cars were shapes, antennas crusted white, tires gone from sight. I walked the line, brushing off lights and thumping tires by habit though the wind stole most of the sound.

Rebecca walked beside me, hands in her pockets, shoulder brushing mine, when a gust shoved us both the same direction. We didn't say anything, laughed once about it. Snow had worked its way down my collar, cold running between my shoulder blades. Rebecca's hair and hat were dusted white, flakes caught in the knit like they were hanging on for dear life. She walked close enough that our sleeves brushed now and then, not hanging on me, but matching her stride to mine like we'd been doing this run for years instead of days.

For a second I pictured us from the highway, two small shapes cutting a path between buried trucks, and it hit me how little we were against all that weather and steel. Little, but not alone.

Back in the cab, I keyed the mic. "Before we roll tomorrow, top off your tanks, all of us. Don't play games. We might have to go straight to the ferry if we can thread the needle through this mess."

Clicks came back one by one.

"Copy that."

"Roger."

"Copy."

Everything went quiet except for the wind humming between the mirrors. I grabbed the phone. "Katie, you watching the radar?"

"I was," she said. "Then I stopped before it gave me nightmares. You guys okay up there?"

"We're parked. That's about the best kind of okay there is right now."

She sighed. "Figured. I wanted to hear your voice, make sure you weren't out there trying to play hero."

"I already played hero once," I said. "Didn't pay worth a damn."

She laughed soft. "Mom used to say that too."

"Yeah," I said. "She was usually right."

A beat of quiet. Just the heater and the wind.

"You eating?" she asked.

"Had something that looked like chili and acted like regret. It'll do."

"Try not to die of cafeteria food before the storm clears, okay?"

"I'll do my best, kiddo."

"I love you, Dad. Tell Nat I said hey."

"Love you too, Katie. I will. Get some sleep."

"I'll try."

The call clicked off. The cab felt quieter than before, like the world had exhaled and forgot to breathe back in. I sat there with the phone still in my hand, watching frost creep along the lower edge of the side glass.

Katie has Maggie's timing for calling right before I do something stupid. She was small when I first started hauling the big stuff, used to draw my truck in crayon and tape it to the fridge with hearts around the tires so I would see it before I left. Now she sits in a warm house I barely helped her enjoy and tracks weather on her phone, calling to remind me that parked and alive beats brave and gone. Funny kind of circle. The kid guarding the parent's blind spots.

The CB popped once more.

"Mercer Ops, Harley. State called it. No movement 'till ten hundred tomorrow at the earliest. They'll start plowing hard at four."

"Copy," Natasha said. "We'll be ready."

I settled in for the night, hung my wet parka on the passenger grab handle, laid out tomorrow's clothes on the seat, and slid my boots under the floor vent to dry. Gloves and orange beanie went across the defroster. I plugged the phone and handheld into the inverter, turned the CB down to a murmur, set two alarms, and cracked the bunk curtain so the heat from the sleeper would reach the windshield. The engine idled steady and warm.

The heater pushed steady across my boots. In here, the truck still breathed and the stories kept my hands warm. Out there the storm owned the road and the border; out there I could hear other engines idling through the storm, a rough little choir of iron and diesel keeping back the cold one gallon at a time. It wasn't much, but it was ours. Tomorrow can come when it's ready. I'll be here.

Journal Entry 9

Parked all day; felt wrong down to the bones. Border shut, plows blind, wind pushing snow sideways hard enough to sandblast paint.

Café turned into base camp. Coffee that could wake the dead.

Too many accidents rolling over the TV screen today. Showed the kind of pictures that make you glad you stayed put.

We told stories to keep the walls from closing in.

Rotated to the pumps one at a time, spotters in the white-out, drifts to the knees at the island.

Harley and Billy Bob kept eyes on the lot, voices steady, their parking lights assuring like a lighthouse.

Customs pushed us to ten hundred tomorrow.

Katie called. Reminded me Maggie would be thankful I stayed grounded.

We didn't roll an inch, but we kept everybody warm, fed, fueled, and safe.

Tomorrow, if the plows win, we go. If not, we wait and keep each other human.

—Pops

Chapter 11

NORTHBOUND SHADOWS

The yard was alive all night. Diesels idled in rhythm, exhaust drifting under the floodlights. Nobody shut down; cold that deep does not forgive.

By 0530 the café was half-full of road crew thawing out, boots dripping, plates steaming with hot food and the smell of coffee and biscuits coming through the vents. TV played the morning news low, a weather map sliding east with the anchor reporting, "Bands pushing toward Moncton through mid-day." A ticker crawled along the bottom about ferry delays and school closures.

Since we were still stranded for the time being, Rebecca pulled her digital recorder out. She started with me, of course. "What keeps a convoy together?" she asked.

"Teamwork and habit. It's kinda like muscle memory," I said. "You do not want to be the one who breaks the rhythm. Everybody is counting on the guy in front and behind to hold the line."

She nodded, a pen and pad sitting near her elbow. "So it's more than following orders?"

"Orders are the easy part. What keeps it together is trust. You trust that everyone has secured everything right, read their permits, and knows when to speak up. You cannot fake that."

A radio behind the counter crackled through a song, then a weather blip: "Highway crews report slick bridges between Saint John and Moncton, salt trucks out."

The waitress passed with a coffee pot and said to no one in particular, "Bridge by Exit 12 is a skating rink, watch yourselves."

Rebecca glanced at the window where headlights cut through the snow. "You've been doing this a long time?"

"Most of my life. Started hauling farm loads when I was too young for the insurance company to like it," I said. "After that, never stopped. Got married, raised a family, built a company, lost a few good friends along the way. The work doesn't change, only the faces."

"And you still like it?"

"Some days," I said. "It's hard work and it wears on you. But it fits me. I know the job, I trust the people I'm with, and I am where I'm supposed to be."

"That's probably the most honest answer I've heard," she said, a little smile at the corner of her mouth. She clicked the recorder off and gave me a look I hadn't seen in a long time. Not flirt, nothing loud. Just someone actually listening. It caught me a little sideways. Most folks hear what truckers say, not what we mean. She caught both, somehow. Then she went right back to her notes like it never happened.

"Honest is all I've got," I said, finishing my coffee.

A pair of plow guys in orange jackets stamped snow off their boots and slid onto the stools. "If you folks are heading north, watch the drifts past Oromocto. That wind has teeth."

The other added, "They're talking about holding the afternoon ferry if the line of vehicles is long, but don't bank on it."

"I'm gonna go bug Ron and Ducky and let you finish breakfast." Rebecca stood.

I waved her off. "Good luck. They'll talk your ear off."

Ron and Ducky were working through pancakes and coffee. Hockey highlights flashed on the TV screen—the horn of a goal and the roaring crowd muffled under the newscaster's voice.

"All right, gentlemen," she said, sliding into the booth and flipping the recorder back on. "Can I get your name, how long you've been driving, and the worst storm you've ever been through?"

Ron wiped his mouth and leaned back. "Ron Calhoun. Thirty-one years behind the wheel. Worst one was Pennsylvania, 1996, ice storm. It was so cold my truck froze to the ground. I had to take a torch and a hand sledge to the brakes to get moving again."

"You were stuck how long?" she asked.

"Two days," he said. "Slept in the seat, ate crackers, and listened to the radio."

She turned to Ducky. "Your turn."

He grinned. "Donald Carver. Twenty-five years behind the wheel. Worst storm? Take your pick. I have seen Wyoming close the same highway three times in one day. Once I was chained up for so long, I forgot my wife's birthday."

"You actually forgot your wife's birthday?"

"Yep. Couple of days. She reminded me when she called to chew me out for not calling her."

Ron snorted into his coffee. "He's lucky she didn't change the locks."

The counter radio squawked with a quick road update in French. The waitress translated without looking up. "Accident cleared near Sussex, all lanes open."

Rebecca checked her notes. "All right, last one. Why do you keep doing it?"

Ron shrugged. "I still like the view."

Ducky added, "Beats sitting still. Besides, somebody's got to move this stuff."

"That's a better answer than most people give," she said.

Ron smirked. "It's the only one that makes sense."

At 0800, Bret stood by the window, clipboard in one hand, coffee in the other. Natasha sidled up beside him with her tablet. "All right, quick brief," he said. "The storm is ahead of us, moving northeast. Roads to Moncton are passable but greasy. All info is on your tablets for the push to the ferry, last truck on by twenty-fifteen local. Top every tank, mains, auxiliaries, whatever we've got. No exceptions."

Natasha added, "Check your paperwork before we roll."

A local in a knit cap pointed at the TV ticker and called over, "They're saying wind picks up after lunch. If you're going, go."

Bret nodded. "That's the plan."

By 0830 everyone was outside, shoulders hunched against the wind. Plows passed in pairs, throwing snow in waves. We hit the small fuel island. Pumps moved slow in the cold, handles icy, hoses stiff. You could smell the winter additive sharp in the air.

Bret walked the line, checking caps and straps. Our temperature gauges in the cabs crept upward. At 0945 he came over the radio. "Line up for customs. All lights on for inspection. Stay sharp."

"Copy," I said, easing forward. The rigs moved nose to tail toward the row of booths, amber flashers cutting through the gray.

Customs opened at 1000 hours on the nose. Harley idled at the lead; Billy Bob bracketed the tail. Natasha and Rebecca went inside with the paperwork while the rest of us waited in the inspection lane, mirrors checked, undercarriages scanned, officers polite but slow.

Nat came back out ten minutes later, muttering, "They want a form they have never asked for before." She dug through the binder and jogged back inside. Everything was suddenly fine when she returned. Rebecca followed a step behind her, smiling just enough to make you wonder.

By 1115 we were cleared into Canada, trucks staged in the holding lot waiting on stamped packets. Bret paced between cabs, radio clipped to his collar. "Now that it's almost time to stop for lunch, we are good to go," he said. "Let's roll north. Storm is still ahead of us, but the roads are open."

We eased onto the Trans-Canada Highway under a low silver sky. Snow flurries rode the wind across the lanes, curling ahead toward open road. The ferry wouldn't wait for us.

The convoy eased out in order, Harley up front, Billy Bob trailing Bret's dually. All lights on. Natasha called roll from the van; Bret echoed the check over the radio. The ferry manifest said last truck on would be 2015 hours local time and even though the road looked open, every one of us knew the clock was already breathing down our necks.

The flurries turned to a cold mist, heavy enough to coat mirrors but light enough to fool you into thinking the storm was done. It wasn't. Radar said the real wall was sitting north of Moncton, waiting for anyone dumb enough to come looking for it.

···◆◆◆···

Rebecca leaned her camera on the dash. The wipers brushed a slow rhythm against the glass. "You mind if I record while we roll?"

Nat smiled. "Sure. Just don't catch me swearing at permit forms. Makes me sound like a lunatic."

"I'll edit out the evidence," Rebecca said. "How long have you been in dispatch?"

"Officially? Six years," Nat replied, eyes steady on the road. "But Pops started testing me way before that. Used to hand me route charts and ask which states needed banners or escorts. I think he wanted to see if I could read his handwriting."

Rebecca chuckled. "He sounds a lot like my dad. Always had me solving problems to keep me busy."

Nat shot her a grin. "Military type, too?"

"Yeah. Army, then private contracting. Couldn't retire if you paid him."

Nat raised a brow. "Didn't you say he was Navy once? Rescue swimmer?"

Rebecca hesitated, then smiled thin. "Briefly. Before he switched branches. Long story."

Nat nodded, letting it go. "That's dedication."

The CB crackled, Harley's voice coming through. "Bridge clear. Rolling steady."

"Copy," Nat answered into the mic.

Rebecca thumbed off the recorder. "Nice start, Nat. I'll catch Bret at the next stop."

Around noon the traffic thinned. Salt trucks laid clean stripes, and the world went from wet gray to white again.

At the rest area, Rebecca hopped out of the van to go interview Bret. Nat didn't mind the quiet.

Bret had the hood up on the dually, a flashlight wedged under his arm checking a coolant line. He looked up when Rebecca walked over. "Hop in before you freeze."

She climbed into the passenger seat, tucking her notebook beside the coffee cups and buzzing about wanting a mechanic's eye view. "How long you been with Pops?" she asked.

He smiled. "Since before I knew what I was doing. I used to run a bowling alley in town. It burned down, total loss. Pops rolled in that night hauling a D9 dozer, saw the mess, and stuck around. Next day he offered me a job."

"So he recruited you?" she asked.

"More like rescued me," Bret said. "Mercer was already rolling, but he needed somebody who could keep pace. Figured I was too stubborn to quit. He was right."

"You two sound like family," she said.

"Out here, you act like it or you don't last," Bret said. "Pops gives people chances. Most of us try not to waste them."

She smiled. "Sounds familiar."

Bret tilted his head. "What does your family do?"

"Operations work of sorts. Different kind of freight, I guess."

He chuckled. "Long as it keeps the lights on."

Rebecca laughed, watching snow swirl across the windshield. "Something like that."

··◆◆◆◆··

It was mid-afternoon on the run toward Moncton, road flat and open across the snowfields. I had the Kenworth settled at fifty when the pyro started creeping higher than it had any reason to, nine hundred, nine fifty, a thousand on flat ground. I checked the dash. Water temp was edging up, not hot, just wrong. Then the truck coughed once, hard, and a streak of gray smoke rolled out of the stacks.

"Bret, she is not right, smoking bad."

"I see it. Ease over."

We coasted onto a plowed turnout about five miles from Moncton. The smell hit first, raw diesel, thick and bitter. I eased to the shoulder, hazards on, gray haze curling out of the stacks like a warning flag. The idle stumbled, felt like one cylinder dead.

I set the brakes, dropped her into neutral and climbed down into the cold. By the time I walked up along the driver's side, the miss was something I could feel in my ribs. I grabbed the fender and pulled the hood open. Now I could hear it, uneven thump, smoke rolling out heavy from the stacks and hanging low in the cold.

Bret rolled up and was out before his truck stopped. He came around to the driver's side and stood shoulder-to-shoulder with me by the steer tire, both of us listening.

"Smoke's the wrong color," he said. "Unburnt fuel. Does she clear up at all if you throttle up?"

"Nah, she gets worse."

"Kill it," he said. "Sounds like an injector or two. No sense pumping fuel into the oil and spinning a bearing."

I climbed back in, shut her down, then stepped out again. For a second it was the tick, tick, tick of cooling metal and our breath in the cold.

Bret leaned in with the flashlight and checked around the fuel filter and lines for leaks. "Any codes?"

"Nothing lit."

"Okay," he said, backing off. "Let's find a shop and someone who knows N14s." He jogged back to the dually, climbed in, and started searching. A beat later he keyed the CB. "Nearest shop is—wait for it—Redneck Rocket Science and Diesel Therapy. You can't make that up!"

Ducky came over the CB. "Sounds like my kind of place."

"Yeah," Bret said. "If they have parts and coffee, I'll send them a Christmas card."

He got them on the phone. "Yeah, hi, this is Bret with Mercer Hauling. Got a Kenworth W900L with an N14 Cummins about five miles south, coughing its guts out, heavy white/grey smoke will not clean up when I step on the throttle. We're on a tight schedule. Any chance you can squeeze us in?"

Voice on the phone: "Could be a fuel filter coming apart, maybe the pump is acting up. Worst case, you've got an injector or two sticking. Won't know till I get my hands on it. Where exactly are you parked?"

Bret: "Plowed turnout near the 114 junction past the green Moncton Recycling sign. We've got several trucks behind us and need to keep the convoy together if possible. You have room for all the rigs to park?"

Voice: "I can fit the tractors in my lot, but the support trucks need to head up the road. Bluebird Motel on the west side of 114 across from the Irving diner. The owner is used to truckers parking there. Tell her I sent you."

Bret: "Copy that. I found your place online, Redneck Rocket Science and Diesel Therapy, red metal building with old hoods hanging on the fence, right?"

Voice, laughing: "That's the one. I'm Eddie. Big gravel lot out front, two bays, and just enough heat to keep the coffee from freezing. Don't let any grass grow. I am a busy man."

Bret: "Appreciate it, Eddie. We're rolling your way now."

We limped the five miles to a squat cinder block shop with a crooked sign that read, REDNECK ROCKET SCIENCE AND DIESEL THERAPY: If It Smokes, We'll Fix It... Eventually.

Eddie met us at the door, wiping his hands on a rag. He listened for ten seconds, then shook his head. "She's over-fueling. At least one injector stuck open, maybe two," he said. "I'll call the parts house in town. If they're short, I may have to fly parts in out of Argentia."

Bret frowned. "That's where the ferry runs from, right?"

Eddie nodded. "Right. Airstrip is close. If I have to fly anything in, it won't cost you much in time."

"All right," Bret said. "Let us know what you find out. If you need parts, get 'em coming as quickly as possible."

We rolled the truck into the bay and set the chocks. Eddie waved a hand. "Let's open her up." Floodlights snapped on as his crew pulled the hood over. Eddie pulled the dipstick, rubbed the oil between his fingers, and sniffed. "That's not oil anymore, it's diesel." He slid under the truck, cracked the drain plug, and watched the thin diesel-washed oil pour into a catch pan. He whistled. "You shut her down just in time."

He climbed out, wiping his hands. "We'll flush it, change filters, refill with fifteen forty. House brand is what I've got." He nodded toward the injector rail. "I'll ohm the injectors next. If the parts house has them, we're fast. If not, I'll get them flown in."

Eddie stepped into the office, made the calls, and came back two minutes later. "Local has one on the shelf, second can be here on a courier by twenty-two-hundred from Argentia. If nothing slips, I can have you buttoned up by oh-six-hundred."

Bret turned to me. "Good. Now we have an ETA. Let's get the crew fed. Nat will call in the update from the diner."

Rebecca stood beside me, flakes drifting sideways through the yard light. "Does this happen often?" she asked.

"Not to me," I said. "But trucks are like people, they act up at the worst times."

She smiled faintly. "Then I guess she's human."

Inside the bay, Eddie's crew worked under the lights. Tools clattered, air hissed, and every minute scraped a little more off our margin. Bret clapped my shoulder. "Go grab something hot, Pops. I'll stay here with Eddie."

"Copy that." I took one last look at my truck, hood open and thin diesel-washed oil spattering into the drain pan, then we all piled into Natasha's van or shotgun in the pilot cars and headed toward the diner up the street, racing the storm and the clock.

The café was half lit and smelled like fried onions, coffee, and wet coats. The kind of place that had seen more winters than customers. I ordered stew. The waitress poured coffee that could strip paint and she left the pot behind, muttering something about the roads icing over.

Outside, snow thickened under the streetlights. Through the window I could see the glow of Eddie's shop two blocks down, our trucks lined up like tired horses.

Bret finally arrived, dusted in snow, and hung his coat on a rack that leaned like it was giving up. "Eddie's got the injectors coming on a freight hop out of Argentia," he said, rubbing his hands. "They'll land at the airfield around midnight and he can get started before daylight."

I nodded. "How bad?"

"He said we caught it early. Fuel thinned the oil, but you shut her down before she ate herself."

Natasha sat at a corner booth, ferry schedules glowing on her tablet. "First available sailing is ten-hundred. If Eddie finishes by seven, we can make staging."

Rebecca looked up from her notebook, pen tapping the page. "You ever think about how much of this job is waiting?"

Bret grinned. "It's all waiting. We charge by the mile to make it feel like we're working."

Chad bowed his head. "Lord, bless this food, the hands that made it, and keep us steady through the storm ahead. Amen."

Ducky snorted into his cup. "Amen and maybe throw in some pie while you're at it."

Ron jabbed his fork toward me. "You realize if we miss that ferry, it's coming out of your cut, Pops. You're the one who broke first."

"Yeah? Next time I'll let her melt down on the highway and we'll see who makes the ferry then."

Harley, sitting by the window, watched the snow. "I'm glad it's your rig in the shop and not mine. I'm allergic to wrenches after dark."

Billy Bob raised his mug. "Here's to breakdowns happening somewhere with food, coffee, and indoor plumbing. Beats fixing one in the middle of nowhere."

The waitress stopped by with refills. "You all headed for the coast?"

Bret smiled. "If the trucks behave."

"My cousin runs freight up that way," she said, setting down a basket of rolls. "Said the ferry crews are running behind, ice buildup near the docks. He's stuck at the terminal with a bad attitude and a load of lumber."

Natasha looked up. "When was that?"

"Couple hours ago," the waitress said. "They were hoping to start moving again by morning."

Nat glanced at her tablet again then back to me. "That delay might actually work in our favor. I'll send the update up the chain, let them know our timeline is holding for now."

She slid the tablet aside and pulled out the satellite phone, voice steady but quiet.

"Command, this is Mercer Dispatch. Mechanical delay south of Moncton, injector replacement in progress. Local shop expects completion before oh-seven-hundred. Terminal reports ferry operations delayed by ice, next sailing currently posted for ten-hundred. We expect to make that sailing if repairs stay on track. Will advise immediately if ETA changes."

There was a pause, then a muffled voice on the other end. "Copy, Mercer. Monitor repairs and keep us updated."

"Copy," she said. "Mercer Dispatch out."

We finished dinner in the low hum of locals talking hockey and weather. The space heater in the corner rattled, trying to keep up with the cold. By the time we paid the check, the snow outside was falling straight down, heavy and quiet.

The café emptied. Outside, snow drifted in lazy sheets under the streetlights. Rebecca slung her duffel over her shoulder and jingled the van keys. "I'll take first watch," she said, looking over at Natasha. "You boys get your sleep. I can nap in the morning when we're back under way."

Bret frowned. "You sure? It's cold enough to freeze a rumor out there."

"I've done worse," she said. "Besides, someone should keep eyes on the trailers."

By twenty-one-hundred support crew and I had checked into the little motor lodge Eddie mentioned. The heat barely kept up, but it was dry and close. I called it a night, boots by the heater, phone on the nightstand. Wind worked the window seams in a slow moan, same rhythm as a reefer cycling on a cold dock.

···◆◆◆···

Over in Eddie's lot, Rebecca idled the ops van near the line of stationary giants. Ron, Chad, and Ducky were hunkered down in their sleepers, engines idling. Diesel throb echoed off the motel wall. She cracked the window to keep the windshield clear, tuned the AM band until a talk radio signal came through fuzzy, local news, then an old country song that came from another century. She poured coffee from a thermos, steam curling through the cab, and unwrapped a bag of pretzels. The smell of diesel and cold, damp dark hung in the air.

Around twenty-three-thirty, a pair of headlights turned off highway 114 and bounced across the snow-packed lot. Rebecca straightened in her seat, watching a small box truck ease up to the shop. The side read "Eddie's Diesel, Field Freight Division."

Eddie stepped out of the bay, breath smoking under the lights. He waved the truck in with two short sweeps of his hand. A young guy hopped down, mid-twenties maybe, parka half-zipped, cap backward, worn thin from the drive.

"Would you sign this already?" the kid said, shivering. "It's cold enough to make the ink stop dead. Parts house boxed everything up, I double checked the contents, got both injectors, seals, and filters."

Eddie clapped him on the shoulder. "Good. Let's get them inside before they freeze."

Rebecca cracked the van door enough to hear the exchange. Diesel and cold air rolled in together. The kid carried a cardboard box marked 'Fragile, Fuel System Components' into the bay. As he passed, his eyes drifted across the line of Mercer trucks, nothing pushy, just a little too curious for someone dropping parts. When the door thudded shut behind them, she poured more coffee and watched the glow from the shop windows.

A few minutes later, the driver came back out pulling on gloves. He climbed into the truck and idled a moment before backing toward the road. Rebecca stepped out into the cold and walked toward the bay. Eddie looked up when she poked her head in. "Everything came in, right?" she asked.

"Yeah," he said. "Courier was late. Said the highway north of Sussex was half-closed with drifts. But I've got both injectors now. I'll button her up before I grab any sleep."

"Good. I wanted to make sure nothing got missed."

Eddie grinned. "If it did, I would blame my cousin, Rob."

She smiled, stepped back out, and let the door close behind her. The box truck's taillights faded up the highway, pausing at the intersection longer than it should have. Something about it tugged at her attention, maybe how it turned north instead of west.

Pulling her hood drawstrings tight, she grabbed a flashlight from the van and walked the line of trucks, checking straps, covers, and the slow vapor drifting from each stack. Everything looked fine, tight, untouched. Still. The hair on her neck would not settle.

Back in the cab, she jotted a note in her pad. Courier truck arrived twenty-three-thirty, departed twenty-three-forty-two. White box truck, Eddie's Diesel lettering, headed north. Then she switched off the dome light, sipped her coffee, and watched the road until the snow swallowed the last of the taillights.

Around zero-one-hundred, headlights washed across the lot again. A cruiser eased in slow, tires crunching the snow. Rebecca watched the reflection sweep across the dash. The driver's door opened, and a uniformed officer stepped out, flashlight in hand.

She rolled the window down halfway. "Evening, Officer."

He leaned toward the beam of light, breath fogging in the cold. "Evening, ma'am. Everything all right?"

"Fine, sir. Just keeping an eye on our trucks. One's in the bay, hoping to roll out at daybreak."

He nodded, scanning the quiet line of rigs. "Figured it might be you folks. Eddie mentioned you had equipment parked over here. Just doing my rounds."

"Appreciate it," she said. "Didn't mean to spook anybody."

"No trouble," he said, then added with a hint of a smile, "We don't get many folks sitting in parking lots with the interior lights on this late. You from around here?"

"Texas," she said. "We stop in every winter to make sure you all remember what hard work looks like."

That earned a laugh. "Fair enough. Need to see some ID if you don't mind."

Rebecca passed it through the crack in the window. He took it, glanced at the photo, then handed it back. "Looks good. Long way from home, Ms. Lane."

"Tell me about it. I've been in warmer morgues."

He grinned. "Can't argue that. Eddie keeping it warm in there?"

She raised an eyebrow. "If by warm you mean the lights are still on, sure. He's probably working in gloves."

"Yeah, that sounds like him. Man runs that heater like he's charging by the degree." He tilted his head toward the trailers. "Mind if I ask what you're hauling?"

Rebecca didn't miss a beat. She let her eyes flick to the mirror, then to the trailers, small, plain, unmarked crates glinting under the floodlights, and back to him. The officer followed the look, a quick, professional glance, then back to her face.

"Nothing I am allowed to talk about, Officer," she said evenly. "Safer for everyone if we keep it that way."

He studied her for a second, then exhaled a breath that sounded like acceptance. "Fair enough. Sounds above my pay grade."

"Most things are," she said with a wink.

He chuckled, brushing snow from his hat. "All right, Ms. Lane, I'll let you get back to your stakeout. You need anything, call dispatch. I'm around all night."

"Appreciate it, Officer. I'll be here, guarding the world's most boring view."

"Try the AM band," he suggested. "That's where we hide all the excitement."

She smiled. "Already on it."

He tipped his hat, stepped back into the cruiser, and rolled off into the snow, taillights fading red down the road.

Rebecca poured another cup of coffee and adjusted the gap in the window. The night smelled like exhaust and freezing air. She leaned back, listening to static and an occasional song through the rumble of idling engines, thermostat clicks, and an occasional plow truck in the distance. The world reduced to small, steady sounds. The AM station shifted between a hockey recap, farm price reports, and a late-night host talking about the best way to fry cod. She smiled at that, turned the volume down, and finished her coffee.

By a quarter past two, the thermos was empty, and the cold was winning. She fired the van into gear and eased out to the main road, headlights slicing through the drifting snow. The Irving, half a mile up still glowed against the white, an island of fluorescent light and slush.

Inside, the clerk looked up from a crossword. "Cold night to be running deliveries this late."

"Tell me about it," Rebecca said, shaking off her coat. "Coffee still hot?"

"Depends on your standards."

"I'll risk it." She slid a few bills across the counter and pointed toward the back. "Restroom still open?"

"Always. Watch your step. The plows came through, and folks tracked in a lake."

She returned a few minutes later to steam curling from a fresh thermos fill. The clerk was by the window now, looking at the plowed snow lining the street. "You folks parked down by Eddie's?" he asked.

She nodded. "He has one of our trucks in the shop."

"Good man, Eddie. Grumpy as a badger, but he gets it done."

Rebecca smiled. "Seems like the kind you want turning the wrenches."

He chuckled. "That's him. And be careful on that bridge heading back, it's slicker than glass tonight."

"Appreciate it." She climbed back into the van. The heater was struggling but steady. By the time she eased into Eddie's lot again, powdery snowdrifts had blown an extra dusting on the hoods of every truck. She parked where she had been, lights dimmed, radio back to low static and slow music.

At zero-three-hundred she keyed the handheld. "Nat, it's Rebecca. All secure. No movement except a plow and one local patrol. Temps are dropping, but the trucks look good."

"Copy that," Natasha's voice came back, scratchy from sleep. "Maintain watch. Call in again at oh-four-thirty."

Rebecca scribbled a note and sipped the steaming coffee, watching Eddie's shop light hold its place on the horizon. The night moved slow. She dozed in short fits between checks, the warmth of the thermos heating a small patch on the outside of her thigh and the radio murmuring like company.

At zero-four-thirty she keyed up again. "Nat, Rebecca again. All secure. No change."

"Copy, Rebecca. Continue monitoring until daylight."

She leaned back, rubbing her eyes. The sky started to smudge pale at the edges. When the first mechanics' steps sounded over at the shop, she gave the line another sweep with her eyes. Snow stacked on the hoods, everything looked untouched, nothing out of place. She zipped her coat, locked the doors, and headed for the bay.

··✦✦✦✦··

I woke up before five. The lot at the Bluebird was a white sheet under a pale moon. Out by the highway, Eddie's shop lights were already burning. I could hear the faint hiss of an airline and the bark of a wrench on metal.

By six, the support crew and I had drifted back to the shop: Bret with coffee, Natasha with breakfast sandwiches. Rebecca was bundled in her coat, filming the activity. Eddie waved from under the hood. "She's buttoned up. Oil is fresh, filters new, injectors in three and four replaced. Fire her when you're ready."

Bret looked at me. "You want the honors?"

I climbed in, keyed the starter, and she fired right off, no hesitation, smooth and even like nothing ever happened. Relief rippled through the lot. I held her at an idle while the temps came up.

Eddie wiped his hands. "No leaks on the rail. Let her warm and keep it easy till everything's hot."

Bret said, "You got an invoice for us?" Eddie passed him the paper. "Canadian or U.S.?" Bret asked.

"Canadian is easier," Eddie said. "If you have U.S., I'll write the rate on the slip."

Bret handed him an envelope. "Here you go, and a little extra from the group for the quick turnaround."

Eddie nodded. "Appreciate it. Roads are open to the ferry but keep your lights on. They're still plowing shoulders."

Natasha checked her watch. "If we roll now, terminal by oh-nine-thirty."

"Copy that," I said. "Let's move."

Engines settled into a fast idle, stacks breathing white in the cold. The storm had blown itself out before midnight, leaving the world scrubbed white and quiet. Harley rolled first. I fell in behind her, then Ron, Ducky, and Chad. Bret followed in the dually and Natasha drove the ops van with Rebecca riding shotgun, seat reclined a little and half dozing after her night watch. Billy Bob set the tail.

"Fuel checks," I called on the radio. "I want a read before we hit the highway."

Ron said, "Three quarter. Good to the boat."

Ducky said, "Same. She'll drink a little once we're rolling, but we're good."

Chad said, "Seven eighths. We're fine."

Harley said, "I'm good to go."

Bret called out, "All support vehicles circle back to the Irving by the motel and top your tanks. Harley, make sure all fuel cans are full in case anyone needs a splash later."

"Copy. No stops till the terminal. Keep it tight," Harley answered.

AM radio hissed low in my cab, farm prices, a weatherman half asleep saying the bay was open and roads were salted to the ferry. An old song faded under him, steel guitar thin as ice.

Eddie stood by the bay door while we filed past, phone up for a quick picture and the other hand waving a tired circle. He looked like a man who had wrestled a bull and kept the horns. I gave him a little air horn tap. He tipped his cap and pocketed the phone, eyes lifting toward the highway like he was still working on some problem in his head.

We rolled out in single file. Sun broke under the cloud shelf and turned the snowfields gold. Out past the fences a school bus idled, headlights haloed, breath from a lone horse smoking in the field. The plows had carved the shoulders high, lane paint showing like a fresh shave.

"Irving fuel stop has open pumps, filling all tanks," Bret said.

Natasha said, "Copy. Two minutes to grab coffee, then we're back on your tail."

"Copy," I answered. "Hold the lane until we're clear of town."

The convoy eased past the Bluebird motor lodge; that was when I saw the van parked by the far pumps. Black. No decals. Glass dark enough to see yourself in and almost nothing behind it. Two men stood at the rear doors, shoulders hunched, one with a fat duffel that looked like it belonged at an airfield more than a gas station. Plenty of folks wait on freight runs, but the way they watched us didn't sit right.

Billy Bob came up on the channel, easy as breathing. "Ops, you get that van at the Irving?"

Bret said, "I see it."

Harley said, "Plate looked Newfoundland. Too far from home for a casual stop."

"Copy that. Eyes on but keep rolling," I said.

We cleared the ramp. Highway ran level and clean, frost glittering in the median like ground glass. AM radio slid to classic rock, snare drum sounding like a door slamming in a cold shop. Ducky started in about breakfast. "I can smell the bacon from here," he said. "Might be my imagination."

Chad said, "Pray for self-control."

Ron said, "Pray for the ferry coffee to be drinkable."

"Save the sermons for now," Bret said. "Support is topped. Transfer cells full. We've got a cushion if anyone needs a splash before the ferry."

"Copy, Bret. Hold the rear till we're past the river bridge," I said.

We ran sixty-five, no reason to push. Sun climbed and flattened the shadows. A grader sat dead on a side road, orange paint glowing, operator sipping from a thermos and giving us a chin lift as we passed. The world looked peaceful. Nobody seeing us roll by would guess how hard yesterday fought us, or how ready we were to move again.

Fifteen miles from the terminal, Rebecca keyed up. "Van ahead, right shoulder, same make, same tint."

Harley said, "Visual."

Bret said, "Copy. Parked behind a plow truck. Two inside this time."

I saw it as we came up, a black rectangle in the corner of my eye, idling. No one stepped out. It stayed put till we went by, then nosed in behind a tanker like it was shy.

"Let it go," I said. "We aren't here to make friends."

"Roger," Harley said. "Next sign for the ferry in two."

Wind found us once we crested the last rise. You could smell the water before you saw it, salt and iron and something like cold pennies. The bay lay slate blue under the morning sky, streaked with whitecaps and the slow churn of tugs moving in for the next load. An ice shove crushed along the edges where the tugs had worked the night, crackling as the tide turned.

Harley took the lead lane like she had done it a hundred times. I swung in behind her, then Ron, Ducky, and Chad. Bret and Rebecca pulled up along the fence. Billy Bob tucked in last, hazard strobes ticking slow and bright.

Terminal crews in reflective jackets were already hustling like the clock owed them money. Breath fogged in thick bursts as they jogged between lanes, radios clipped to collars hissing with half-overlapping instructions. A yard boss in a hard hat walked the line waving a clipboard like a sword, shouting times nobody believed. You could feel the backlog before you saw it, rows of trucks inching forward, drivers leaning out windows waiting for somebody to tell them the ocean had decided to cooperate. We waited too.

A dockhand motioned us ahead with sharp, fast swings of his glove. No small talk. A woman in a knit cap pointed us toward the line of commercial vehicles, her gloves white with salt spray, muttering into her radio about "two hours behind and sliding toward three." A pair of deckhands dragged a stubborn hose reel across the pavement, cussing like they had been born doing it.

Natasha had the tablet up, giving confirmation codes to a checker who barely looked up. He ticked boxes and waved, eyes already on the next rig. Drivers stood outside their cabs, boots planted in slush, coffee steaming in one hand, paperwork flapping in the wind. One guy up the line kicked a tire like he was expecting it to apologize.

Rebecca stepped out long enough to get a few pictures and stretch. She scanned the lot like she could read a story in the way people moved: frustration, nerves, boredom, all of it simmering under the cold.

I kept the Kenworth at a high idle, gauges steady. Eddie's work felt good under my boots, no stumble, no haze, oil pressure right where it ought to be.

A gull dropped out of the sky and screamed at a dockhand. He screamed back and kept walking. Seemed about right for dock diplomacy.

Around us, the morning was boots on gravel, radios talking over each other, dock crews pushing late freight into tighter piles, and impatient drivers watching a whole lot of nothing happen slower than it should. Someone slammed a pallet jack so hard it echoed across the lot.

Out in the fog, the loading bridge clanged home against the berth, a hollow metal slap that said, "Wake up, get moving, we're already behind!"

The ferry horn answered, low and annoyed, tired of waiting on the humans.

"All trucks staged and parked," Harley said. "Just waiting on the orange vest ants running around the dock to wave us into their ant hill."

"Copy that," I said, settling the idle a notch lower. The world smelled like salt and exhaust; a choir of people coming from every direction, trying to catch up to a schedule that was already ahead of them.

Journal Entry 10

A long twenty-four hours for all of us.

The Kenworth coughed halfway to Moncton, fuel in the oil, and smoke out the stacks. Caught it early, thank God.

Eddie and his crew at Redneck Rocket Science and Diesel Therapy worked like they had something to prove. Had her breathing again before dawn.

We waited out the repairs at the diner up the street. Locals talked about hockey and weather.

Rebecca stayed up all night on watch, eyes sharp like she was lining up a target.

My engine fired right off in the morning, no hesitation, every gauge right where it ought to be.

We rolled for the coast. Eddie waved us out like a man sending his kids off to college.

It didn't feel like victory, relief more than anything.

We made it to the ferry at North Sydney.

Next, whatever waits beyond it.

—Pops

Chapter 12

TRAVELER ON THE OCEAN

The horn off the bay moaned once, low and tired, as the morning came gray over the lot. Wind cut through the line of trucks parked nose to tail. Bret had everyone circle up by the van.

Natasha stood beside him with the tablet open to the ferry manifest, hood drawn tight, coffee steaming in one hand.

"All right, listen up," Bret said. "We're loading in thirty. Ferry crew wants trucks on first, then the RVs and cars. Pilots will stage on the upper deck so they can roll ahead when we dock. It's about a sixteen-hour crossing, four-hour rotations."

He looked down the line, counting faces.

"Pops and I have first shift down by the trucks. Ron, Chad, Ducky, you're second watch. Harley and Billy Bob take third. Rebecca and Nat bring it home. We'll meet in the restaurant up top before we start our rounds."

He scrolled the tablet. "We've got five berths paid. Split them as needed for rack time. When we hit the other side, we top off fuel before anything else. All tanks, jugs, and cells full. Then a nine-hour run to final, and the weather's turning. Forecast says the storm's pushing ahead of schedule."

161

Bret looked up. "Merritt wants status reports at each leg. Keep comms disciplined."

Then he added what he didn't like saying out loud. "Lockbox stays in my truck. One armed per shift. Pops, Chad, Harley, Rebecca, you're cleared. Sidearms only." He closed the tablet. "That's it. Let's get this show on the water."

Harley fired up her pilot car and rolled toward the gate, hazard strobes cutting through the fog. Billy Bob fell in behind her.

The dock chief stepped out, clipboard in hand, motioning the two pilots toward the upper ramp. "Pilots go top deck, first off at landing," he said. Harley gave him a thumbs-up and peeled right.

"Convoy trucks, hold formation," Bret called. "We're lower deck. Follow the wands."

I eased onto the bridge. Tires rang on steel. Salt, grease, and paint hung in the air. A deckhand in a knit cap stepped in front of my bumper, palm down, directing me left a foot, then right half that. Hand up, stop. I set the brakes, dropped into neutral, and let her settle.

The deck foreman came over with a tablet and folding stick, pencil behind his ear. "Need your numbers, driver. Gross, axle spacing, where the weight sits."

"RGN. Gross one-zero-eight. Steers twelve, drives forty, trailer fifty-six. Eighty between drives and first trailer, forty between trailer axles. Center of gravity about a third back on the deck."

He crouched, measured kingpin to axles, checked my tag, and tapped in notes. "Any liquids? Slosh risk?"

"Truck fuel and cells only. Cargo's dry."

"Copy. You're port two. Extra chain on the frame. She'll want to walk if we get a corkscrew."

He glanced at my securement. "Chocks next, then ship chains to frame and neck. Don't touch the brakes till I clear you."

"Copy."

I sat tight. A deckhand shoved rubber chocks tight to the drives, rope tails tucked. "Clear!"

I set the brakes, stepped down, and started my walkaround: kicked the chocks, tugged my chains, killed everything but markers, and finished walking the perimeter. Everything sat the way it should.

Ron came up next. Same drill, weights, spacing, center of gravity, then waved starboard two to balance me. Ducky rolled in behind. Foreman quizzed him on spare rubber and loose gear, then flagged him port abeam me. Chad followed, mirrors close to the steel uprights and got sent starboard with two extra lashings over the trailer frame. Bret's dually and the ops van went inboard as ballast.

Above us, Harley and Billy Bob eased onto the upper car deck with the RVs and sedans. Harley keyed her mic, voice easy through static. "Pilots set topside. We'll stake out a table in the restaurant."

"Copy," I said.

Ship crew moved fast, chains low and wide. A rigger thumped my frame, slipped a protector under the web, threw a chain through the RGN neck, then spun the turnbuckle until it sang. Another ran a surge pair fore and aft on the trailer frame. "If she takes a bad roll, she won't walk," he said, more to the steel than to me.

Bret walked the lanes, writing who was port and who was starboard, checking chain angles and tension.

Ron: "Brakes set, chocks in, extra chain starboard."

Ducky: "Brakes set, chocks in, surge pair added."

Chad: "Brakes set, chocks in, frame double-lashed."

"Copy," I said. "Set here, walk around complete."

The foreman gave a last nod. "Good spread. We're level." He waved forward. "Close her up."

I took one more pass, brakes set, chocks set, lashings tight, wraps on binders, nothing loose. The trailers wouldn't walk when the ferry started moving.

Boots rang on the catwalk overhead, then the horn rolled through the hull, long, steady, heavy enough to feel in your chest. The outer ramp started to lift, dock light narrowing to a thin gray slice, then gone. The ship shifted underfoot as ballasts moved and the screws bit.

Bret keyed the handheld. "Deck's satisfied. Grab your bags and head topside. Restaurant before first watch."

I patted my fender once, the way you thank a good horse before you leave it for the night. The hold echoed with the rattle of chains, the hum of pumps, and the low grind of the sea getting its hands on the hull.

Steel hummed under my boots. Somewhere past that gray horizon another trek was waiting, also pointing northeast.

We left the lower deck through a narrow stairwell, the metal handrails cold enough to bite through gloves. The smell of oil and salty spray clung to everything. Every few seconds a loud clang somewhere below echoed like a hammer in a drum, and the floor trembled under our boots.

Halfway up, a blast of cold air came through an open door. We could see the docks fading behind us, lights shrinking through the fog, snow blowing sideways under the floodlamps. Fifteen degrees, maybe less. Out here it felt closer to zero, the kind of cold that gets under your collar and stays there.

The ship's intercom cracked to life, the speaker above our heads buzzing. "Good morning, folks! Captain MacLeod speaking from the bridge of Marine Atlantic's Ala'suinu. Welcome aboard. We're departing North Sydney bound for Channel–Port aux Basques, with an estimated crossing time of sixteen hours. Seas are rough today through the Cabot Strait with strong northeasterlies and freezing spray on the decks. For your safety, please remain seated while we clear the harbor, and use handrails on all stairways and corridors. Hot food and beverages are available on Deck Three. Outside gangways are open but slippery. Vehicle decks are closed for the crossing. On behalf of the crew, thanks for sailing with us. Ala'suinu means traveler on the ocean. Settle in, hold on, and we'll do our best to give you a steady ride."

"Traveler on the ocean," Bret said, shouldering his way up. "Let's hope she's in a good mood."

The door to Deck Three opened into a wall of sound. Hundreds of voices, fryer hiss, utensils clattering. The smell hit next: cheap food, wet coats, burned coffee. The cafeteria was packed end to end, condensation fogging the windows so bad you couldn't tell sea from sky. Every now and again, a slow tilt slid coffee in its cup.

"Looks like boat food," Bret said, staring at the line.

"Yeah," I said. "In winter."

He nodded once like that settled it.

We merged into the line. Three registers up front, two tired kids behind them, a hot bar steaming like a high school lunch line. Burgers, fries, something pretending to be stew. Plastic cups. Napkins that dissolved on contact. A sign said Beer $9 and Wine $10, explaining why some folks looked calmer than they ought to.

Ron pointed with his tray. "That soup alive?"

"I hope not," Chad said.

Ducky elbowed through, grabbing double fries and a cup of coffee. "Thick as gear oil," he told the kid behind the counter, his voice fading into the noise.

Harley and Billy Bob came in last, snow still melting off their jackets. "Smells like a truck stop had a baby with a cafeteria," Harley said.

Natasha and Rebecca arrived behind them, both working their phones like they could bully a signal into existence. "Comms tablet won't connect," Nat said. "GPS is bouncing all over."

"Good," Bret muttered. "Means nobody can call us."

My coat cuffs were still stiff with frost by the time we found an open table near the back wall. Outside, wind howled against the hull loud enough to make the glass hum.

Harley lifted her beer. "To not dying on a boat tonight."

Rebecca smiled without looking up from her notes.

Natasha shook her head. "Insurance doesn't cover seasick drivers, in case you're wondering."

Everybody laughed, then went quiet as the ship pitched once hard enough to rattle cups across tables. The lights flickered. You could feel the wind outside, heavy and mean, pressing at the walls like it wanted in.

"Maybe they're switching generators," Rebecca said.

"Yeah," I said. "Still sounds like she's working."

I watched faces a second. Tired. Cold. Good people trying to act normal. "Eat," I said. "Then rack out. Four-hour watches. Bret and I start, Ron and Chad after, Harley and Billy Bob take dusk, Rebecca and Nat bring us in. Ducky, you stick with second shift and keep the van radio open."

Bret pushed back from the table, stretching. "Copy that. Everybody else, find your berths or whatever passes for one. First shift, meet me by the stairwell in fifteen."

We headed down.

The restaurant noise fell away step by step until it was just the hull talking, low and steady like a truck frame with a load on. The lower deck felt colder than outside. Breath hung in the beam of my flashlight. Yellow work lamps marched down the lanes, throwing wet shine across steel and chain.

The ship's heartbeat came up through my boots, steady, then just a shade uneven, like a diesel thinking about dropping a cylinder and changing its mind.

Bret went to work. "Frame chains tight," he said, tapping each turnbuckle until it sang. "No slack. No twist. Protectors in place."

I ran the other side, chocks set, brakes set, wraps right, nothing rubbing.

A deckhand in an orange parka passed with a flashlight and a clipboard.

"Afternoon," Bret said.

"If you can call it that," the man said without stopping. "Port ballast tank's reading heavy again. Chief's on it."

"How heavy?" Bret asked.

"Couple tons high. Might be the gauge. Might be air. We'll reset it. You guys aren't supposed to be down here."

"We have clearance."

He gave us a questioning look and disappeared into the shadows like he'd never been there.

We finished the line. My trailer sat solid. Ron's RGN sat rock-steady starboard with extra chain where it should be. Ducky's surge pair was holding. Chad's frame was double-lashed just like the foreman wanted.

Everything said "good."

The floor under us said "watch it."

Bret wrote time and notes on his pad. "Log that little engine dip. You hear it?"

"Yeah," I said. "Half a beat off."

We started back. Halfway to the stairs the ship shuddered once, not hard, just a loud snap through the hull that made every hair on my neck stand up for a moment. Then nothing.

Bret stopped and looked back. "That didn't feel like the ocean."

"No," I said. "It didn't."

I climbed into the ops van long enough to warm hands while Bret walked off to grab coffee. Heater barely did anything, but it took the bite off my fingers. Ducky was already in the back tucked in a ball on the bench seat, sound asleep.

I keyed the handheld to test the signal and caught static, then a voice I knew better than my own.

"Hey," Katie said. "You still floating?"

"Floating and complaining," I said. "How's the office?"

"Quiet for once. I paid the three squeaky wheels and told the rest to call tomorrow. How's the boat?"

"Busy. Noisy. Feels like a parking lot with a propeller."

She laughed, soft. "And the crew?"

"Hungry and tired. Doing fine."

I heard shuffling papers and keys rattling in the background. "That reporter still tagging along?"

"She's with Nat," I said. "Sharp. Keeps Nat on her toes. Good person to have in a storm."

"So, good person to have around, huh?" Katie said, stretching the words like she was smiling. "You like her?"

"Don't start," I said, but it came out warmer than I meant.

"Okay, okay," she said. "Just be careful, old man. Storms and romance don't mix."

"Maybe not," I said. "But they make a story."

"Call me when you get a bar again."

"I will."

The line cracked once and went dead.

Bret ducked into the driver's seat with two cups of joe. "You tell her you're moonlighting for the advice column?"

"She heard something she wanted to hear," I said. "Not my fault."

"Sure isn't," he said, handing me a cup. "Just don't let Nat hear first. She'll have you registered and monogrammed before we hit the ramp."

I shook my head. "Very funny. Get your laughs in now."

Bret looked past me at the lane lights. "You ever notice how quiet it gets before the bad stuff? Not the good kind of quiet. The waiting kind."

"I noticed," I said. "Let's hand it to second watch."

We keyed up.

"Ron. Chad. Your turn. Chains tight, floor feels twitchy, port ballast gauge been acting up. Log anything you don't like," Bret said.

"Copy," Ron came back.

"Copy," Chad echoed.

Bret reached behind the seat and wrestled Ducky's foot until he woke up. "Ducky," Bret said. "Stick with them on the van radio."

"Copy," Ducky yawned.

I sat there a second longer than I meant to, listening to the ship through the windows. It wasn't panic—just a feeling you get when the air changes.

Then we headed up to rack out. Just before I attempted some shut eye, I jotted notes in my journal.

Journal Entry 11

Port aux Basques run under way.

Ferry packed tight, air cold enough to taste.

Trucks solid, chains tight, crew steady.

Engine hums a little off-beat, might be nothing, might be something.

Katie called. Good to hear her voice.

Bret's right, quiet feels like the waiting kind.

We'll see what the night brings.

—Pops

······◆◆◆······

The ship kept moving, but the radios weren't cooperating.

Static chewed up everything past a mile. The automatic identification system (AIS) blinked once, then went dark. GPS drifted, snapped back, drifted again. The crew didn't say much about it. They just wrote it down and stayed vigilant on the bridge.

On land, silence meant something else.

Colonel Merritt stood alone in a dim operations room, jacket still on, coffee untouched. Screens glowed dull blue and green. Weather overlays stacked. One icon blinked where it shouldn't have, then disappeared.

He tried to make contact. No answer. Tried a secondary relay. Nothing. He waited thirty seconds and tried once more. Still nothing.

That was enough. He stepped aside and dialed a number he had hoped not to use tonight.

Katie answered on the second ring, voice steady but sleepy. "This is Katie."

"Miss Mercer," Merritt said. "I won't take much of your time."

She was quiet now. Awake.

"I've lost contact with the ferry," he said. "Could be weather. Could be equipment. At the moment, I don't know."

"How long?" she asked.

"Minutes," he said. "Not hours."

She let that sit. "And my dad?"

"He's aboard. He's with his people. If anyone can ride out silence, it's him."

Another pause. Paper moved on her end. A chair squeaked. "What do you need from me?" she asked.

"Nothing yet," Merritt said. "If the line stays quiet, I'll call again. If it doesn't, you'll probably hear from him first."

"Yes, sir," she said. "Thank you for calling."

Merritt ended the call and stood there a moment longer than required, watching empty water on a screen that refused to explain itself.

Then he turned back to work.

The ship was still out there. So were the people who mattered.

Chapter 13

TRAVELER DOWN

Maybe I drifted off for an hour. The ship's roll had a hitch in it, too long between crests, then a hang to port like she meant it, enough to make the coffee cup on my nightstand walk an inch or two. Bored and sleepless, I pulled on my coat and went up to the bridge. The first mate, O'Rourke, caught me at the door. "Passengers aren't allowed up here."

"I'm not really sightseeing," I said. "It feels like something's wrong. Captain MacLeod, can I assist in any way? I can hold a heading on anything with a wheel if someone points me in the right direction. If you don't want the help, I'll go back down and mind my trucks."

MacLeod looked me over, jaw working, red alarm light painting the bridge in pulses. The inclinometer needle—a dash gauge that shows how far the boat is leaning off level—eased to eighteen, then twenty. He gave a tight nod. "Stand by the chart table. You don't touch a thing unless I tell you."

"Got it."

He leaned into the intercom. "Engineering, report."

Static, then O'Rourke: "Port ballast three won't isolate. She's sucking the ocean straight into the tank."

"Counter—the ballast starboard," MacLeod said. "Buy us a few degrees."

The deck shuddered. Down in my bones I felt another tone, deeper, slower. Not waves. Weight moving where it shouldn't.

My handheld crackled, then Ducky's voice came in thin. "Ops van. I've got odd noises between the rigs." He stopped for a beat. "Correction, odd noises and a flashlight down lane two. That's not crew down there."

The ship dipped hard enough I had to catch the chart table.

MacLeod's mouth flattened. "Security to the vehicle deck. Now!"

I keyed Bret. "You hear that?"

"On my feet," he said. "Halfway to the stairs."

The horn moaned, then the ship went black. A moment, then the generators kicked in and emergency lighting broke the darkness, emergency strips lit the walkways in red. The ship rolled further and held. Twenty-three degrees.

"Engines?" I asked.

"Spray in auxiliary space," O'Rourke responded. "Main switchboard tripped. Emergency generator's carrying alarms and lights. Propulsion is down."

Water was blowing into one of the equipment compartments below decks, packed with wiring and pumps. Saltwater and electricity don't share space for long.

"Rudder?"

"Hydraulic follow-up lost," the helmsman said. "No response."

The steering gear had dropped out. Without hydraulics pushing the rudder, the ferry was a victim of the waves and sea instead of driving through it.

I keyed the deck channel. "Bret. Get Rebecca and Nat. You three don't move without a crew lead. Offer your brains and keep it respectful."

"Copy," Bret said. "Moving."

··•✦•··

He took the mid-ship stairs two at a time, boots hammering metal steps as the ferry rolled under him. Rebecca grabbed the rail and kept pace while Natasha stayed tight behind them, one hand braced against the bulkhead, the other already pulling her gloves back on.

They hit the vehicle-deck hatch just as it slammed half-shut and rebounded with the ship's tilt. Cold air rushed up through the opening, smelling like diesel, saltwater, and hot wiring.

A bosun stepped into the doorway and threw an arm across it, blocking them.

"Passengers stay upstairs."

Rebecca didn't slow. Her breath fogged in the cold as she stepped into the red emergency glow. "Electrical and mechanical," she said, jerking a thumb toward Natasha, then herself. "You're losing pumps and steering. Let us help before it gets worse."

The bosun studied them, eyes flicking from Rebecca's boots to the grease under Natasha's fingernails, then back to Bret behind them. The deck shifted again, a slow roll that made everyone grab something solid.

"Do you know about ship systems?" he asked.

"Enough to keep water out of wiring and power moving," Rebecca said. "And enough to listen when your crew gives orders."

He held her stare one second longer than anyone liked in that red, tilting light. Somewhere below them, steel groaned as the ferry took another wave. He stepped aside.

"You stay with me," he said. "You do exactly what I tell you. Don't touch live panels unless my sparky clears it."

Rebecca nodded once. Natasha was already moving.

They splashed through ankle-deep brine. Water ran toward the scuppers in sheets. Chains hummed. The trucks groaned. They have a different sound under stress, like an old dog wailing in its sleep.

Ducky stood by the ops van with his light sweeping low. "Port aft seam is weeping. Not bilge. Taste that."

Rebecca caught a droplet on her glove, touched it to her tongue, then followed with a furrowed brow. "Salt. That's the sea, not tank overflow."

The bosun bristled. "You can't know that by taste."

"Pressure and taste," she said. "Bring me your ballast manifold sketch. And clamps."

Nat had a breaker box open with the ship's electrician beside her. She glanced up. "The emergency board's dry on this side. I can borrow a lighting feed and wake one ballast pump. It'll be ugly."

Nat snapped the panel shut a minute later. "I've got a plan. Temporary power, one pump. It'll either buy us time or it won't."

"Ugly may keep us upright," the electrician said, handing her tape and a panel key.

Up on the passenger deck, Harley hit the cafeteria first, Billy Bob and Chad right behind her. With the rough seas and Ala'suinu struggling to stay level, all passengers had been called to the muster station and were gathered on level three.

"Everybody up," Harley said, voice sharp enough to cut through panic. "Grab your kids and move to the inner stairwells. Do not open outside doors. Do not go on the gangways."

A woman pointed at a locker. "There's blankets in there."

Billy Bob kicked the latch and shouldered it open. Emergency gear tumbled out, foil blankets, lifejackets. He and Harley started handing them down the line.

"Jackets on," Harley called. "Strap them but don't pull them tight unless the crew tells you."

The ship rolled again. A coffee mug slid. Somebody screamed.

Chad stepped up onto a table bolted along the inner wall. The ferry rolled again, hard enough to rattle trays and send a few loose cups sliding. He planted his boots wide and grabbed the edge of the wall until the sway passed.

He didn't shout. He waited, let the noise settle just enough for people to notice someone wasn't losing their head. "Hey folks," he said, voice steady but not loud. "Look this way for a second." A few faces turned. A few stayed buried in their hands. He nodded like that was fine. "The crew's working on it. The ship's still upright. Right now, the best thing we can do is stay seated and keep each other steady so the crew can do their job."

He eased down into a crouch instead of standing over them. Made himself seem smaller, easier to listen to. "I'm gonna say a prayer," he added, simple as that. "You're welcome to listen. You're welcome to join in. Or just sit quietly."

He bowed his head and rested one grease-stained hand against the wall, fingers spread like he was grounding himself through the steel. "Lord, we could really use a steady hand right now," he said. His voice stayed low, conversational, like he was talking to a friend instead of a crowd. "Watch over the crew working this ship. Give them clear heads and sure footing. Keep this vessel sound and pointed in the right direction." The ferry shuddered again, a deep metal groan rolling through the hull. Chad paused, waited for it to pass, then continued without rushing. "Help us keep fear from running the room. Help us look out for the person sitting next to us. Keep our families safe wherever they are tonight." He drew in a slow breath. "If this storm's a way for you to love us in a way we don't really understand, please be with us, comfort us and wrap us in your loving arms. Amen."

He lifted his head slightly but didn't stand yet. He stayed crouched, not breaking the moment, just breathing steady. Around the room, hands found other hands. Some passengers bowed their heads. Some just leaned shoulder to shoulder with the person beside them. A child across the aisle copied Chad's slow breathing, her mother following a second later.

The noise didn't stop. The ferry still rolled and creaked and complained about the sea but the edge came off the room. Panic loosened its grip and settled into shared quiet. Chad slid off the table and sat against the wall with them like he belonged there.

Continuing his shift, Ducky swept his light across the deck again. He slowed near Ron's trailer. Even from a few feet away, it looked wrong. He lifted the chain. Cut clean.

"Bridge," he said. "The chain across the container door on Ron's trailer is cut. Not failed, cut clean. Looks like an attempt at getting a peek at what we're carrying."

"Either someone's down here… or they were."

The ship lurched hard.

Rebecca's voice came through the radio. "Ducky, where are you?"

"Vehicle deck," he said. "There is a seam leak, port side."

Nat watched the pump another second, listening past the engine noise for the rhythm to stay steady. The temporary feed she'd borrowed held, wires taped and zip-tied where they had no business being permanent.

She keyed her radio. "Electrical's holding. Pump's online. Passenger deck—stay put and follow crew instructions."

On Deck Three, heads lifted slow and unfocused, people blinking like they'd been dragged out of bad dreams. Some were drunk. Some green from the seas. Most were scared enough they didn't know where to look.

The floor shifted again, a slow roll that turned level into suggestion. Plastic cups slid across tables and bounced on the floor. A phone skittered off a seat and cracked against the deck. Someone grabbed for a chair back and missed at first when it slid from under their hand.

Crew finally arrived and their voices cut through the noise, sharp but controlled.

"This way, folks. Stay off the outer rail."

"Hand on the wall if you need it."

"Take the inside stairwell, nice and easy."

A steward knelt beside an older man who couldn't get his balance, talking him through each step like they had nowhere else to be. Two deckhands moved shoulder-to-shoulder through the aisle, guiding people with open palms instead of pushing.

The air smelled like coffee, diesel, and rising panic trying not to break loose.

Passengers shuffled toward the inner stairwells in uneven lines, gripping railings, clutching strangers, moving because standing still felt worse.

On the bridge, MacLeod keyed the ship-wide speaker.

The horn blew once, short and angry.

The inclinometer needle held around ten degrees, then edged higher. Heavy steel started thinking about moving whether you wanted it to or not. Bret met Rebecca and Ducky at the ramp.

"The flooding's real," Ducky said.

Bret looked down the ramp. "If we lose that deck, she'll roll."

"Then we don't lose it," Rebecca said. "Get the others!"

Bret thumbed his handheld. "Harley. Billy Bob. Get your tails up here! We're taking on water; bring lights!"

"Copy," Harley answered.

On the bridge, O'Rourke called over alarms. "Port ballast breached. Intake valve jammed open!"

"Shut it at the manifold," MacLeod barked.

"Trying. She's fighting pressure!"

"Counter—the ballast starboard," MacLeod shouted. "Keep her on her feet!"

The needle kissed fourteen, then stopped, then eased back like the ship was thinking about it.

"She's holding for now," O'Rourke said. "But we're not winning."

Down below, Nat bridged power under the electrician's direction, hands shaking, breath clouding in the cold. Sparks popped, the pump coughed, then settled into a steady whine.

"You've got power!" she yelled.

Rebecca cracked a line, bled the return, cinched clamps, then looked up at the deck speaker bolted to the bulkhead like it could hear her. "Bridge, try steering now."

MacLeod eased the wheel. It pushed back like a stubborn mule, then gave him a little bite.

The helmsman's shoulders dropped an inch. "We've got follow-up."

"Into the wind," MacLeod said. "Hold her there."

"Copy."

They bought minutes. Then more minutes.

Pumps whined. Plates complained. The deck stayed nasty, but the bow quit jerking around and started tracking again.

Harley and Billy Bob worked the passenger deck like it was a crash scene. Jackets on. Kids wrapped in blankets. People seated against inner walls. Outside doors blocked. No hero nonsense.

··✦✦✦✦··

At 3:15 a.m. O'Rourke's voice came through, rough and tired. "Emergency board stable. One main generator relit. We can give you a little thrust."

"I'll take it," MacLeod said. "Port shaft, dead slow. I only want a nose."

Vibration returned under my boots, thin but real. I looked at the captain. "She's acting differently."

"She's listening now," he said.

The needle kissed thirty degrees once and slid back like it changed its mind. Twenty-five. Twenty-two. Twenty-one and easing off.

MacLeod keyed ship-wide again, voice steady. "Bridge to all decks. We have partial power. Steering recovered. Heel steady at twenty-one degrees and easing. Lifejacket issue continues at muster points. Lifeboat crews stand by. Outer gangways remain closed. Remain seated and secured."

You could feel the whole ship exhale.

Dawn came in as a gray smear behind a curtain. The red strips felt less like an emergency and more like tired lights in a truck stop. Fifteen degrees. Twelve. Holding.

The carrier-waves sputtered, then a blessed voice cut through. "Ala'suinu, this is Halifax Rescue Two Zero Three. Radio check."

MacLeod closed his eyes for half a blink and keyed the mic. "Halifax Two Zero Three, Ala'suinu hears you five by five. Position mid-passage, under own power at limited thrust, flooding contained, requesting escort on approach."

"Two Zero Three copies all. Hold that heading, Captain. We're on our way."

By 6:30 a.m. we were crawling past the length of the coast. Seas still ugly, wind still barking, but the horizon had definition again. Gray rock. White surf. Something solid.

Below, our trucks sat ice-crusted under work lights, chains humming soft with the vibration.

I ran a hand across my steer tire, feeling for heat through the rubber like I always did after a bad ride.

Ducky stood, checking binders with bare fingers like he'd lost his mind, wrapped in a foil blanket somebody shoved at him. "Thirty-two chains," he said. "Thirty-two tight. Lost one binder handle, snapped when she listed."

"Fair enough," Bret said. "Keep it that way."

Ron was straightening a sedan that had broken loose and wedged against a bulkhead. "Some kid's rental car," he grunted. "Poor bastard's gonna find salt in his air vents forever."

Rebecca crouched near the port wall, tapping the plate with a wrench. "Still sweating through the seam, but slow. Pumps are buying us time."

Nat sat beside her with the tablet. "Battery's at thirty percent. I rerouted both pumps to the dry bus. We've got a window if nothing else shorts."

"Let's use it," I said. "Get to land, unload, fix it right."

Ten miles out, the Coast Guard cutter slid alongside, white hull riding waves like it was born there. They signaled with a handheld lamp, checked our situation, then fell back to shadow us in.

When the first mooring line hit the bollard, it felt like the world stopped moving.

Rebecca let out a breath like she'd been holding it since midnight. "That's the best sound I've heard in a week."

The stern ramp came down slowly, steel grinding against steel, steam rolling out into cold daylight. Salt streaked everything. Our trucks looked ghost-gray under the coating. We walked the line one last time.

Chains solid. Brakes set. Every binder where it belonged.

A Coast Guard officer photographed the cut chain link, then looked at us. "That wasn't random," he said. "We'll have divers inspect the hull and rudder gear once she's unloaded. If someone got below decks, we need to know how far they went."

I didn't answer. I just looked out at the sea, gray and flat now, like it hadn't just tried to kill us.

Journal Entry 12

Didn't think we'd see land again.

Ballast stuck, power out, steering gone, and somebody cutting steel in the dark.

But she held.

And so did we.

Rebecca and Nat turned that engine room into a miracle, one with more sparks than sense, but it worked.

Bret, Ron, Ducky, every one of them earned another stripe tonight.

Harley and Billy Bob kept the passengers calm while the deck tried to roll them into the sea.

Chad found a prayer that quieted a cafeteria full of scared people.

MacLeod ran his ship like a man who refused to quit.

We'll remember the sound: metal straining, chains humming, pumps whining.

Docked under sleet and gray skies, hull bruised but standing.

Coast Guard called it luck.

I call it mercy mixed with diesel, salt, and stubborn hands.

The ocean tried to take us last night.

She didn't get her way.

—Pops

Chapter 14

HARD MILES

The ramp slammed into place with a metallic boom that echoed through the hull like thunder. Chains rattled, deck hands shouted, and the smell of diesel and saltwater filled the lower deck. Engines idled, ready.

"Lead pilot rolling," Harley crackled over the radio. "Ramp's slick, tread easy."

"Copy," I said, easing the rig forward. Tires chattered over the wet steel. A gust hit as we cleared the hold, sleet coming sideways.

We filed into the queue outside the port yard at Port aux Basques. The dark sea behind us and a pale dawn thinking about it. Pilots guided us off the ramp and onto slick tarmac.

"Convoy eastbound, stay tight," Bret called. "Fuel stop next two lanes only."

Downtown was still waking. We rolled toward the Irving / Circle K on High Street and found what everyone off the ferry already knew—two diesel lanes, both jammed, trucks stacked three deep, mirror to mirror.

"Figures," Bret muttered. "Same idea as the whole island."

We shuffled forward a truck length at a time. Pumps spit diesel as fast as they could. Men stamped cold out of their legs.

I shut down in line, stepped into the wind, and zipped my coat to the chin. That's when I saw it at the far side of the lot—a black van, no markings, glass too dark to be friendly. Parked where it could watch both diesel lanes without being obvious.

I climbed back in. "Bret, you got eyes on a black van by the car pumps?"

"Copy," he said, voice gone flat. "Saw it in the ferry line, too."

Rebecca on ops: "Plate comes back clean." A beat. "Too clean."

"Fuel and go," I said. "No wandering."

We topped everything: main fuel tanks, auxiliary fuel cells, jugs. Support filled too. Coffee, water, new rags. No souvenirs.

The black van blinked its lights once and slid out ahead of us, tires spitting slush.

"Convoy rolling," I called. "No more stops till Deer Lake."

We pulled back onto the Trans-Canada. Ten minutes out of town, then a last flash of blue light as a local cruiser peeled away and the Coast Guard pickup turned for the docks. After that it was us and the weather—steady snow with white-out bands blowing across the highway, wind blowing out of the cut valleys and slapping us awake.

Katie rang my cell through the truck's hands-free. "Quick check-in. You off the boat?"

"Off, fueled, moving," I said. "How's home?"

"Warmer than you. Everything's fine. Tell Nat I said 'hi.' And don't be a hero."

"Copy that." I hung up before she could hear the gust hit my door.

Harley kept a steady forty-five, letting plows make the first mistakes. Billy Bob ran rear guard and called out bridges and drifting. We kept the pace and talked like drivers talk when the road wants to wander counter—steer if she kicks, don't chase the trailer, easy on the throttle.

Chad keyed up, voice calm as a Sunday. "Lord, keep this crew steady, give us eyes for the slick spots and the sense to ease off when we should. And if there's bacon in the next world, save us some. Amen."

Ron snorted. "Pray for coffee that isn't charcoal."

"Save the sermons," Ducky said. "I saw the black van again back there, on the shoulder, two inside."

"Copy," I said. "Eyes up."

Nat keyed the sat phone. "Command, Mercer Dispatch. Black van from terminal sighted twice, fuel stop and the shoulder twenty miles from the terminal. We're north bound, maintaining speed." She listened, then: "Copy. We'll keep you posted."

The snow thickened. We may as well have been in a dust storm, it was so dark. Traffic bunched up behind a snowplow then spread out again. We caught white-out bands near the open water and drove by feel for ten seconds at a time, road markers disappearing then reappearing.

"Next services, thirty miles," Harley said. "Wind's cutting across the road from left to right."

"Let it," I said. "We'll take it the best we can and turn as much into it as possible."

The road undulated with stretched, deep rolls the closer we got to St. George's. We could make out through the snow a few scattered lights twinkling in the distance to our left and right. We hit a long, empty stretch that was black as midnight and, without warning, a shape appeared where there shouldn't be one. A black van sat perpendicular in the lanes, hazards flashing red through the snow like trouble. A sign glowed ahead through the sleet—Midway Motel—but it felt like we were in the middle of nowhere.

"Harley! Move to the left, slow to a crawl," I said. "Everybody move with her. Something stinks like last week's coffee."

"Copy," she said, voice already smaller.

The black van straightened just enough to look helpful then lunged as Harley tried to ease past, boxing her in. Another vehicle, an older pickup with a plow on the front, barreled out from the motel driveway to close on our right. A classic squeeze move.

"Stop. Full stop," I said calmly, because I had to. "Take up all lanes and set your brakes. Bret, grab the lockbox. Rebecca, you're with him. Nat stays in the van."

"Copy," Bret said. "Rear secure. I'm out on foot."

Harley's voice came quiet. "I've got room to my right if I have to punch it."

"Hold," I said. "Don't give them a wreck to sort out."

The two vehicles idled in front and right, doors cracked. I cracked mine enough to step down into the sleet. Bret met me behind my bumper with the keyed black box and flipped it open. "Same three guys we've been seeing the last few days," Bret said, low. "Pops, Chad, Rebecca," he continued, handing us the sidearms, just like the order said.

I nodded, pistol holstered. Ron slid up with a tire iron nested under his coat and Ducky wielded a twenty-inch Maglite. Billy Bob eased his pickup across the lanes behind our trucks to block the road, strobes slow and steady.

The van's side door slid open. Two men stepped out—dark coats, hoods. One raised a pistol and fired a warning shot into the sky. The sound cracked and died in the wind and snow.

"Don't," I said, not shouting. "Bad night to be stupid."

They moved anyway.

I took the right, Chad went left. Harley had stepped out of the pilot car, door open and peering through the window, while simultaneously looking back and throwing hand signals. Rebecca came up fast from the ops van, posture all business. Bret held position near my truck bumper, pistol in hand, and eyes on our flanks.

Then it happened. The play we didn't want but trained our nerves for: the black van gunned its engine and headed straight at Harley to shove her off the road.

I shouted without thinking. "Nat!"

But Natasha didn't wait for permission. The ops van jumped the curb and rammed the black van at the right rear, spinning it to the left and away from Harley. The two vehicles ground together, bumper to fender, sliding over the packed snow. I heard the ops van's windshield crack with the blow. The right mirror ripped from the door frame, passenger-side glass shattered, and the front-right tire hissed flat when it caught the snowplow. A hole appeared in the passenger door—maybe a bullet—finding sheet metal but nothing else.

The black van fishtailed into the snowbank and stuck.

I moved. The man with the pistol tried to re-sight but met the side of my bumper with his shin as he stepped out, and down he went. He stayed there with my firearm pointed at his chest.

The second guy took a swing at Chad, but he ducked and knocked the guy into the slush with a quick shove of his shoulder and then leapt on top to restrain him. Ron kept the left clear like a shepherd with that tire iron and Ducky lit up the inside of the second vehicle's cab with the flashlight beam. The driver froze like a deer in the headlights and Ron ripped open the driver's side door, pulled the guy into a snowbank and tried to secure his arms behind his back.

Ducky flew across the hood of the van and subdued him with a crack to the temple from his light. "Anybody got a zip tie?"

"Don't," Rebecca warned the third man as he was exiting the pickup, her voice even and firm. He eyed her and the end of that muzzle, then gave a sideways glance at the snow and decided on the softer of the two landings. She walked over, flipped him face down, put a knee in his back and zip-tied his wrists.

Thirty seconds was all it took, but it felt much longer. We all stood there breathing in sleet and the smell of hot antifreeze from the ops van.

"Clear," Harley said, voice steady. "I'm good."

"Nat?" I called.

"I'm good," she answered through the hole in the window. "Van's wounded but should run. The radio mount snapped clean in two. I can fix the comms with Rebecca's help."

Bret was already on the sat phone. "Royal Canadian Mounted Police. We are south of St. George's at the Midway Motel entrance. Attempted hijack. Suspects are subdued and restrained. Our ops van is damaged but drivable. We're securing the scene and then we gotta move. This storm's building momentum and we have to roll."

The entrance to the motel opened a crack. An elderly woman with a wind-burned face and enough lines on it to make a new road map stepped out in her thick cardigan and rubber boots. I jogged to the office with Rebecca while Bret and Chad finished zip-tying ankles and checking pockets for any surprises.

"Ma'am, we need warm rooms for these fellas until the RCMP show up to collect them," I said. "We'll pay whatever you're asking."

She looked past me at the trucks and the snow and the black van sitting sideways in the ditch. "Laundry room's warm and has a lock on it, and close to the office," her voice rasped, as she was reaching for a ring of keys. "Blankets are in the closet right there, along with towels for you to dry off with. I'll put coffee on so you can warm up a bit. I'm Mae."

"Appreciate it, Mae."

We carried the three detainees into the laundry room and sat them against the wall on folded wool blankets. Zip ties tight, ankles cinched, gags improvised from clean shop rags and duct tape so they'd stay quiet. One started to bluster; Rebecca looked at him once and he went quiet.

Next to the laundry room was Mae's office; the coffee maker sat on a small filing cabinet in the corner, giving off that divine aroma. Something on the corkboard by the door caught my eye—a few curled flyers and a bright poster for Redneck Rocket Science & Diesel Therapy. The same red logo I'd seen glowing over a cinder-block shop in Moncton.

"Eddie's place," I said.

Mae followed my look. "You know Eddie?"

"He fixed one of our rigs down in Moncton. He saved our run."

She gave a small, careful nod. "That'd be my nephew. Calls when he remembers my number. Good with engines, not always with company."

Rebecca glanced over. "Bad company?"

Mae shrugged. "Big heart, bad friends. Hard mix in a small town. Coffee's almost ready. You folks look like you could use a cup. If those troublemakers try to run I'll lock the outer door," she said. "But I doubt they'll run far in this."

"RCMP are on the way," I said. "Roads are ugly."

"I know," Mae said, checking the window. "I listen to the scanner. You folks finish whatever you're doing and get a move on. From the looks of it, this one's going to close the road soon."

Back outside, Nat had the van hood up, right fender creased but tire changed. Windshield cracked but holding. She'd already secured the broken mirror and had a black, plastic contractor bag taped over the broken window. The dash was half apart with radio/GPS leads spliced back to life with a bit of wire and tape from Bret's kit.

"Van will pull to the right," she said. "Alignment's off a hair."

"Good enough," I said. "You and Rebecca swap. Nat drives, Rebecca rides and watches for more trouble."

Bret rejoined us, breath fogging. "RCMP confirmed they'll take custody when they can get a unit through this weather and roads. Let's leave a written statement with Mae and roll."

"Do it," I said. Then I keyed the convoy. "Everybody chain up. Now."

Side boxes opened and chains came out. We did it the way winter demanded: one chain per drive dual set on the tractors, both sides; a single drag chain on one trailer axle to hopefully keep the trailer from walking; the dually and support vehicles got chains on their drive tires too. Bungee cords were criss-crossed on the outside of every chain to tighten them and we checked the clearances and slack, had each driver roll a quarter turn, re-tensioned, then set them again.

"Forty miles per hour is the cap with chains on," I said into the mic. "You push harder, you'll sling one and wreck a fender—or worse."

"Copy," Ron said, already down checking his bungees.

"Copy," Ducky said.

"Rear ready," Bret added. "Van's patched. Billy Bob, you good?"

"Good," Billy Bob said from the pickup. "I'll watch for strays."

We left Mae a short note with times, our names, and the RCMP case number Bret pulled from dispatch. As we headed out, she watched with the door cracked and held it so the warm air stayed where it needed to. She nodded once and set the note by the kettle.

We formed up again at the edge of the road, iron rattling soft, engines low. Nat took the driver's seat with Rebecca beside her scanning for any signs of trouble. Harley eased out first, tested a lane change, gave us the go.

"Roll out," I said.

Engines came up in a roar. We nosed back onto the Trans-Canada, chains ticking, snow thickening. The motel sign swinging behind us in the wind like a clock that didn't care about our schedule. The storm took us into its throat, and we went anyway.

The storm nearly swallowed the road whole. Chains clattering as they gripped the roadway, snow hammering the windshield in sheets. The wipers beating time like they were mad about it. The dash lights looked dim and the world past the hood was a tunnel of white and the faint red glow of Harley's taillights leading us east.

"Visibility's down to about a hundred feet," Harley called over the CB. "Drift buildup between lanes. Take it slow through here."

"Copy," I said. "Forty max. Keep those chains on."

Billy Bob's voice came in from the back. "Rear's clear. Got one four-wheeler half-buried on the right shoulder. Looks like they hit the drift sideways."

Harley answered first. "Anybody in it?"

"No movement, windshield's iced solid. Doors shut, no flashers on. I'll call it in when we get signal."

"Copy that," I said. "We'll keep rolling."

Ron came on, steady as a metronome. "Bridge ahead, see the markers? It looks slick. Watch for the seam bump at the far end."

Harley eased across; I followed. You could feel the grip change under the tires—iron biting the ice, then slipping, then catching again. Every truck hit it a little different. The chains singing louder for a beat.

"Everybody good?" I asked.

"Rear's good," Bret said. "Van and pickup both running steady."

Nat came in from the ops van. "Copy. Visibility holding at two hundred feet."

The wind came harder as the highway climbed upward. Snow blew sideways in walls. The kind that makes you think the world's turned on its side. The plows had carved a narrow path, berms stacked high on both shoulders. One wrong move and you'd be part of the scenery 'til spring.

Ducky broke the quiet. "Got a car up here, nose down in the median. No flashers, can't see a driver."

"Roger," Harley said. "We're not stopping in this. We'll call it in if we see a cop."

"Copy," Ducky said. "Poor bastard picked the wrong day to test his winter tires."

Chad laughed once. "Ain't a tire made that beats an ice slick."

Billy Bob keyed up from the rear pilot. "Still getting cross-winds back here—blowing snow across the lane. Can barely see your trailer lights."

"Copy," Bret said. "Hold spacing, twenty count gaps. Everybody keep an eye on the taillights in front of you."

Rebecca's voice slipped in next, low from the ops van. "Visibility dropping again up ahead. Looks like the whiteout is stretching another five miles."

"Copy," I said. "We'll crawl it if we have to. Nobody hammers the throttle."

The world shrank to headlights, gauges, and radio chatter. Every voice kept the others awake.

Harley: "Truck coming southbound—fuel hauler, slow moving, lights dim."

Ron: "Got him. Right lanes clear."

Ducky: "Chains holding, but she's bouncing hard."

Chad: "Same here. Trailer's walking a little."

Me: "Ease out of your throttle through the turns."

Harley again: "Passing another plow convoy. Two wide, staggered. They're throwing snow high and to the right. Stay dead center behind me."

We dropped our speed to thirty and hugged the plow wall until their lights faded in the mirrors. For a moment it was silence and the constant clank of our chains on the snow.

Then the radio came alive again, Billy Bob this time. "Rear good. Two more cars in the right ditch, one nose down, one sitting high. Locals. They look fine, waving us on by."

"Copy," I said. "Keep your eyes scanning. They're the lucky ones tonight."

We rolled another ten miles in second and third gear. The snow thickened, wind blowing across at an angle that made it hard to tell what was road and what was open ditch.

"Anybody else's defroster fighting the snow?" Ron asked.

Ducky: "Mine's losing ground. Bottom corners frosting up quickly."

Natasha: "Ops van's fogging up too. Roll down the passenger window a hair."

Bret: "Roger that."

I adjusted the defroster, cracked the driver's window just enough to let the sleet sting my ear. The cold kept me sharp.

That's when Harley's voice went up a notch. "Look out ahead, something in the road! It's big!"

Through the wash of snow, I saw it: a dark bulk lurching out of the median, broad as a truck hood, then another, and another. Moose! A whole herd crossing, eyes glowing like dull lanterns.

"Brake! Hold your lanes, and do not honk your horns!" I shouted.

Chains screamed on ice. Harley's pilot car slid sideways but stayed on the road. I eased pressure on the brakes, felt the weight pushing me. The trailer slid a bit. One bull turned at the last second, missing my bumper by inches.

Behind me came the sound of the impact, a thud. The heavy grunt of weight meeting steel. "Ron, report!" Bret's voice snapped through.

"Clipped one!" Ron yelled. "Right headlight gone dark, I think the bumper is shoved into the steer tire!

"Copy," I said. "Everybody else?"

"Ducky clear," came the reply.

"Chad clear."

"Clear," Harley added.

"Van's fine," Nat said.

The herd scattered into the trees, shadows dissolving into the storm. Through the crack in the passenger side window came the stink of wet fur.

Ron and I pulled to the shoulder and stopped, hazard lights cutting the white. Bret came up behind, blocking my lane while Billy Bob turned the pickup crosswise to slow anyone dumb enough to try passing.

Ron stayed in the driver's seat as we all piled out into the storm. His right fender was shoved back into the steer tire, sheet metal cracked, chrome bent, headlight smashed to powder.

"Does the wheel turn free?" I asked.

He shrugged. "Barely. I can feel the fender rubbing the tire when it turns."

"Getting the saw," Bret said.

He was already at the dually with the toolbox open. Ducky and Chad used their flashlights and headlamps while I held the fender steady. The saw threw orange and blue sparks into the snow as Bret cut the twisted metal. Steam rose off the exhausts and hung around us like smoke.

Rebecca's camera light flicked on, catching just enough glow for her photo. She didn't say a word, just filmed the repair so there was proof it happened.

"Cut through," Bret said, stepping back. "Check your tire clearance."

Ron spun the wheel. "Good enough to roll."

"Bumper will need replacing later," Ducky said.

Ron grinned. "So will my nerves."

Nat came on over the radio. "RCMP logged the report. They'll send a note to wildlife department. Road's still open, but visibility is dropping again up near Deer Lake."

"Copy," I said. "Everybody load up. No delays, we'll do a full inspection at the pullout east of town."

We climbed back in, shaking snow from our collars. The convoy rolled out again, one by one into the blowing snow. The chains found rhythm, engines climbed back into their low song, and we followed Harley's taillights through the storm.

A yellow MOOSE CROSSING sign flashed past on the right, half-buried in a drift. Ducky keyed up, voice dry. "Well, that would've been nice to know two miles back."

Ron came over the line, laughing. "Yeah, little late for the memo."

Even Bret cracked a grin.

Snow still fell hard, but the glow of Deer Lake's city limits began to show through the blanket of white.

Nat came on once more, calm as ever. "Estimated Deer Lake arrival in fifteen."

"Copy that, Nat," I said. "Everybody hold steady. Once we hit the pullout, we'll check chains, lights, and nerves."

Ahead, the highway signs loomed out of the blizzard: Deer Lake—ten km. I let out a slow breath. "Almost there, boys."

The glow of Deer Lake crept closer—orange halos from light poles and the faint smear of traffic lights through blowing snow. It looked like civilization, but it felt like we'd rolled in from another planet.

"Lead to convoy," Harley said. "There should be a pullout half a mile ahead. Hopefully it's plowed."

"Copy that," I said. "We'll use it. Everybody ease off and follow her in."

The exit ramp was slick, half-buried in slush, but wide enough to swing the rigs through. Chains clattered as we turned into the rest area—a windswept lot with one dead streetlight, two porta johns half buried, and a snowbank tall enough to hide a small car. We parked in line, brakes set, lights dimmed. The snow bounced off the hoods.

Bret keyed up. "All stop. Let's check chains, lights, and fenders. Five minute stretch before we roll again."

I stepped down into ankle deep powder. The air felt heavier here closer to the open water and the storm that still clawed at the coast. My breath fogged thick as I walked down my truck and trailer.

Ron was already crouched under his fender, checking the cut edge where Bret's saw made a clean cut. "Tire's holding, no rub," he said. "I call that a win."

"Good," I said. "hopefully it will stay that way."

Ducky came up, flashlight beam sweeping his tires. "All my chains are tight. Left rear trailer chain stretched a bit, but still holding, I added another bungee to secure it."

Chad was standing on his trailer checking his tarp and straps, ice hanging from his beard. "Upper corner loosened again," he called down. "Wind's been chewing at it."

"Pull it tight again," Bret said. "We can't lose a tarp this close to the end."

Billy Bob pulled the pickup alongside, window down, grin showing behind the steam of his breath. "Rear's good. I think Bret's dually has more ice than paint now."

"Adds character," Ducky said.

Harley walked the front, pilot car lights on and flashers still ticking. "My right rear's packed solid with slush. I'll clear it before we roll."

Rebecca climbed out of the ops van, camera tucked away for once, walking and looking. "Everyone holding up?"

Ron shrugged. "Still breathing."

She smiled a little. "That counts."

Nat was inside the van, tablet glowing in the dark. "Weather radar shows partial clearing near Corner Brook," she said through the open window. "We'll have a short lull if we move quick."

Bret leaned against the dually door, rubbing his hands. "Fuel check?"

"Seven eighths on mine," I said.

Ron: "Same here."

Chad: "About three quarter."

Ducky: "Little over three quarter."

Harley: "I'm over three quarters."

Billy Bob: "Good here. I'm over three quarters as well."

Nat: "The van's around seven eighths."

"Copy," Bret said. "We'll keep rolling. Up around South Brook, about fifty miles, we'll stop long enough to top off the coffee cups before we head further east."

Snow swirled around us, thick but lighter than before, like the storm was finally running out of steam.

Ron kicked the bent chrome bumper. "You think the moose learned anything tonight?"

Chad laughed. "Doubt it. Probably bragging to his buddies."

Bret smiled, barely. "I'll pass on a rematch."

I looked down the row of trucks, chains snug, exhaust drifting steady, lights burning through the mist like dying campfires. Tired faces, stiff hands. We'd been at it too long to lose our rhythm now.

"All right," I said, keying the mic. "Five-minute check is up. Everybody button up and get ready to roll. Keep it slow through the next set of grades, there's ice under powder."

"Copy, Pops," Harley said. "I'll call out the slick spots."

"Rear ready," Billy Bob added.

"Ops ready," Nat said.

I climbed back in, stomped snow off my boots. Gauges read normal. Radio was clear. I glanced in the mirror—every rig behind glowing through the haze, each driver sitting there with the same tired focus. "All right, Mercer Hauling. Let's put some miles behind us."

Harley's headlights swung onto the ramp, taillights barely visible in the drifting snow. I eased out after her. The convoy falling in behind me, chains ticking, engines rumbling low, our own small storm moving east.

The first ten miles east of Deer Lake crawled by under a bruised sky, but the worst of the storm finally eased. The defroster started hissing again—there was a fine powder instead of full sheets coming out of the sky. I could see Harley's taillights more than a ghost flicker now, steady against the white.

"Visibility's coming back," Harley called over the radio. "I can see the next hill for once."

"Copy that," I said. "Hold forty. Let's enjoy it while it lasts."

The land opened around us, pine trees climbing on both sides of the road, dark shoulders mounded with snow. Power lines followed the highway, sagging under ice, and every few miles a side road carved away toward houses tucked behind trees—rooflines holding up piles of snow, chimneys ghosting thin smoke into the cold air.

For the first time all evening, it felt like the world existed again.

Ducky's voice cracked the quiet. "I can see stars through the breaks. Either that or I'm hallucinating."

Chad chuckled. "Could be both."

Rebecca came over the CB, voice calm but lighter now. "Satellite feed shows the front pulling north for a few hours. We've got a window before the next one builds past Grand Falls."

"Copy," Bret said. "We'll take the mercy."

We fell into the rhythm drivers live for, steady hum under the seat, chain tick soft and even, engines working easy in the cold. The storm's roar faded behind us until all that remained was wind over mirrors and the low murmur of radios.

Pines closed in again near the twenty mile mark. Drifts built high against the rock cuts, half-buried reflectors marking the edge of reason. Every few miles a frozen river slid under the highway, ice dark blue where the snow had blown clear.

"Bridge ahead," Harley warned. "slick but clear. Watch the bump on the far end."

"Copy," Ron said. "Holding my lane."

The truss bridge crossed a river that had a dull gleam under the moonlight. Ice fog rose from cracks where water still ran. For a heartbeat, it looked almost peaceful—steam rising, tail-lights glowing red across steel.

Beyond that came the highlands before South Brook—low rolling grades that lifted us above the tree line for a few minutes. Up there the sky widened, showing streaks of stars and the faint green smear of aurora at the horizon.

Ducky keyed up. "Now that's something! Didn't think we'd get fireworks tonight."

Bret answered. "Don't tempt it. We're due for payback."

The descent toward South Brook showed lights again—a scatter of yellow from porch lamps and one bright glow ahead where a sign leaned into the wind: PINE RIDGE TRUCK PLAZA — CAFÉ • DIESEL • SHOWERS.

Harley said. "Pulling into the plaza lot, right side. Looks plowed."

"Copy," I said. "Everybody ease in. Watch your swing."

We rolled in single file, chains hissing and stacks steaming, parking along the outer edge by the pumps. The air smelled like diesel and salt—heaven on a night like this.

Bret keyed up. "All stop. Ten, maybe fifteen minutes."

Drivers shuffled around stamping warmth into their boots. Inside the café, the floor was wet with melted snow and the walls yellow with old photos of snowplows and fishing boats.

Ron came out first with a tray balanced in one hand. "Six coffees, a bag of sandwiches, and something pretending to be soup."

Ducky followed carrying two thermoses. "Refills for whoever's about to fall asleep."

Chad leaned against his step, unwrapping a biscuit sandwich. "Best five bucks I ever spent."

Natasha and Rebecca stood beside the ops van. The tablet balanced on the hood. "Winds have shifted east," Nat said. "We'll have a tailwind again till we get past Grand Falls. Nothing nasty yet, but it's rebuilding."

Rebecca handed her a coffee. "Then let's not linger."

Bret glanced at me. "Everybody got food, drink? We'll run another hour before we check chains again."

Billy Bob stuck his head out the pickup window, grinning. "I bought all the jerky that wasn't nailed down. Anyone hungry later, holler."

"Copy that," I said. "Let's roll before this place freezes over."

We climbed back into our cabs. The world beyond the lot was quiet but not friendly. Snow still drifted in lazy sheets under the lights, enough to coat windshields before wipers finished one pass.

Harley rolled first, easing onto the ramp. "Drifts ahead but manageable. Stay centered."

"Copy," Billy Bob said. "Rear following."

The convoy fell back into order, Harley's amber strobes in front and Billy Bob's headlights steady in my mirrors.

For twenty miles the world held steady. The snow fell soft, visibility a good three quarters of a mile. The forest pressed close on both sides, black trunks banded with white. Hills rose and fell like slow waves, and every descent felt like sliding into a dream.

"Nice stretch through here," Ducky said over the mic. "Almost peaceful."

"Don't get used to it," Bret answered. "Radar says it's winding up again near Notre Dame."

By the time we reached the flats east of Grand Falls–Windsor, the first gusts hit—light at first, then harder, pushing the snow across the asphalt.

"Drifts are forming in the right lane," Harley warned. "It's shallow now, but it's growing."

"Copy," I said. "Stay left through it."

Light flakes at first, the horizon started shrinking to a gray tunnel. We climbed another rise and the wind found us full on the side.

"Here we go again," I muttered.

"Convoy, heads up," Bret said. "Drifting lanes, low visibility ahead. Stay centered."

The storm's breath gathered itself once more. By the time the sign for NOTRE DAME JUNCTION flashed past in the snow, visibility had dropped to a quarter mile and falling.

The snow built fast after the junction—flakes thickened in the beams and slapped the glass like wet sand. The wind came crosswise through the trees, pushing the rigs sideways on the open stretches. The road was more guesswork than lines now, two faint grooves in the white.

Chains hissed and clapped under the tires. The convoy moved like a train—each truck trusting the blur of taillights in front of it. The snow swallowed the landscape until the world was a gray tunnel with a sound.

Billy Bob said, voice rough, "Wind's pushing hard from the left."

"Copy," Bret answered. "Keep your lane and your patience."

We climbed a shallow grade where the highway curved east. The snow turned dry and sharp. The kind that squeaks when it hits glass. I caught glimpses of power poles leaning in the wind, flashes of drifted spruce tops, then nothing again.

Ron keyed up. "This is getting dumb. I can't see squat."

"Stay in it," Bret said. "We're twenty out from Gander."

"Feels like two hundred," Ducky muttered.

Harley called out from up front. "Bridge ahead—slick road, no rails on the right."

We eased across, tires clattering over steel. A single streetlight marked the far end, its glow a suggestion through the white. Beyond it the grade dropped and leveled into open bog—no shelter, raw wind.

The snow came sideways again, a solid wall. The windshield wipers struggled and froze mid-stroke. I leaned forward, hands easy on the wheel, watching the faint red blur that was Harley's car.

Then a voice cut through the static—Chad's, low and tight. "This is stupid. We need to stop. We can't see a thing."

No one answered right away. Just the rush of static and wind.

"Hold your thoughts," I said finally. "Ops, what's the radar show?"

Nat's voice came through from the van. "Worse east of here. You've got two, maybe three hours before the system stalls over the highway. If we stop, it'll bury us."

"Still safer than playing pinball with semis," Ron muttered.

"Copy that," Bret said. "Nat, patch us through to Merritt."

There was a pause, static crackling. Then the line clicked open and the Colonel's voice filled the cab—steady, unhurried, that clipped calm that meant the decision was already made.

"Mercer Convoy, this is Colonel Merritt. Situation update: Base command initiates a full weather lockdown at twelve hundred hours. At that time every perimeter gate closes—no inbound, no outbound, no exceptions until further notice. Your freight must be inside the fence and staged for internal convoy movement before that deadline. Miss the window and you'll be parked outside for three to four days while this system blows through. I'm authorizing double hazard pay for completion under these conditions, effective immediately. But you cannot stop. The road stays open as long as you do. Merritt out."

The channel went dead.

Nobody spoke for a full ten seconds. The only sound was wind thumping the side of the cab.

Bret finally broke it. "Well… there's our vote."

Ron exhaled hard. "Double pay doesn't fix dead."

Ducky: "Speak for yourself. I'll take my chances. I need a new set of drives."

Chad: "You can't spend money if you're upside down."

Harley's voice came steady but tired. "We'll stop in Gander. Check straps and chains, catch our breath. Then we decide if we're that stupid."

"Copy," I said. "Ten mile push. Everybody hang on."

We crawled the last stretch toward Gander; the storm clawing at every inch. The town's glow showed ahead like a ghost-orange halo behind curtains of white.

"Lead to convoy," Harley said. "Exit ramp's coming up. It's half-drifted but passable."

We followed her down the ramp and into the lot of a small all-night stop—Trailside Diner & Fuel, a handful of pumps and one sagging sign with half the letters missing.

We parked nose-out, wind still howling. Drivers climbed down their steps cautiously, shoulders hunched, lights reflecting off the ice-coated hoods. The air was so cold it made your teeth ache when you breathed.

Nat stood beside the ops van, phone still in her hand, Merritt's voice probably echoing in her head. Rebecca handed her a thermos, and she took it without speaking.

Ron stomped over, hood up, eyes red. "We should hole up right here. Let it pass."

Bret shook his head. "You heard him. We're the only ones moving freight that still matters."

"Doesn't mean we have to die for it," Ron shot back.

Harley leaned against her car, arms crossed. "We've been through worse. Maybe not colder, but worse."

Ducky grinned under the frost. "He said double pay, right? That's twice the stupid tax."

Chad's breath fogged as he spoke. "I'll roll if Pops rolls. But maybe say a prayer before we leave."

I looked down the line at the tired faces, every one of them covered in ice and grit. The trucks idled steady, chrome buried under white. The dark sky above was a swirling mess of snow and a sodium glow.

"We don't have to like it," I said. "But we've come too far to park now. Chain checks, strap checks, ten minutes. Then we roll."

Nobody argued this time. They nodded and moved.

Ron hammered ice off his fender. Ducky cleared snow from the steps. Harley scraped her headlights clean. Bret wiped the cameras and checked the tool truck doors. Rebecca filmed quietly from under the hood of her parka, breath fogging the lens.

Nat's voice came soft over the radio. "Weather's red across the whole region. Wind gusts forty-five and rising. But the road's still open east of town."

"Then that's where we're going," I said. "Let's earn that double pay."

While everyone was loading back up, I hurriedly scribbled notes into my journal.

Everyone climbed back in one by one, cab lights snapping off down the line. The convoy rolled out into the white again, engines groaning low, lights cutting short beams into the storm.

The wind swallowed the world.

Journal Entry 13

Black van shadowed us off the ferry.

Irving fuel stop jammed and busy; topped mains, cells, jugs—no souvenirs.

Midway Motel—black van tried to highjack us. Nat rammed the van into them and won.

Ops van: windshield spidered, mirror gone, front right tire was flat; still drivable after a quick field repair.

Mae from the motel made room to secure the hijackers and coffee to go; RCMP en route.

Chained everything.

Whiteout bands, bridges are slick; drove by taillights and prayer.

Moose herd west of Deer Lake, Ron clipped one; we sawed the fender free of the tire and rolled.

Deer Lake pullout: chains re-tensioned, straps checked, nerves counted.

Short mercy window to South Brook, quick stop for inspection and coffee at Pine Ridge.

Past Grand Falls the wind found us again, snow drifting badly.

Merritt called it: base lockdown by twelve hundred, double hazard pay, no stopping.

Gander at last—Trailside Diner & Fuel, teeth aching from cold, crew tired, frustrated, and wanting to stop till storm ends.

One mountain left.

—Pops

Chapter 15

LOCKDOWN RUN

The Trailside Diner faded behind us like a rumor, trees closing in on both sides. Snow hammered sideways. The wipers kept time with the radio, barely audible with the outside noise. Wind off the water cut through the seams, shoved the truck half a lane, then let go to see if I was paying attention.

Harley: "Drifts getting deeper. Two lanes down to one in spots, watch the buildup in the middle."

Me: "Copy that. Keep your lane; we'll follow your tracks."

Bret's voice came from the back, steady and dry. "Holding twenty-five. If I go any slower, I'll need snowshoes."

Ron chuckled. "Traction control flashing. You sure this highway still goes east?"

Ducky: "Either that or we're headed for Narnia."

Laughter crackled through the static, thin, quick, but it helped.

We rolled past a semi nosed into the ditch, trailer half-buried. The driver's door hanging open.

Me: "Anybody see a driver?"

Bret: "Negative. Cab looks empty. Door's hanging open. Probably rode out with a plow crew."

Chad: "Lord, keep whoever was in that truck warm tonight."

Me: "Copy that."

The snow thickened—wet flakes slapping the windshield like gravel. The road dipped, then climbed just enough for the wind to hit us broadside. Chains clattered. The trailers shifted with every gust.

Harley: "Wind's crossing left to right—you'll feel it on the bridge ahead."

Me: "Copy."

The bridge was slick as owl shit. The trailer wandered, but we made it through, eyes locked on Harley's taillights glowing faint amber through the blur.

Nat: "Radar's lit like fireworks. Heavy band ahead ten klicks to the next break."

Ducky: "Define break."

Nat: "Less snow, more wind."

Ducky: "Comforting."

Rebecca: "Visibility down to ten meters from the van."

Bret: "If we make it home, we'll sell the script to the Weather Channel."

A few more miles. The road wound between rock cuts, snow filling every hollow. A sedan sat crosswise at a turnout, headlights dimmed to a yellow blink.

Harley: "See anyone?"

Me: "Negative."

Bret: "Empty. No tracks. Been here a while."

Then the grade changed; Harley called it before I could.

Harley: "Sign says Steep Hill—Next three kilometers. That'd be our welcome mat."

Me: "Copy. Ease to the turnout before the climb. We'll regroup."

We rolled into a plowed pull-off that hadn't seen a plow since breakfast. Snow waist deep at the edges, wind swirling hard enough to blur the truck in front of you.

Me: "All right, boys, if it glows, turn it on. Load lights, fogs, every chicken light you've got. I want to see each of you even when I can't."

One by one the world lit up, white, amber, red, blue.

Ducky: "Looks like a rolling carnival."

Me: "Good. Maybe the storm'll let us buy a ticket to let us pass."

Wind roared down the hill like a freight train.

Harley: "You still want to take it?"

Me: "Got a deadline. We climb."

Bret: "Tighten the gaps and keep your eyes open. This is where stupid meets expensive."

I smiled despite the tension and eased into gear. Amber lights ahead swayed in the snow like lanterns guiding us into the teeth of it.

Halfway up the third climb Harley's voice cracked through static: "Voltage light lit up, I'm losing lights. Hold what you got!"

Her Jeep drifted right, nose first into a drift.

Me: "Convoy, hold your lane!"

Engines idled against the wind. Snow hissed like sand. Billy Bob stayed back in the blind curve, hazards flashing.

Rebecca: "Radar still solid red, two more climbs before it breaks."

Up ahead Harley was already out, hood up and spray bottle of some liquid in hand.

Five long minutes. Belt screamed once, then caught.

Harley: "Alternator was soaked. Hit it with alcohol to dry the belt."

Me: "Copy. Ease back in."

We'd started creeping when Billy Bob's voice tore through the static.

Billy Bob: "Bret, you're too close to the edge! You're sliding—stop! … He's going down! Smoke down the hill!"

The wind shoved crossways on the crown, and we all watched as Bret's dually disappeared over the side.

I stopped and grabbed my gloves and threw open the driver's door. Over the radio I yelled, "I'm going down!"

Without hesitation, Harley spun her Jeep around with the winch facing the edge of the road, set the brake, jumped out and anchored the jeep to a nearby tree. Rebecca grabbed a pair of gloves, dropped from the cab of the ops van, and ran towards the edge of the road.

We used the winch cable as a handline, boots skidding, snow to the waist. Bret's dually was wedged between two spruce trees, rear wheels slightly hanging in the air. Steam rolled from under the hood and the sweet smell of hot coolant blew through the wind. The trailer had broken loose from the dually and slid a hundred yards farther down the hill, sitting sideways in the snow. I yelled for Bret.

Bret: "I'm here. I can't move my leg and have blood running down my face."

The door was jammed by the trunk of the tree it was against.

Me: "Harley, feed me some more line."

Cable rattled through branches. I hooked the winch cable around the pendle hitch using a short chain to make the connection, tugged twice and yelled, "Winch it!"

The Jeep's winch motor whined; bark tore; the truck slid enough to take weight off the door frame.

Rebecca: "The door's still stuck."

Me: "Breaking the window—watch your eyes, Bret!"

I drove my elbow through the glass and cleared the sharp edges with my gloved hand. We cut the seat belt and eased him out, trying to keep the bad leg straight while Bret growled with pain. Rebecca looked at the cut above his left eye and said it would be ok till we got him up top.

Ducky and Ron tossed straps down. We fashioned a sling out of the straps and got Bret into it. We clipped the winch cable to the sling and began hauling him up a foot at a time, ice breaking under every step.

When we got to the top everyone helped carry Bret to my truck where we hoisted him into the sleeper and laid him across my bunk. Rebecca climbed in right behind him with her medical bag from the ops van and splinted his leg with one of my queen-sized pillows and duct tape, then tended to the cuts on his face and hands.

Ron: "I radioed the base and their medical team is standing by."

Me: "Copy. Let's finish this hill."

By the time we rolled again, the snow was a wall. It wasn't falling anymore, it was flying sideways, thick enough that Harley's taillights were the only color left in the world.

Rebecca, headset half-on, stayed with Bret, talking to him and listening to him gripe about his leg and head.

Harley: "Sign says eleven percent grade next kilometer."

Me: "Copy. Everyone keep the guy in front of you in sight."

We crawled past the warning sign and the road fell away. Transmission growled, drives whined, wind hammered from both sides. Tire chains bit and slipped.

Billy Bob: "Back's clear, but it's gettin' greasy. Visibility maybe twenty feet."

Me: "Hold your lane."

The grade eased for half a mile, then pitched again even steeper. Another yellow diamond warned: TWELVE PER-CENT GRADE NEXT 1 KM.

Harley: "Switchback left. Shoulders gone. Stay in the middle of the road."

Me: "Copy."

Her strobes pulsed through the white; they were the only thing keeping us from driving blind.

Rebecca: "Base confirms radar still solid red. Snow band extends another eight kilometers."

Me: "Then through it we go. Ride it out. Don't break down now—it will be a cold night."

The slope of the road dropped and bent to the right. Weight shoved the truck through the curve. With hands locked and eyes on Harley's strobes, we were driving a frozen roadway, white walls of snow on both sides.

Billy Bob: "Mirror full of nothing but snow you boys better—"

Chad: "Lord Jesus! Billy Bob ran into me!"

Me: "Talk to me!"

Chad: "Billy Bob lost traction, came around sideways and hit my trailer right at the rear axles. Right rear corner of the trailer dropped. Load still seems tight, maybe slid a bit to the left."

Me: "Copy. Everybody stop! Set brakes. Nobody moves 'til we check the damage and Billy Bob."

Harley stopped in the middle of the road. I stopped and stepped into the wind. Downhill through white blur I could see that Billy Bob's pickup sat nose-first in a drift, rear jammed against Chad's step-deck. Headlights buried.

Me: "Billy, you alive?"

Billy Bob: "Yeah. Airbags popped out and saved me. Looks like the frame is twisted, motor died. I tried to start her but it made all kinds of racket, but I'm walking."

Rebecca: "He's moving. No smoke. Leave it, get him in with Chad."

Me: "All right. Billy Bob's pickup looks totaled. Chad, can you roll?"

Chad: "Maybe. Rear axle is sitting a bit sideways, but she'll make it if I baby it."

Me: "Do it. Keep it under twenty. We are too close to quit."

We rolled again, slow enough to feel every link of the tire chains slapping the road.

Chad: "Load looks like it's walking left a foot, maybe more."

Me: "Ducky, you have eyes on him?"

Ducky: "Load still looks tight from here, but one binder's swinging loose on the right rear."

Chad: "That's the one that probably took the hit. She'll hold 'til the bottom."

Wind screamed between the trees, whistling through stake pockets like a pipe organ. Every bump worked against that broken axle until a metallic pop echoed, another chain gave way.

Chad: "Load's moved more left. But the remaining chains seem to be holding."

Ducky: "Keep it straight, and slow as you go around the corners, she should hold."

Me: "Eyes ahead so no one gets lost out here."

Through the wall of snow, Frostline's towers appeared, yellow lights cutting the fog.

Natasha: "Base perimeter coming up in four miles."

Me: "Looks more like forty miles. Stay in the throttles. We're almost home. Keep them slow and watch the edges. Don't want to lose anyone else to this mountain."

Ron: "This is so stupid! Why the heck didn't we wait for this storm to blow over."

Me: "We're almost there! Stop worrying about things we cannot change."

Chad: "Dear Lord, please keep our hands steady, our minds clear, and the trucks upright."

Me: "Amen!"

Two miles later, Chad called out: "Something let go! I'm dragging to a dead stop!"

A metallic crack, then the grind of steel. His lights dipped; trailer dropped.

Chad: "Looks like the axle folded under. The right rear is buried!"

Ducky: "I'm on him. The axle is cocked sideways; load shifted about twenty-four inches left. We're done where we sit."

Natasha: "Base says we're within visual."

Me: "Tell 'em we'll bring it in one way or another. I'm headed for the base and will drop my trailer inside the fence and come back. Chad, Ducky, hold what you got."

Ducky: "Copy."

Me: "Harley, take point. Ron, stay on my bumper."

Harley: "On it."

Rebecca: "Bret seems to be stable for the moment, he's awake enough to cuss."

Me: "Tell him to save it."

The perimeter towers grew through the storm, floodlights painting yellow arcs. MPs waved us in, parkas snapping.

MP: "That pad is clear to the right and medical crew is waiting by the hangar."

Me: "Copy."

I pulled over to the pad where the MPs directed me. The medical crew ran over to my truck and helped Rebecca get Bret out of the sleeper. While they were unloading Bret, I jumped down and, moving as fast as I could, pulled the fifth wheel pin, dropped the airlines between the truck and trailer, jumped back into the cab, then hit the switch to dump the air out of the truck airbags to drop my trailer inside the outer fence. Then I turned back into the storm.

Five minutes later I found Chad and Ducky's strobes again. Chad's trailer sat nose-high, axle twisted under the deck. I helped Chad drop his trailer and Ducky, Chad, and I grabbed the chains from all our headache racks and we shoveled two trenches between each truck and laid out two parallel runs of three-quarter inch, grade one hundred chain, five twenty-footers each, joined with one-inch anchor shackles. We threw a blanket over each leg near mid-span to kill snapback if any part of this setup thought about giving way.

Front truck hookup: Chad's rear pintle hook on the rear of his tractor connected to Ducky's front tow hooks, crossed to stop side loading. Ducky's DOT trailer bumper connected to my front tow hooks, also crossed once to stop side loading. We ran our gloves over every link, checked clearances and double-pinned each shackle. Ducky put wheel chocks behind Chad's good axle to ensure it didn't roll backward.

Me: "Radios up so we don't miss a single command. Test pull, inch it forward."

Chad eased out on the clutch; links went tight, then he set the brakes.

"Hold," I called. We walked the line again—no twists, no kinks. I took the rear, Ducky climbed back in the middle, Chad up front.

"On three," I said. "Release your brakes, clutch out. Roll the smoke."

Chad/Ducky/me: "One … two … three."

Three throttles slammed to the floor at the same time. The mountain shook and the noise was deafening. Chad's Kenworth lunged first, rear suspension slammed to the stops, stacks coughing black. Ducky came in behind him, tires clawing through slush, trailer chains snapping tight. My W900 jerked forward hard enough to slam my shoulder into the belt.

Every link stretched like piano wire.

Between us we were throwing roughly seventeen-hundred horsepower and more than five thousand pound feet of torque into over a hundred thousand pounds of dead weight.

Every gear tooth in the drivelines screamed under the load. Turbo whine built into a steady howl, turbo boost gauge needles pegged and vibrating.

The smell of clutch lining hit first—sharp and bitter—followed by raw diesel. Black smoke boiled against white snow. Steering wheels shook in our hands as driveline slack snapped tight. Suspensions squatted low, tires biting just enough to keep from polishing the ice slick.

For three heartbeats nothing moved. Then the trailer twitched a few inches.

Ducky: "She's crawling!"

Chad: "Don't lift—don't you dare lift!"

The trailer broke free—snow and sparks in the same breath—and the whole line started crawling uphill toward the gate.

The air filled with sound that wasn't sound anymore; it was pure pressure, a solid wall of mechanical fury that shook the valley. Turbos howled to full song. The deep hammer of open exhaust cutting through the storm. Diesel haze rolled thick and black, coating the inside of every cab with the taste of soot. The smell of clutch lining, gear oil, and hot antifreeze bit through the cold. Gauges pegged—EGT > 1,400° F, coolant approaching the red line, transmissions cooking in their own oil, rear ends mercifully cool.

Rebecca: "We see you—two miles out!"

Base Ops: "Mercer, lockdown active. You have two minutes!"

Natasha: "Pops, one and a half miles and closing!"

Me: "Copy! We're still dragging the mountain behind us, don't close that gate!"

Chad: "Boost pegged, temps climbing, I'm stayin' in it!"

Ducky: "Traction lights flashin' like Vegas—don't stop, don't breathe, pull!"

I could smell oil in the cab; feel it slick on my gloves.

Base Ops: "Ninety seconds!"

Rebecca: "They're coming in hot! If that gate closes, they're done!"

The MP's voice crashed over them: "Requesting delay on lockdown countdown, convoy still outside the perimeter!"

Merritt: "Denied. The sequence is preset; we couldn't stop it even if we wanted to. No override!"

Chad shouted, "We're past the first tower! Don't back off!"

Then the first deep knock came from under my hood, a solid bang like a hammer on a drum. Oil pressure dropped. Temperature pegged.

"Give 'em everything you got," I roared, voice breaking over the radio. "Even if they blow!"

I slammed the throttle flat on the floorboard. The 550 roared once, coughed, and detonated with a single metallic crack that shook the whole truck. Black smoke rolled out of the stacks like tar. The cab filled with the smell of burning oil and metal cooking itself alive.

A burst of flames shot from my exhaust stacks, the driving snow attempting to extinguish them. I held the throttle flat praying for another few inches knowing she'd given me everything she had.

Rebecca: "Pops, you're on fire! Let off!"

Me: "Can't! Not now!"

Base Ops: "Lockdown one minute!"

Rebecca: "One mile! You can make it!"

Ducky: "Keep it alive!"

Chad: "Pull, baby, pull!"

I could see the floodlights looming now through the snow. The gates closing. Natasha hollered, "Thirty seconds!"

The MP yelling: "Gates in motion! Repeat gate closing!"

Merritt, distant but firm: "Get them inside whatever it takes!"

The three trucks screamed like dying animals. Chains had no slack but were jumping and snapping like rifle cracks as Chad and Ducky's trucks were now dragging me too. At about twenty miles per hour, snow boiled under the drives, spraying sideways in white geysers. The smell of ozone and hot gear oil turned the cab metallic.

"Ten seconds!" Rebecca shouted.

Ron yelled from behind the gate, "Don't stop!"

Ducky's truck roared.

"Five seconds!" Natasha's voice broke the static.

The floodlights hit us full on. The base walls loomed silver and black through the storm.

Chad's rig finally broke the threshold followed by Ducky's step-deck scraping the edge of the concrete apron, tires shrieking. The gate hydraulics whined, metal doors closing like jaws.

My poor, dead Kenworth and Chad's crippled trailer pulled like an anchor, but the impact of the solid gate rammed the tail of this broke-down train over the threshold with dragging metal screaming, chains snapping like gunfire, and sparks scattering through diesel fog.

The roar of engines drowned everything until the sound collapsed all at once. Chad and Ducky's air brakes hissed. The engines were silent against the storm; the ticking of hot metal and the thin whine of cooling turbos was but a whisper.

Rebecca's voice came over the radio, half disbelief. "Gate sealed. Convoy secure."

I keyed the mic once. "That oughta do it."

Steam and smoke drifted from hoods and stacks. Ducky sat motionless, both hands still white-knuckled on the wheel. Chad leaned forward over the dash, breathing hard, the glow of his gauges flickering low. Snow and wind still pummeled our trucks but somehow it felt warmer on this side of the fence. Beyond it, the road was gone, buried in snow and silence.

Inside the gates of Frostline, the floodlights seemed to burn a little brighter, like they knew we'd make it. For a moment nobody moved. The world breathed steam and silence. Then the quiet broke.

Sirens rose under the wind; the kind that carry through cold air. Two base fire trucks appeared with red lights flashing dull through the snow, followed by an ambulance and a pair of Humvees with MPs riding shotgun. Tires crunched over packed snow; exhaust fog rolled around their bumpers. Medics piled out before the engines even stopped.

One team came straight for my truck and another toward Chad and Ducky. The smell of diesel and burning clutch mixed with the antiseptic from their kits, a sharp, strange smell. A medic slapped a gloved hand against my door. "You Mercer?"

"Yeah. I'm okay—go check on the other two."

I took a minute to journal a few notes sitting here in the dead quiet of my truck.

Journal Entry 14

Made the gate under blowing snow. Took all three trucks chained together to drag that crippled trailer.

Trucks screaming, temps over the top. My engine blew sky high just shy of the gate, but Chad and Ducky's momentum got us over the finish line before she completely gave up the ghost.

Bret to medical, leg splinted, ribs taped, forehead bandaged. He joked anyway.

Harley's Jeep in the motor pool.

Parts trailer and Billy Bob's pickup are still six miles down the mountain, buried. Rigs shut down.

Base called Lockdown Delta. They'll move the trailers into the hangar and unload them.

We'll all sleep indoors tonight, in beds, with heat. The base will be a bustling city of activity overnight as rigs, trailers, and cargo are relocated to the safety of the giant indoors but I don't think we'll notice.

—Pops

Chapter 16

PROJECT IRON REACH

Morning. Snow hammered the bay doors like the mountain wanted its freight back. Each gust shook the panels and sent a new sheet of white sliding down the seams. Inside, heat shimmered off the rigs, turning the air into fog that smelled of diesel, antifreeze, and the kind of sweat that comes from doing something nobody should have survived.

Two forklifts were moving the twisted frame of the trailer we had dragged off the mountain. Chains groaned; hydraulics hissed. With the light of day it looked worse than I thought. Nose caved, frame bowed, decking scarred where our chains had bit in. The rear axles sat cockeyed. The wiring torn and hanging like veins. Rebecca, standing beside me, folded her arms.

"Think it'll roll again?"

"Not that one," I said. "She's done. Gave us everything she had."

Ron brushed a glove across the broken rail. "Scrap metal now."

"Hell of a eulogy," Ducky said. Nobody laughed.

The guys drifted off to check their trucks. Habit. None of us knew yet that none of them were going home.

I turned toward mine. She sat dead center in the bay, streaked black and gray like a burned-out stove. The stacks were charred halfway up, oil running down both sides and puddling under the steps. One headlight hung by its wire, still dripping meltwater. I pulled the latch and the hinges squealed as I yanked the hood open. One look told the story.

There was a hole the size of a football in the side of the block, edges clean and shiny where a rod had punched through. Oil and coolant had sprayed everything in reach. The belts hung slack, half-burned. Twenty years of miles staring back at me in silence.

Rebecca, beside me, hands in her pockets, took notes out loud. "She's sitting high on the left. Frame's bent. Fifth wheel's twisted too."

"She's not scrap yet," I said. "She's been with me twenty years. Seen her share of near-death experiences. Always bounced back."

Rebecca didn't argue. She nodded, eyes on the hole in the block. We moved down the line.

Ron's Peterbilt wore the fight on its face, hood crumpled, bumper bent from the moose, one fender missing, a chunk of fur still stuck to the grille.

The mirror was gone and the hood latch hung by a bolt on Chad's W900.

Ducky's old W9 sat next to them, spotless except for road salt, like it had cruised through a storm meant for somebody else.

"See?" he said, running a rag down the fender. "The Lord protects fools, drunks, and professional drivers."

"Lucky for you, you tick all three boxes," Ron muttered, and for the first time in hours we laughed.

The other trailers didn't look much better. Scraped sides, bent rub rails, marker lights missing, and a few flattened air bags causing them all to sit crooked. Natasha went by with her tablet, jotting numbers and shaking her head.

We ended up in a loose circle between the trucks. Nobody spoke for a long minute. Just the sound of the wind beating on the doors and the steady hum of the generators buried somewhere behind the wall.

Chad set his cap against his chest. "Before we start patching, we need to say thanks."

He looked around at each of us, eyes red but steady. "Every one of us made it off that mountain alive. Engines can be replaced. Friends can't."

He bowed his head and prayed. Simple, quiet. The way truckers talk to God when nobody else is listening. When he finished, nobody moved. Even Ducky kept his mouth shut for once. The forklifts idled out. The bay doors thudded closed. For the first time since Florida, we were standing still.

When Merritt came in, Rebecca was walking the line, moving slow and careful the way you would around something holy, camera strap around her wrist. Every few feet she would crouch, snap a shot, check the screen, and move again. She never pointed toward the far end of the bay where the cargo sat tarped and sealed. She knew better. Just our trucks, our damage, our ghosts.

Merritt's boots echoed across the floor. The man looked like he hadn't slept since we hit the gate, but his eyes were steady.

"Morning, Mercer," he said.

"Still feels like more of the same night to me," I told him.

Walking beside me, hands behind his back, we both watched Rebecca work. "She's got a good eye," he said.

"Yeah," I answered. "Sees what matters."

We passed my wrecked truck first. Hood still up, oil dripping to the floor. Merritt studied the hole in the block, then the burn marks along the stacks. "Hell of a pull," he said quietly.

"Cost me a motor," I said.

"Cost you more than that. But it kept the mission alive."

He stopped at the broken trailer, the one the forklifts had parked like a casualty of war. Snowmelt pooled beneath it. He ran a glove over the twisted decking and sighed.

"Per the contract," he said finally, "all rolling stock remains on site. Cargo, trailers, tractors. The works. Property of the United States now."

I felt that one land deep.

"Would've been nice to know that before I rebuilt half of it on the road."

He gave a small nod. "It was buried for security reasons. If anyone had gotten word of what you were hauling, it would have been compromised."

Rebecca's shutter clicked somewhere behind us. The sound felt like punctuation.

Merritt turned back to me. "Command's doubling the contract. Straight from Washington. Your company's already flagged priority payment."

I stared at him. "You serious?"

He nodded once. "After what you faced out there, ambush, weather, mechanical losses, they said it was the least they could do. And you will all have full medical coverage until you are cleared to travel."

I leaned against the fender and wiped my hand across my jaw. "Speaking of that ambush," I said, "Who were they? Any idea yet?"

"Contract shooters," he said. "A private firm that went dirty. We've encountered them before. Ex-military. Flexible morals."

"So not random bandits."

"No. Someone tipped them that a classified payload was moving north under civilian cover. They thought they could intercept and sell it."

"What's in the boxes worth dying for?" I asked.

He paused, choosing words. "Something we can't talk about yet. You'll get the full brief once Command signs the release. We'll have a full debrief later today. For now, all you need to know is they didn't get it."

I nodded slowly. "That'll do."

"Whatever kicked this off didn't start here," he said. "You walked into the middle of something bigger than any of us."

For a long moment, neither of us spoke. The bay lights buzzed overhead; somewhere in the distance a generator coughed.

"Appreciate it," I said finally.

"You earned it."

He looked toward the bay door where Rebecca was lining up another shot, camera raised, hair loose from its tie. His voice changed, lower, softer.

"You know she used to go by my name."

"I figured it might be something like that," I said. "Didn't want to pry."

"She took her mother's maiden name before she joined the Marines," he said. "Didn't want help. Wanted to stand on her own. I didn't take it well." He rubbed a thumb along the edge of his glove, eyes still on her. "Her grandfather's here too. Retired rescue swimmer. She wanted to see him after everything."

I kept quiet as I put the jumbled pieces together in my head. Some stories don't need commentary.

He drew a slow breath. "I thought maybe if I got her close to this assignment, she would start to understand why I stayed in uniform so long."

"I'm sure she understands," I said. "She just needed the miles to prove it to herself."

Merritt smiled barely, but it was there. "You have a good crew, Mercer."

"Yeah. I've had better engines, but not better people."

He offered his hand. "You will have my thanks on record."

I shook it. "Thanks is good. Parts and engines would be better."

"We'll see what we can do," he said, and walked toward the offices, boots echoing until the door shut behind him.

Rebecca lowered her camera and came over. "Everything okay?"

"Yeah," I said. "He said we'll be getting paid double."

Her eyes widened. "Double?"

"Guess the paperwork fairy smiled down on us."

She smiled back, small but real, and looked toward the wrecks. "Good. Maybe we can afford new prayers next time."

"Or at least new trucks," I said.

She slipped the camera into her pocket. "Mind if I get a few shots of the bay before they rope it off?"

"Go ahead," I said. "Just don't catch me crying over the old girl."

We pushed through a side door a little later, leaving the noise of the bay behind us. The hallway to the medical wing smelled like antiseptic. White light, gray tile. The kind of place that never knows night. Rebecca trailed behind me, camera off now, both of us walking quietly while the wind outside threw itself against the metal skin of the base.

Bret was in the second bay on the right. The door stood half open, warmth rolling out into the corridor. Stainless-steel carts, instrument trays and remnants of bustling medical staff were evident from the night before. The nurse was re-wrapping his arm.

He looked half-mummified, right leg encased in fiberglass from thigh to ankle, bandages wrapping his ribs so tight you could see them rise and fall. His arm was stitched and taped, skin blooming in purple bruises. Butterfly strips ran along his temple where a dozen neat stitches closed the cut that nearly went to his eye. Someone had cleaned the blood from his hair but left a curl of dried blood behind his ear.

"How's your head?"

Bret's voice came out rough but alive. "Feels like I lost the argument."

"You won the important one."

"Guess I'll need some rest," he rasped. "Somebody find me a wrench and a coffee."

The nurse snorted. "That's not rest, that's denial."

"Denial's cheaper than morphine," he muttered.

We all laughed and for a second the room felt human again. The monitors beeped soft and steady and the nurse left, leaving Bret pale and breathing under the lights.

Rebecca slipped her hand over mine and whispered, "He's tougher than he looks."

"Yeah. Always has been."

Through the glass wall we could see the snow curling past the floodlights outside, white against white. Somewhere in the distance, a forklift clanked and the echo carried down the corridor like a heartbeat under steel.

"Get some rest, Bret. We'll keep your seat warm."

He gave a lazy salute without opening his eyes. "Don't scratch my toolbox."

We left him under the hum of machines like another piece of busted equipment the base was trying to put back together.

After lunch with the crew and some down time to catch up on life, Rebecca and I walked down the hallway to a small debrief room off the main corridor. It was 4p.m. and most of the crew were already there, scattered around the table nursing their coffee and bandages. It wasn't the big command debrief, just our crew, so we all heard the same story and the same numbers.

Concrete walls, humming heater, a coffee pot that smelled more like metal than caffeine. Ron had scrounged up a marker and was using the whiteboard to sketch parts lists that nobody would ever order. "Front bumper, hood, fender, moose parts optional," he muttered.

Ducky leaned back in his chair. "You oughta bill the moose for damages."

Harley sipped from a Styrofoam cup. "You would never collect. No fixed address."

Bret would be arriving via wheelchair. Natasha kept glancing toward the door like she expected him to roll in any moment. Billy Bob was balancing sugar packets into a pyramid and Chad was scrolling through his phone, muttering prayers and looking for frame shops.

"I'll tell you right now," Chad said, "I'm gonna need a hood, a door, a mirror, and about twelve square feet of luck."

"Luck's backordered," Ducky said. "Tried to buy some last week."

Ron pointed the marker at him. "You don't need luck. You need soap. That truck's the only clean thing in this base."

"Jealousy," Ducky said. "Pure jealousy."

The laughter came easy, thin but honest. The kind that comes when nobody's sure whether to cry or joke, so they do both.

Natasha looked over her notes. "Fuel cells, air lines, maybe brakes on two of them. Pops, what's your truck need besides an organ transplant?"

"Motor, frame check, fifth wheel, and a miracle."

"Good news," Billy Bob said. "Miracles are government issue around here."

Rebecca grinned, perched on the edge of the table with a mug between her hands. "If half these trucks roll home under their own power, I'll eat my notebook."

"You'll need ketchup," Ron said.

The door opened and Merritt stepped in, clipboard under one arm, parka half unzipped. The room straightened. A medic wheeled Bret inside. Cast propped, head bandaged, tablet on his lap.

Merritt nodded once. "Command has confirmed full completion of Mission Iron Reach. Contract paid in full, doubled for extraordinary conditions. You are all authorized medical coverage until you are cleared to travel."

Silence dropped across the room. Only the heater kept humming.

Merritt gestured toward Bret. "You have the numbers?"

Bret tapped the tablet awake. His voice came out dry but steady. "Base contract, five hundred thousand dollars. Four tractors and trailers, one hundred fifty thousand each. That's six hundred thousand. Three support vehicles, fifty thousand each for a total of one hundred fifty thousand." He scrolled. "Double bonus and reimbursements put it at about two and a half million dollars. Each person gets the money for their equipment. Then we split a million seven ways. Comes out to about one hundred forty two thousand each. Not bad for ten days of work if you ask me. Plus expenses for the company." He looked up. "That sound right, Colonel?"

Merritt nodded. "Every dime authorized."

For a second nobody moved. Then Ducky grinned. "Guess I can buy chain by the pallet. And pay a kid to carry it so my back quits complaining."

Ron snorted. Harley laughed. Bret tried and clutched his ribs.

Billy Bob leaned back, chair squeaking. "I'm buying brakes and coffee before the Lord thinks up another test."

That brought another round of laughter.

Bret looked over at Rebecca. "We ought to peel off enough to put her in a proper pickup. One that starts when she asks it to."

"Put fifty on paper for that," I said.

Rebecca blinked. "You're serious?"

"Yeah. Earned it fair and square."

She smiled, shaking her head. Natasha rubbed her eyes and pretended it was the light.

Ron looked up. "Wait. Why are they paying for our equipment? They're covering the damage, right?"

The room went quiet. I sighed. "They're not fixing anything. They're buying it. Everything we brought up that hill stays here."

No one spoke. Then Ducky let out a low whistle. "Well, that explains the bonus."

Chad shook his head. "I'd rather have my truck."

"Yeah," I said, "me too."

Merritt cleared his throat. "Before anyone turns in tonight, medical needs each of you for a full evaluation. Cuts, frostbite, anything that hurts. Report it. I want everyone cleared before lights out. That's an order."

We nodded. Nobody argued.

I looked around the table. Bandaged, bruised, half awake, but alive. "Money's good," I said, "but that isn't why we came. We finish what we start."

Bret set the tablet aside. "Then we're rich and stupid."

"Speak for yourself," Ducky said. "I'm stupid."

"Yeah," Billy Bob said, "but at least now we can afford to be stupid in comfort."

The room cracked up, low, easy laughter that loosened every knot in our shoulders.

Merritt smiled at the door. "Get checked and get some rest. Command wants the full debrief tomorrow morning. This was to cover money and damage."

Then he was gone.

We sat there for a while longer, no road, no orders. The storm pounding the walls and the sound of men and women who had somehow made it all the way north and were still here to laugh about it.

Bret's orderly arrived to return him to his room and drivers drifted out one at a time, most of us heading toward the medical wing to get our full physicals. At dinner, we told big fish stories about what we'd do with the money.

I laid down but sleep didn't come. Snow was still howling outside and wind hit the walls hard enough to make the steel groan. Most of the crew had turned in after dinner. The base lights were dimmed, half the hangar dark except for a few service lamps glowing over the trucks.

I couldn't sleep. Too much noise in my head.

I found myself back in the bay, walking the line of rigs we had nearly died for dragging them up that mountain. Every one of them looked asleep. Shadows of engines, chains, and oil. My own truck sat near the center, hood still up, frame bent like a tired shoulder.

Rebecca was there too, sitting on a crate near the RGN, camera hanging at her side, hair pulled loose, staring at the hole in the block like she could still hear it run.

"Couldn't sleep either?" I asked.

She looked up and smiled softly. "Tried. The wind won."

"Yeah. It's louder when you close your eyes."

I sat beside her. For a minute we didn't talk. Just watched the snow creep down the windows and listened to the metal rattle.

She finally said, "I keep thinking about what it took to get here. Every mile, every breakdown. Part of me feels proud. The other part feels empty."

"That's the hard part," I said. "You fight so long to get somewhere that when you finally stop, you don't know what to do with the quiet."

She nodded. "My dad used to say quiet was where you hear yourself lying."

I chuckled. "Merritt still say things like that?"

She smiled. "All the time. We used to argue about everything. He thought I should stay in uniform. I wanted to fix things with my hands. Machines make sense. People don't."

"Guess we both picked loud jobs for quiet reasons," I said.

She studied me then, long enough that I felt it. "You never talk about yourself, Pops. You talk about the work. The crew, your daughter. But not you."

"Ain't much to tell. Started driving before I could afford tires. Married the one woman patient enough to stand me. Lost her too early. Tried to raise a daughter without screwing it up."

Rebecca leaned forward. "Sounds like you did all right."

·"Some days," I said. "Others I can still hear Maggie's voice telling me to slow down and appreciate the small things."

"She sounds smart."

"She was."

The lights in the bay flickered and everything went dark; came back on a second later.

Rebecca spoke softer. "You know why I came on this run?"

"I figured you drew the short straw."

She shook her head. "I heard rumors about Iron Reach. I knew my dad was involved. I wanted to see if he still believed in the same things he used to. I thought maybe if I did something impossible, he would see I wasn't a mechanic or a reporter with a chip on my shoulder."

"And?" I asked.

"And somewhere between Fort Liberty and that mountain, I stopped caring what he thought." She looked at me then. "I started caring what you thought."

That one hit hard. I opened my mouth, closed it, and tried again. "I think you're one hell of a woman. Smart. Stubborn. You can fix a heater with a butter knife and some wire. And you kept this crew together when we were hanging by a thread."

Her voice almost cracked. "You kept me together."

She reached over and took my hand. Her fingers were cold. Mine were rough. It still fit.

"I don't know what happens when we leave here," she said. "My dad will stay. The crew will go home. And you…"

I looked toward my broken Kenworth. "I can't rebuild her," I said quietly. "But maybe I'll find another one like her and start over. See if I've got another road left in me."

She smiled faintly. "You could rebuild something else too."

"Like what?"

She squeezed my hand. "Your life."

The wind outside roared against the doors, a low howl that rattled the rafters. For the first time in years, I didn't feel alone in it.

"Rebecca," I said quietly. "This road's been long and ugly. I'm not sure what's left of me is worth holding onto."

She turned to face me, close enough that I could see the green in her eyes. "I'll decide that," she said.

We sat there a heartbeat longer. The space between us shrinking until there wasn't any.

No words. Just the storm outside as she leaned in and I met her halfway.

The kiss was quiet, steady, certain. Two people who had been running too long and finally stopped in the same place.

When we pulled back, her forehead rested against mine. "Guess that counts as rebuilding something," she whispered.

"Yeah," I said. "And this time I'm not letting it fall apart."

Outside, the wind backed off a little for the first time in days. Rebecca brushed her fingers across my sleeve, then stood. "We should try to get some sleep before morning."

"Yeah," I said, though neither of us moved right away.

Finally she smiled, tired and real, and started toward the door. At the threshold she turned back. The dim light catching her hair. "Good night, Pops."

"Night, Rebecca." Her footsteps echoed down the corridor until the door closed behind her.

I sat a while longer beside the broken truck, listening to the wind die out. For the first time in a long time, I wasn't listening for ghosts. Maybe the sun would come out tomorrow.

Later, Rebecca told me about the talk she had with her dad and her grandfather in the medical wing.

······◆◆◆······

The medical wing was warm and smelled faintly of coffee and iodine. Her grandfather sat by the window, blanket over his knees, watching snow blow across the runway. Merritt sat beside him, tablet in hand, uniform jacket unzipped, posture tired.

When Rebecca stepped through the door both men looked up at once. Her grandfather smiled. "Morning, kiddo."

"Morning, Pop." She hugged him, then glanced at her father. "Hey, Dad."

Merritt stood, almost formal, then eased back. "Glad you came," he said. "We were talking about how I ended up frozen to a mountain base."

Her grandfather chuckled. "He was telling me the sanitized version. I want the real one."

Merritt sighed. "Iron Reach started as a logistics trial. Civilian interface with a secure transfer line. I volunteered because I thought I could keep it from becoming another bureaucratic mess. And because it meant staying close to the Atlantic. Close to you." He looked at Rebecca. "I knew you were out there on the coast. Writing. Fixing trucks. Refusing my calls."

She crossed her arms. "I wasn't refusing. I was done. There's a difference."

The air went still.

Her grandfather looked at her. "He told me you used to say I was your dad. That true?"

Rebecca hesitated. "Yeah. It was easier that way."

"Why?" he asked.

"Because I was mad," she said. "Because every time I looked at a uniform I thought of him choosing it over me. Mom's funeral, graduation, my first deployment, he was always somewhere else doing something important. So when people asked who raised me, I said you. You taught me how to hold a wrench. How to breathe underwater. How not to quit when something hurts. That seemed more like a dad than a phone call once a month."

Merritt swallowed hard. "You're right. You were angry and you had every right. I told myself I stayed in uniform to give you a name that meant something. Truth was, I didn't know how to come home. Every time I tried, I saw your mother in your face and I couldn't stand the reminder."

Her grandfather nodded. "That's the curse of our kind. When I was a rescue swimmer, we used to say the ocean always keeps a piece of you. You drag men out of waves that are trying to kill you, and part of you stays out there. You come home dry, but never whole. The people waiting don't understand why you look past them when you walk through the door."

He turned to Merritt. "You left pieces of yourself in too many storms."

Then to Rebecca. "And your storm was being the one left waiting. Different sides of the same wave."

Nobody spoke. Snow slid down the glass outside.

Rebecca finally said, "You could have told me that."

Merritt's voice cracked. "I didn't have the words. I spent my life learning how to brief missions, not daughters."

Her eyes softened. "That you did. I don't think you or me or mom knew that was gonna come with the job. I understand. Rough on everybody."

Her grandfather smiled faintly. "Good. Now you can stop talking around the truth and start talking to each other. I'm too old to referee another round."

Merritt rubbed his temples. "You staying a while?"

Rebecca nodded. "Yeah. I think I need to. Help with the reports. Maybe tinker in the hangar so I don't drive anyone crazy."

Her grandfather grinned. "Start with that busted Kenworth. Looks like a challenge."

"I was planning on it," she said.

Merritt chuckled. "You always liked fixing things that looked past saving."

Rebecca met his eyes. "Guess I get that from you."

For the first time in years they all laughed together. Quiet. Real.

···◆◆◆◆···

By noon the storm had thinned to lazy flurries. Sunlight pushed through the gray and threw bars of light across the bay. The smell of diesel and disinfectant mixed with melting snow.

I was making notes for the debrief when Rebecca walked in, bundled in her base fleece. Her eyes looked clearer. "Morning," I said.

"Morning." She leaned on the rail beside my truck. "Dad says the med team wants everyone for follow-ups before supper."

"Guess we earned a check-up and a meal."

"They promised food first this time."

I set the clipboard down. "You get things straight with them?"

She nodded. "Yeah. It wasn't easy. But it needed to happen. I think he finally heard me."

"Good," I said. "Some bridges are worth the rebuild."

She traced the scarred metal on my truck. "He told me about the first time he saw Granddad after the accident that grounded him. Said it took two stubborn men ten years to admit they missed each other."

"Runs in the family."

She smiled.

"We've got the debrief tomorrow morning," I said. "After that I'll find out what happens next."

"Home?"

"Eventually. Depends what the brass has to say."

She nodded. "Whatever they decide, you did your part. All of you did."

"Maybe. Still feels unfinished."

"Most good stories do."

The hangar door cracked open. Harley yelled, "Chow line's open before the docs get us."

Rebecca laughed. "Saved by the cavalry."

We joined the others in the corridor. Ron limping but grinning. Ducky joking about trading his boots for hospital slippers. Chad arguing with Billy Bob about who ate the most rations during the storm. For the first time in days their laughter didn't sound forced.

They filed through the mess line, plates steaming. The room filled with warm clatter and relief. Afterward the medics pulled us in one by one. Checking pupils. Re-bandaging scrapes. Listening to lungs full of cold air.

Bret was last. Leg in a full cast. Stitches along his arm and forehead. He still looked half dead but managed his grin. "You all look worse than I do," he said after exiting the clinic.

Ron snorted. "You're a liar and we've got proof."

Bret chuckled. Winced. "I'll be prettier after the meds."

The orderly helped him back to bed and we all gathered round. No speech. Just the quiet that comes when everyone is thinking the same thing and doesn't want to break it.

Rebecca touched my arm. "Get some rest tonight. Tomorrow will be a long day."

"Yeah," I said. "One more mountain to climb. Paperwork this time."

She smiled and headed down the hall toward her father's office. Her boots echoed against the tile. For once the sound didn't feel like goodbye. Just distance waiting to close again.

Journal Entry 15

Snow kept hammering the walls like it was trying to take back what we hauled.

Engines cold, hearts colder, but the lights held.

Spent the morning watching forklifts drag what's left of our tractors and trailers inside.

One's twisted past saving. Mine's not far behind. Rod through the block. Frame bent. Hood hanging like a broken jaw.

Still smells like diesel and stubbornness.

Merritt gave the briefing. Said the contract doubled, payment cleared, and everything on this floor now belongs to the government.

Didn't sting until he said it out loud. Twenty years in that truck and I can't even drive her home.

Crew banged up but alive. Bret's stitched up and casted, still managing jokes.

Ducky swears divine intervention spared his paint. Ron's still blaming the moose.

Chad led a prayer. Even the wind shut up for a minute.

Rebecca's been taking pictures. Quiet kind.

We talked later. Just us and the storm outside.

Didn't fix the world, but it took the edge off the silence.

For the first time since Florida, nobody's rushing to roll.

We're here.

Tired. Breathing. Still standing.

Maybe that's enough for tonight.

—Pops

Chapter 17

PROJECT IRON REACH:
THE DEBRIEF

The hangar was brighter than it had any right to be. Sun bounced off the snow outside and filled the bay through the open doors. Everything felt washed out and tired, like a shop right after a long night shift.

Soldiers moved in rows, doing their jobs without wasting motion. Forklift alarms beeped. Chains clanked. Radios hissed. Nobody talked unless they had to.

Ducky and Chad were walking the step decks with two MPs. Seeing those trailers in full daylight wasn't pleasant. The mountain wasn't kind. Chad's trailer had a deep twist in the rear frame, enough that you could see daylight under one corner. One side of the rub rail was peeled back like somebody had hooked it on a guardrail. Ducky's had a front fender bent and the driver-side toolbox hanging open where the latch had given up. Both decks still had mud frozen into the crossmembers.

Ron stood near his RGN, staring at the gouge in the neck where that chunk of ice had kicked back near Deer Lake. "Didn't look this rough in the dark," he said.

"It usually doesn't," I told him.

Bret's dually sat crooked on a dolly line. Once the storm had eased up, the military was able to drag it and the trailer off the mountain side, with Billy Bob's truck also in tow. His rear fender was taped and the side panels dented from the wreck. The parts trailer behind it looked worse. The right side was torn open near the front corner from where it bounced through the trees. You could see where hits had shoved the storage boxes inward and twisted the front wall. Tarps and chain pockets were scattered across the floor from where they had fallen out during the drag to Frostline.

"Looks like it came down the mountain sideways," Bret muttered from his chair.

"It basically did," I said.

A sergeant with a clipboard approached. "Mercer, they're ready to load your tractor now."

My Kenworth, or what was left of her, was parked by the door. Hood removed. Stacks scorched. Engine bay was empty where they had lifted the motor. She didn't have a start in her. Soldiers had run a heavy winch line through the bumper and were threading it back to a floor anchor on the government RGN they had staged.

Rebecca had been there a while, hands in her coat pockets, watching the whole thing like she was trying to memorize it.

The winch pulled slow and steady. The Kenworth inched up the deck, tires chirping on the steel. Two spotters walked alongside calling corrections. They ratcheted her up until the steers cleared the breakover point, then laid her down square on the main deck.

"Good," the lead rigger said, waving the winch crew to stop. "Chain her front and back. Keep the lines low."

I walked up next to Rebecca. She kept her eyes on the truck. "She looks rough," she said quietly.

"She earned it," I told her.

Rebecca nodded, still watching the riggers connect the binders. "She'll run again," she said. She didn't say it like hope. She said it like a fact.

I looked at her. "You sound pretty sure."

"I am," she said. "Some trucks are worth fixing."

Not poetic. Just plain. And it landed.

Across the bay, Ron called out to Bret, "Your parts trailer might need last rites."

"Don't joke," Bret said. "It can hear you."

The line of soldiers kept moving equipment toward the far gate. Our trailers, our trucks, anything with wheels or welds. It felt strange watching it all roll away after hauling it across half the continent.

Rebecca stood beside me long enough that we didn't have to say anything. She watched the Kenworth disappear behind a snowbank like she was seeing both ends of the road at once.

Merritt appeared with a stack of forms. "We'll take care of it," he said. "All of it."

He wasn't talking about the trucks.

We moved into the conference room the same way we moved through the whole mission: tired, automatic, falling into old habits. Boots squeaked on the floor. Chairs groaned. Nobody sat tall, like they were finally allowed to sag.

Natasha took a seat near the end, eyes rimmed red but sharp enough to cut glass. On the wall monitor, Katie appeared from Mount Pleasant. Headset on. Papers stacked high. Hair pulled into that tight knot she used when she meant business.

"Nat and I pulled an all-nighter," she said, voice crackling through the speakers. "Payroll, settlements, medical, everything's wrapped. When y'all land, every account's already in the bank. You can actually go home and rest for once."

Natasha snorted. "If another form shows up on my desk, I'm setting it on fire."

That pulled a real laugh around the table. First one in days.

Merritt came in with Rebecca and two officers. He didn't bother with an introduction, set a tablet on the table and pulled up an image. Looked like a satellite photo. Military facility. Armed perimeter. Rows of vehicles I didn't recognize.

"You deserve straight answers," he said. "Iron Reach was a decoy."

The room went quiet.

"Your convoy moved in the open to pull fire away from the real shipment. Identical containers, same weight, same manifest codes, same security protocols. We needed someone to draw heat while the actual cargo moved dark."

Nobody spoke. Just waited.

"What was the real shipment?" Bret asked.

Merritt tapped the tablet. The image shifted to something that looked like a secured compound, heavy fencing, guard towers.

"What we told the intelligence community you were hauling," he said, voice flat, "was prototype guidance systems for hypersonic interceptor missiles. Three units. Two hundred million each in development costs. We leaked that information through back channels. Made sure Russia, China, and North Korea all got wind of it."

He swiped again. Different location this time. Northern Canada. Ice cores stacked in research tents. Scientists in parkas moving between equipment. "What you were actually covering," he said, and his tone dropped like he was finally getting to the part that mattered, "was something else entirely."

I felt the room shift. This was the real briefing.

"Biological samples," Merritt said. "Recovered from permafrost up in Northern Canada three months back. Similar to what those science teams found in Antarctica." He glanced at me and I remembered that morning in my kitchen. The radio crackling about mammoths and military transport planes. "But older. Different genetic markers. Intact cellular structures that don't match anything in the current databases."

Rebecca's eyes widened a touch. "The mammoths. The ones on the news."

"Those were Antarctic," Merritt said. "Public. Flashy. Good for headlines. Ours were Arctic. Classified. And worth a hell of a lot more."

"Why?" Ron asked.

"Because while the Antarctic samples are interesting," Merritt said, "the Canadian samples contain genetic sequences that could change what we know about climate adaptation, disease resistance, extreme environment survival. If the research plays out, we're looking at applications in everything from medicine to space exploration."

"And foreign governments wanted them," I said.

"Desperately," Merritt confirmed. "Russia's been trying to access Arctic permafrost sites for years. China's built an entire program around extinct species genetics. North Korea sees it as leverage, proof they can acquire cutting edge biological research through any means necessary."

He tapped the tablet again. A map appeared, routes highlighted in red and blue across half the continent. "So we gave them a target they couldn't resist," he said. "Hypersonic missile guidance systems, moving overland through populated areas, heavy security, perfect for interdiction. We leaked your route, made sure your convoy was visible on every intelligence satellite, monitored every border crossing. We painted you bright red and waited to see who'd bite."

"While the real cargo moved how?" Natasha asked.

"Two refrigerated box trucks," Merritt said. "Canadian Armed Forces escort. No bells. No whistles. They crossed at a remote checkpoint in Quebec six hours before you hit the ferry. No electronic signature. No satellite tracking. No public permits. By the time those mercenaries set up the ambush at your motel, the samples were already in the cryogenic lab two floors below this hangar."

Ducky let out a low whistle. "So we were bait for the wrong thing."

"You were the shield," Merritt said. "And it worked. Four different intelligence services tried to intercept what they thought you were hauling. Two attempted direct acquisition— your ambush was one of them. One tried to bribe a border agent. Another planted surveillance at three different checkpoints. Every single one of them was chasing missile technology that didn't exist."

"And the real samples?" I asked.

"Secure. Stabilized. Under analysis by a team that's been waiting two years for this opportunity."

He stood up, hands flat on the table like he was bracing himself. "Some freight doesn't make sense until long after it's delivered," he said. "This is one of those shipments. Give it five years, maybe ten. You'll see something in a medical journal, hear about a breakthrough in climate research, and you'll know. That discovery came from what you protected. That technology came from the mountain."

"And if we don't?" Billy Bob asked from the back.

Merritt's mouth pulled into something that wasn't quite a smile. "Then the secret worked exactly as designed."

Nobody said anything for a beat. Just sat there letting it land.

"You didn't haul freight," Merritt said finally. "You hauled the distraction that kept a classified program from turning into an international incident while they were setting up ambushes and tracking your convoy through three provinces. The real cargo slipped through undetected. Russia, China, North Korea—they all spent resources, assets, and credibility chasing something that was never there."

He looked at each of us. "But those biological samples they actually wanted? Safe. The research continues. And because you took the heat without knowing what you were protecting, discoveries that could change humanity's future are now possible."

Chairs creaked. Eyes met across the table. But nobody looked angry. This was the kind of truth that only lands after the danger's past. The kind that fills in the blanks and makes the scars worth carrying.

"Mission complete," Merritt said. "Command is dissolving Iron Reach effective immediately. All convoy equipment is retained for audit under the containment clause. You'll be debriefed individually over the next thirty days, but this is the core of it—you protected something that mattered. You kept it safe. And the work continues because of what you did."

Through the glass wall we could see soldiers sliding the destroyed trailer onto a lowboy. Another crew backed a triaxle RGN beneath my Kenworth. She looked even worse in the sun.

Watching them load her felt like watching someone covering a friend with a sheet.

Merritt read payment lines off a form. Base contract. Hazard bonuses. Doubling clause. Medical coverage. Every number felt unreal.

Ducky whistled. "So that's retirement. Cold wind and too many zeroes."

Chad rubbed his neck. "Bet the bank still finds a way to take its pound of flesh."

Even Bret cracked a grin from his wheelchair. "Save a seat on that jet for my toolbox and this fancy new leg," he said. "I'm charging extra for chrome."

Katie's voice came through the monitor. "Oh, and Ron? Your wife says start packing. She booked a week at Loretta Lynn's Ranch soon as you hit home. And your daughter says she needs three hundred dollars for schoolbooks."

Ron groaned. "Three hundred? For books? She better be studying diesel mechanics."

That broke the last of the tension and everyone laughed.

Merritt waited it out, then stepped over to me. He handed me a thick manila envelope stamped CONFIDENTIAL—PERSONAL RELEASE. The edges were sharp. "Don't open this until you've been home thirty days," he said. "And open it with Katie. You'll know why."

It felt heavier than paper when I slid it into my coat.

We cleared the room by twos and threes. The bay air was cold and clean. Natasha was already back with a clerk, signing things, sealing things, tying up the mission like it was a rescue of its own.

Two Humvees idled outside. Harley up front. Billy Bob behind. "Not my Jeep," Harley said, patting the hood, "but it's got heat and doors that shut."

Billy Bob grinned. "Just point it downhill and pray it's not classified."

Merritt actually laughed. "You'll be headed back to Texas in style," he said. "Secretary Hegseth sent his personal Gulfstream G5 to take you home."

Bret let out a low whistle. Harley raised her brows. I stood there, trying to picture any of this making sense tomorrow.

Rebecca stood beside Merritt, watching the soldiers finish guiding my truck onto the RGN. Slow. Careful. Deliberate.

"They may tear it down," Merritt said to her. "But Mercer will remember what it did."

She looked at him, then at me. "He already does."

I walked over. Merritt offered his hand. "Thank you for bringing her home," he said.

"She brought herself," I told him. "I stayed between the ditches."

Rebecca gave a small smile. "Both of you did."

Merritt nodded. "Safe travels, Mercer."

The Humvees pulled out toward the airfield. Meltwater trickled off the plows. The storm had scrubbed everything clean.

At the gate, a med evac van waited between the Humvees, Bret laughing with the corpsman about the leg that owed him a beer.

I was last. I climbed into the front seat next to Harley. Turned once and looked back.

The hangar was wide open, sunlight pouring through. Cold air rolling out across the snow. My old Kenworth was clearing the far drift on the RGN, chains tight, marker lights blinking red as she faded from view.

··✦ ✦ ✦··

Rebecca stood beside Merritt, wind pulling at her hair.

"Think he'll come back?" Merritt asked.

"If the road bends this way again," she said.

····◆◆◆····

The driver shifted into gear, and we started down the mountain. First clear road we had seen in days.

The G5 sat on the tarmac with its door open and stairs down, engines humming. The flight crew moved with the calm of people who had done this a thousand times. Nothing rushed. Nothing sloppy.

They loaded Bret first. The med evac van backed right to the stairs. The corpsman guided his chair onto the lift. Bret looked around like he owned the place. "Air Force giving me Cadillac treatment," he said.

"You're not special," the corpsman winked. "Just heavy."

That got a real laugh from everyone within ten feet.

We climbed aboard. Warm air hit me first, then the soft hum of the cabin. The seats were too soft for people who had been living in trucks and bunks for two weeks. Everyone sat slow, like their bones weren't sure we had permission to relax.

Ron dropped into a seat across from me, rubbing his neck. "Didn't think I'd ever see the inside of one of these."

"Me neither," I said.

Harley and Billy Bob grabbed a table toward the back. Harley kicked her boots off and let her socks steam in the warm air. Billy Bob attacked the snack basket like he hadn't eaten since Florida.

Ducky sat sideways, staring out the window like the snow-covered ridge was still chasing him.

Natasha closed her tablet for the first time since the ferry. She kept glancing at it like her fingers were trying to wake it back up out of habit. "Feels wrong not having paperwork," she said.

"Don't jinx it," Bret muttered.

The door sealed. The hum deepened. We lifted into the air smooth and easy. No bumps. No drama. Just a clean climb into the blue.

Frostline shrank behind us until it looked like a smudge of white on the ridge. Somewhere below were our trucks, stripped down in the hangar, waiting for whatever the audit teams had planned.

Nobody spoke for a while. It was the first real quiet we had earned.

Jonesboro, Arkansas came fast. The steps dropped. Ron grabbed his coat and stood up slow. He shook each hand like it meant something. That was Ron. No speeches. Just respect.

He paused in the doorway, looked back once, and tapped the bulkhead like a lucky charm.

"Tell Loretta Lynn's Ranch I said hi," I called.

He grinned. "If they got good coffee, you'll hear about it." He stepped down into the morning light and was gone.

We lifted again.

Jackson, Mississippi hit us with warm air the second the door cracked open—felt like stepping into a different world. Harley stretched her back until it popped. Billy Bob wiped his glasses on his shirt twice.

"You two staying out of trouble?" I asked.

"Not a chance," Harley said.

Billy Bob lingered at the top of the stairs. "If y'all need help with whatever they're cooking up next, call me."

"We will," I said. And I meant it. They disappeared into the sunlight.

Back in the air.

The cabin settled into the tired kind of quiet that only comes after a fight you didn't expect to win. Bret drifted off, cast propped on a pillow. Natasha wrote a note to Katie. Ducky finally shut his eyes.

Houston was quick. Chad grabbed his bag, already talking about getting a burger at a friend's spot off the loop. He slapped the side of the plane like it was an old sleeper and walked into a crowd of family who crashed into him like a wave.

Ducky shook his head. "Man didn't even say goodbye to the plane."

"He said goodbye to us," I told him.

"Fair enough."

We lifted one last time. The pilots dimmed the cabin lights. Texas rolled under us in long dark lines. Nobody talked much, didn't need to.

By the time the runway lights of Mount Pleasant came into view, something loosened in my chest. The kind of loose that only happens when you see home waiting.

The G5 lined up on final. You could hear it all the way across town. Mount Pleasant doesn't get jets like that unless a movie star wanders off course, so folks naturally stepped outside to catch a glance.

The wheels touched. Smooth. The door swung open. The stairs folded down. Warm Texas air pushed into the cabin. Jet fuel and sun-baked pavement. Home.

Two trucks pulled up along the fence while we were still unbuckling. Not a crowd. Just locals who lived close enough to hear the engines and got curious.

Old man Carter from the feed store leaned out his window, sunglasses crooked. "Pops Mercer stepping off a rich man's bird. You get lost or win the lottery?"

One of the airport linemen walked over from the hangar, wiping his hands on a rag. "Didn't know y'all were bringing in fancy company," he said. "Boss hasn't stopped staring at that thing since it called in."

Marcy from the diner rolled up behind them, apron still on. "I was rolling dough and saw that jet drop in," she said. "Figured it wasn't one of ours." Got a couple laughs.

Bret came down first in the medic's chair, waving like he had planned it. Carter shook his head. "Boy, you find more ways to get hurt than anybody I know."

Natasha stepped out next and got a nod from the lineman. "Good to see y'all back," he said.

Katie was waiting at the bottom with two steaming mugs. "You look awful," she told me.

"Then I fit right in." She handed me a mug. Real coffee. Real warmth.

The locals hung around for a minute or two, making sure everyone looked upright. Small towns don't crowd. They show up, check the temperature, and drift off like they were never there.

We loaded slow. Bret's buddy hauled him off, still chirping about celebrity entrances. Ducky's brother showed up in a truck held together with hope. Natasha headed out with folders tucked under her arm like she didn't trust gravity.

Soon it was me and Katie standing by her pickup. "You ready to see the yard?" she asked.

"Long as nothing's on fire."

"No promises."

We drove through town. Folks waved from porches. Some-one honked. Kids on bikes stopped to stare. One private jet plus a handful of worn-out faces will do that.

The yard came into view and I caught the differences right away. Fresh gravel. Even spread. The shop doors had a new coat of paint. Clean edges. White trim like Maggie used to like. A couple small flower beds at the fence line. Nothing fancy. Just enough to say someone cared.

"You did all this?" I asked.

"Had a little money left from the parts yard sale," she said. "Figured the place could use a lift."

"It shows."

We walked through the shop. Concrete swept clean. Tools hung where they belonged. The break table wiped down. The whole place felt like it had taken a breath while we were gone.

"Feels different," I said.

"Not bad different."

"No," I said. "Not bad."

I found myself glancing at the road even though I knew better. Katie noticed. "She'll call when she's stateside," she said quietly. "That's what she told me."

I nodded. "I figured."

"No rush," she said, giving me room to think.

Warm air drifted through the bay. Dust floated in the light. The town hummed in the distance. For the first time since the Cape, nothing felt urgent. Just tired bones. A quiet yard.

And the sense that something unfinished was still working its way toward us.

Journal Entry 16

Thirteen days since we rolled from the Cape—feels like a lifetime and a blink.

The hangar is empty now except for wet footprints and the memory of chains. They loaded my old Kenworth onto a government RGN this afternoon and took her slow past the bay. I watched until the taillights went red and the snow swallowed the sound.

The air is clean. Cold enough to bite, honest enough to clear your head. No diesel. No hot brakes. Just mountain oxygen and steel cooling off after too long a fight. The storm is over, outside and in.

Merritt's envelope rides in my coat. Thirty days, he said. Open it with Katie. I will. Some things just need to be with family.

Natasha and Katie tied off every loose end like it was a rescue of its own. Crew is fed, cleared, and laughing for real. Ron is headed to Loretta Lynn's Ranch whether he likes it or not. Bret is promising to charm his therapist and scare his surgeon. Harley and Billy Bob swear they might enlist if Humvees always come with heat.

Tonight, the Secretary's G5 takes us south. Never figured I'd go home from a frozen ridge in a bird with leather seats and a man who calls me sir. Guess miracles come at all altitudes.

We lost steel, but we kept souls. Fair trade. If anyone asks what we hauled, I'll tell them straight. We hauled faith through a blizzard and brought it home in one piece.

The wind is quiet tonight.

So is my heart.

—Pops

THE END

THIRTY DAYS LATER

Thirty days go by fast when you're trying to remember how to sleep in a house instead of a cab. The shop's quiet. The phones mostly stay silent, and the coffee doesn't taste like road dust.

Bret's walking with a limp but grinning about it. Ron swears he's staying retired till next Tuesday. Natasha's catching up on paperwork she swore she'd never touch again. Katie keeps saying the yard feels too empty, and she's right.

The envelope's been sitting in the safe all month. Only Katie's got the combo. Tonight she spins the dial and brings it out, plain manila, still sealed, CONFIDENTIAL—PERSONAL RELEASE stamped across the front.

She sets it on the table between us. "You ready?"

"Thirty days," I say. "Guess that means it's time."

The paper feels like old parchment when I open it. Two things inside, one letter, one smaller envelope.

Katie unfolds the letter first and reads aloud:

"CONFIDENTIAL—PROJECT WHITE REACH. Mercer, what you and your people accomplished under Iron Reach exceeded every expectation. Command has authorized us to continue under civilian cover. You are requested to assemble the same operational team for a controlled logistics evaluation departing Cape Canaveral, Florida within ninety days. Cargo will be designated Data Support Modules: Non-hazardous. I will continue to be your contact. Officially, you'll deliver to a secure testing range in the lower forty-eight. Unofficially, you're being trusted again to carry what no one else can. —Merritt"

Katie lowers the page. "Ninety days. Think he means it?"

I nod. "He knows we'll need it."

She opens the smaller envelope and freezes. Inside is a single check dated today for seven hundred fifty thousand dollars, made out to Mercer Hauling and Recovery.

A note clipped to it, written in quick block print, reads: Get what you need. You're going to need it for this run. —Pete Hegseth, Secretary of War

The kitchen gets quiet. House quiet. Nothing humming but the refrigerator and the distant rush of a pickup rolling down Jefferson.

"Lot to think about," she says.

"Yeah."

"And you know Merritt's not bluffing. Ninety days'll hit faster than we want."

"Yeah."

She watches me for a second. "You gonna be all right?"

"Eventually."

She doesn't push it. She never does.

We clean up the table, put the envelopes back in the safe, and step out onto the porch to breathe a minute. The evening has that soft blue light Texas gets in early spring. Cool but not cold. Yard quiet. Street quiet.

Then I hear a sound I haven't heard in a month. A deep, steady idle. Not loud. Not showy. Just right.

Katie's eyebrows go up. "You expecting someone?"

"No."

The idle drops as something turns onto our road. Headlights sweep across the neighbor's yard first, then the nose comes into view.

My Kenworth. Alive?

Not polished. Not perfect. Passenger-side paint still burned smooth. New mirror bracket. Replacement glass. Primer on the lower panels. Bent step plate swapped with a straight one off the parts pile. Fresh rubber. Hood squares straightened just enough to line up. Someone did real work here, not a showroom rebuild, but a true trucker fix: functional, safe, proud enough to roll.

The truck eases to a stop in front of the house like it knows its way home. Rebecca sets the brakes, lets her idle down a second, then shuts her off. Quiet settles in fast, broken only by the tick of cooling metal.

Rebecca climbs down from the cab and sets the keys on the step. Hair pulled back, jacket zipped halfway. A look on her face that isn't shy or apologetic, steady.

Katie whispers, "Told you she'd call."

"She didn't call," I say.

"Better," Katie says, and goes inside because she knows when to leave a man to handle his own mess.

Rebecca shuts the door gently and walks over. "Hope you don't mind," she says. "I figured she ought to come back under her own power."

I can't speak for a second, which annoys me because I always have something to say.

"How?" I finally get out.

"Base ran the teardown on the tractor fast. Old motor was done. Block damaged, internals scattered. No saving it," she says. "Frostline shops dropped in a rebuilt. I stayed on it 'til they were done and had them bump a few things while we were there. Better injectors, cleaned up the fuel side, a little more pull where you need it. She's not a race truck, but she'll climb better than she did."

"She seems different," I say.

"She is," she says. "And so are you."

That one hits harder than any storm we drove through.

I step closer, run my hand along the fender. Still cool from the evening air. "You didn't have to do this."

"I wanted to." She pauses. "And maybe I needed to."

The ticking from the engine bay fills the quiet between us. "You gonna take her for a spin?" she asks.

"Maybe tomorrow."

"Tomorrow's a good day for new starts."

Neither of us says much after that. We don't need to. Some things settle their own weight without a speech. She reaches past me for the keys dangling over the step. I cover her hand without thinking. She doesn't pull away.

The porch light clicks on behind us, Katie keeping watch without being seen.

Rebecca smiles a little, tired but real. "I was going to grab a room at the inn on Jefferson," she says. "Figured I'd stay out of your hair tonight."

The door opens and Katie answers that before I can. "No, ma'am," she says. "You're not staying at a motel after what you drove. Spare room's made. Truck stays here. We'll get your bag out of the cab and you can argue with him about the next run in the morning."

Rebecca huffs out a breath that's close to a laugh. "Didn't mean to invite myself."

"You didn't," Katie says. "You brought my dad's truck home. That counts for a lot around here."

I take the keys off the step and slip them into my pocket. "She's home," I say. "So are you. That's enough for tonight."

Rebecca nods. "All right. We'll talk tomorrow. About everything."

"I'd like that," I say.

Katie tosses her house keys and Rebecca snags them out of the air. "Come on," Katie says. "We'll grab your duffel out of the bunk and let the old man stand here and stare at his truck 'til his feet go numb."

They walk toward the cab together, talking low.

I walk back up to the porch and stare back a minute longer, looking at the Kenworth sitting quiet under the streetlight, primer scars, fresh rubber, new heart beating under the hood.

For the first time since Frostline, it doesn't feel like the road ahead is something I'll have to face alone.

Some roads don't end. They wait for you to get back on them with the right people beside you.

—Pops

ACKNOWLEDGMENTS

Endless thanks go to my beautiful wife, Rebecca, for her tireless efforts in editing this book. Maybe I created an interesting storyline, but only she was able to see into my vision and make it shine with grammar, punctuation, sentence structure, repetition elimination, and all the other important details that go into making a decent story into a good read. She gets an extra star in her crown for her patience in dealing with me in order to ensure my intended meaning was documented.

Thanks also go to the Kristopeit Girls who added their expertise to the editing process and for their endless support of Rebecca. Liz, for her critical work on formatting, was invaluable and gave the book its professional look. She was also instrumental in ensuring clarity, complete thoughts, and point of view. Deanna, for using her keen eye as a proofreader to capture those elusive typos and oddly worded sentences, and Maria, too, for offering her valuable input and suggestions.

Two additional people I'd like to thank are Kristi Wilkinson and Beth Lottig. Firstly, Rebecca's dear friend Kristi, for being brave enough to write her own stories, giving me hope that maybe I could do it too. Secondly, our publisher Beth Lottig, who Kristi introduced us to and who has been so professional, informative, and helpful, walking us through each step of getting this book published.

Finally, I'm so thankful for God's hand on me, for giving me a creative mind, for helping me develop this story line as I traversed the countryside over the last thirty years in my big rig, and for surrounding me with the support system I needed to help it come to fruition. I don't know where He is leading me, but there's no doubt in my mind He wanted me to get this story down on paper. I couldn't hold it inside any longer!

I sincerely hope you enjoy it.

ABOUT THE AUTHOR

JR Elrod has been a commercial truck driver/owner operator for over thirty years, and he incorporated his wealth of logistics knowledge and plethora of experiences across the forty-eight states and Canada to create this fiction novel.

As an adventure hound, he acquired his private pilot's license in 2019 and has enjoyed the ability to fly for business or taking his family members on trips across the country.

He has been married to Rebecca for thirty-four years and currently operates two companies with her: BAR Transportation and Sunnybrook Logistics. He is the proud father of three grown children and lives in Northeast Texas.

This is JR Elrod's first book in the Iron Reach series.

You can connect with JR at https://www.bartransport.net/frozenfreight or on the following social media platforms:

Facebook–https://www.facebook.com/jrmcelrod
LinkedIn–www.linkedin.com/in/jr-elrod-92357a377

www.ingramcontent.com/pod-product-compliance
Lightning Source LLC
Chambersburg PA
CBHW051311130726
47987CB00004B/1748